OLD SINS

OTHER WORKS BY LYNNE HANDY

IN THE TIME OF PEACOCKS

***

MARIA PELL MYSTERY SERIES

THE UNTOLD STORY OF EDWINA
WHERE THE RIVER RUNS DEEP
OLD SINS

OLD SINS

Lynne Handy

Cover design: William Pack

ISBN: 979-8-83900-390-3 (paperback)

PROLOGUE

In the summer of 1988 when I was ten, I found a baby girl caught in the cattails of a stream running through my parents' property. At first, I thought she was another baby Moses waiting to be discovered in the bulrushes. It was when I knelt to free her from the fronds that I saw her ashen face, her vacant eyes, and knew she was dead.

I see it all in slow motion now: I, in a yellow sundress, scrambling to my feet, knowing something was horribly wrong that a baby had been thrown in the creek. I ran toward my house crying, "There's a dead baby in the creek!"

My academician father was sitting in the porch swing, reading a newspaper. He threw it down and came running. The kitchen door banged behind my mother. "John? What is it?"

I ran to her and pressed my face against her chest. "It's a dead baby," I sobbed. "She's wearing a pink dress."

"A pink dress?"

My mother folded her arms around me and stared after my father, who admonished her to stay where she was. I'm sure my mother looked at the baby afterward, but not on the day that I found her.

No one ever claimed her. No one ever admitted throwing her in the creek. The town called her Baby Doe. The coroner said she'd been alive when she went in the water. She had been a throwaway child. Until finding her, I had not known that children could be so unloved they would be discarded. I was so distressed that my parents sent me to a psychiatrist who told my mother that I had merged my psyche with that of the unwanted infant and feared no one would ever want me.

How many times during my childhood had my mother asked if I knew how much she and my father loved me? Taken literally, it was a difficult question to answer, so I had kept silent. How do you measure love? Fear of abandonment helped form the woman I became, and in some ways, I remained stuck emotionally in my tenth year.

CHAPTER ONE

Coomara, Ireland
April 29, 2016

Bridget Vale was so faithful in her prayers that the nuns selected her as May Queen. On Sunday, she would reign over the village's spring festival. Today was her thirteenth birthday, and my cousin Elizabeth and I remembered with a strawberry frosted cake, balloons, and a pair of gold earrings depicting St. Brigid's eternal flame. Wearing her blue school uniform, Bridget danced on strong-muscled legs among the daffodils and tulips in my garden. Her gracefulness seeded a poem in my mind—*toss of silk-spun hair, gypsy feet....*

Bridget gripped the balloon strings with both hands so they could not fly away and become lodged in the stomachs of terns and sea turtles. Then catastrophe! In the middle of a pirouette, the sky darkened and a sea wind rushed in, batting the balloons against each other, swooping them up, ripping them from her hands. The pretty globes— pink, yellow, and blue—merged into the brew of clouds. I felt a sense of loss.

Before I could pursue the feeling, Iris, Bridget's mother, called to me from the open kitchen window. "Maria, I'm done vacuuming. Do you want me to sweep the front porch?"

"There's rain coming," I answered. "It'll wash the porch clean."

Iris went to the back door. "Come in, Bridget. Time to go home."

As the girl climbed the porch steps, I saw her aura, previously a healthy red, was now tinged with green—a loss of positive energy.

"I'm sorry I lost the balloons, Ms. Pell," she said sadly.

I patted her on the shoulder. "Couldn't be helped. The wind came out of nowhere."

Elizabeth, who had also seen the balloon mishap, sought to distract by asking Bridget to help box up the leftover cake. I paid Iris her weekly wage for cleaning the cottage, and mother and daughter prepared to go home.

"I'll see you at Mass on Sunday," Elizabeth said.

"I'm coming, too," I said. "It's not every day I get to see a queen coronated."

As Bridget walked down the hill with her mother, I saw her aura had not changed and it worried me—perhaps something more was at work in her young mind than the loss of the balloons.

The ability to visualize auras was both a blessing and a curse; it was invasive: perhaps people minded having someone privy to the secrets of their well-being. I had not worked to develop the skill; it had come to me early, perhaps, a result of my self-imposed isolation as a child. Most of the time, my mind was focused on the routines that comprised my life, and especially, my work. I could go days without consciously seeing haloes around people's heads—either that or I did see them as a natural occurrence and did not notice, as one becomes used to floaters in the eye.

I looked at Elizabeth. Her aura was pink. She was running low on energy,

She sighed as she closed the window over the sink. "Too bad about the balloons, Maria. I hope they don't end up in some creature's stomach."

"I hope so, too. Elizabeth, why don't you lie down. You seem tired."

"I may go sit in the garden."

Climbing the stairs to my study, I thought how capricious the weather was. Sunlight, one moment. Rain, the next. No wonder the ancient Celts found divinity in weather phenomena like thunder. So much of life was mystery.

As a poet, I loved mystery, for it tugged at my right brain, inviting possibilities. I'd been granted an eighteen-month leave of absence from my teaching position at Midwestern University in Indiana and was in Ireland on a Lewison Fellowship to study Celtic prehistory. Hopefully, the research would inspire a new book of poems.

The previous year, I had won the prestigious Innisfree Award for *Footprints*, a collection of poems based on the trek of a Celtic tribe from northern France to County Kildare in Ireland. Though I'd won several awards for feminist poetry, *Footprints* had earned the fellowship for me.

Three years earlier, my research for *Footprints* had led me to County Kildare, west of Dublin. I had been overwhelmed by the beauty of the country's landscape—forests and grass-covered hills, monolithic rocks heaved up from the soil, lakes and rivers carved out by long ago glaciers. Mists drifting in from the sea added to a sense of wonder. I felt the pull of history.

While I was in Kildare, Mathieu, my partner of twelve years, began an affair with one of his colleagues, a woman named Zara. All my life, I had been plagued by fear of rejection, and his betrayal sent me into a tailspin of despondency. The Lewison Fellowship allowed me to put an ocean between him and me, and to bury myself in work.

Pausing at the study window, I looked out onto the seaside village of Coomara, which dated to the early fifth century (BCE), when Ireland was carved into unstable tuatha, or kingdoms, with shifting boundaries dependent on the outcome of battles. Coomara, loosely translated as *sea hound,* was probably named for a Viking who came to settle long ago. A mile from my cottage, where the ruins of a thirteenth century castle hugged the ground, was my favorite place to linger. Closing my eyes, I could hear hoof-beats of an ancient army echoing from the earth. Easterly, lay a tumble of pale gray stones—once an abbey.

My five-room rented cottage came furnished and had been built on a promontory overlooking the Irish Sea, yet was within walking distance of the main part of town. Green-shingled, constructed of wood and stone, the house was painted hot pink. Gardens were walled in with a heavy oak gate in front, and a smaller gate in back leading to stone steps descending to the shore. Front and back porches were high enough that I could see into the garden of my neighbor and landlord, Brendan Calloway.

Brendan stood in his garden, looking out to sea. He was an odd sort and I didn't quite trust him. When I rented the cottage, I made sure he handed over all the keys.

Tearing myself away from the window, I sat down at my desk and began sorting through photocopies of mythical stories I'd brought back from my recent bus trip to the Trinity College Library in Dublin, fifty miles north of Coomara. It was the myths that fueled my understanding of prehistoric people, who came in waves during the sixth century (BCE), and with whom, through my late maternal grandmother, I shared a genetic core.

I bent to my work, reading about Dagda, known as the Good God, not because he was particularly moral, but because he was skilled as a warrior, ruler, artisan, and magician. He possessed a cauldron with an inexhaustible supply of treasure for his followers and a gigantic club, which had to be hauled on wheels. Some scholars thought he was a storm god like Thor with his hammer. Others compared him to Hercules.

The wind that had taken Bridget's balloons blew in through my open window and rustled a page on my wall calendar. Glancing up, I saw Elizabeth had penned in her tiny handwriting a reminder of Pearce Mulligan's soiree on April 30. We'd both forgotten about it.

I went to the top of the stairs. "Elizabeth," I called down. "Pearce Mulligan's party is tomorrow evening."

No reply. She must still be in the garden.

Pearce Mulligan was a bore, but I hoped to meet his reclusive poet mother, Margaret. Though I'd been in Ireland for six weeks, her path and mine had not crossed. The public librarian said Margaret had published only one chapbook. I'd read the library copy. Her verses were clever, based on rules of nature.

Rain was coming in my open bedroom window and I rushed to close it. Too many interruptions. My mind could not focus. Putting the notebooks aside, I went downstairs. Soaked to the skin, Elizabeth came in the back door, holding a wisp of pink latex in her hand.

"Part of a balloon," she said, handing it to me. "I found it on top of the wall. At least, this didn't kill some turtle."

I held it in the palm of my hand, thinking it was shaped like a human ear. For some inexplicable reason, I was troubled.

***

The following evening, Elizabeth and I were about to leave on foot for Ravensclaw, the Mulligan family estate, when she was detained by a telephone call from her mother in Indiana. Not wanting to be late, I went ahead. Halfway to the Mulligan estate, I heard Elizabeth shout my name and turned to see her running up the hill.

"Maria! Something dreadful has happened to Bridget!"

My heart lurched. "What? What happened?"

Elizabeth grabbed my hand. "A local boy found her body on the rocks."

"Her body?"

Bridget was dead? I felt as if I'd been kicked in the stomach. Yesterday, Bridget had danced with balloons in my garden. Had she fallen into the sea and drowned? Why had she gone down to the rocks? The village children were well aware of the danger. Signs were posted. Beware: Slippery Rocks.

"Where exactly was Bridget found?" I asked.

"Just below the park dock. A boy found her body when he went to arrange his father's fishing nets."

"And you learned about this how?"

"I was walking past the pub on my way to Ravensclaw when a garda officer pulled Iris and Freddy out of the pub to tell them. Iris..."

I could well imagine Iris's reaction. Years ago, she lost her first child, and now Bridget was dead. With anxious hearts, we hurried down the hill, reaching the edge of the village. As we neared St. Columba's Catholic Church, Judy Moriarity, the priest's gossipy housekeeper, darted out of the priory.

"Did you hear about the Vale girl?" she asked. "What do you think happened?"

She didn't expect us to respond and we didn't.

A mournful chant drifted upward, and I glanced toward the shore where people—possibly latter-day druids—had built a bonfire. They had heard about Bridget. Word of tragedy traveled fast in the village and its environs. On the other side of the street, Daniel Aherne, owner of a pub called Gaelic Earls, broke away from a group of men and waited for a car to pass. He hurried over and fell into step with us.

"Headed for the Vale cottage?" he asked.

"Yes," I replied. "Maybe there's something we can do to help."

A loud, piercing cry tore through the darkness. I could not mistake the source—it was Iris. Elizabeth and I broke into a run. A crowd had gathered at the Vale cottage. The front door was flung open. Iris stood on the threshold, pounding her fists on her husband's chest. Freddy Vale took her blows, tried to comfort her.

Two officers from An Garda Siochána, the Irish police force, stood on the porch. At their feet lay a stretcher holding a body covered with a white sheet.

Why have the garda brought the body to the cottage?

Iris' despair tore through me as if it were my own. I closed my eyes, shrank against a tree trunk to find my bearings. Knowing I could be paralyzed by the strong emotion of others, Elizabeth grabbed my upper arm. I took several deep breaths and nodded, nearly recovered from the onslaught of Iris's grief.

Iris scooped up her daughter's corpse and ran into the house. The officers stared at each other. "Here, here," one said. "We must take the body to the morgue."

Iris slammed the door. The lock snapped shut.

I turned to the officer nearest me. "Why did you bring the body here?"

"Mrs. Vale was with it there at the docks. She refused to let us touch her girl unless we promised to bring her to the house."

Judy seared him with penetrating brown eyes. "You shouldn't have listened to her. Now she'll never give up her girl. She lost her first-born, you know."

"We are Mrs. Vale's friends," I said. "Let us try to talk to her."

The officers stepped aside and we climbed the steps to the porch.

"Iris," Elizabeth called out, "it's Maria and Elizabeth. Please let us in."

Her hair a riotous mess, Iris threw open the door and lunged into Elizabeth's arms. Bracing myself, I reached out to keep them both from falling. Iris smelled of whiskey.

"Not you, Mrs. Clatterfart," Iris yelled at Judy. "I know the wicked-ness of your tongue."

Judy's kewpie doll mouth opened and closed. She stepped back.

I shut the door, but didn't lock it.

"We're so sorry," Elizabeth said. "Bridget was such a good girl. Your heart must be broken."

Her words sent Iris into a paroxysm of weeping. Holding the griev-ing woman against my shoulder, I guided her into the kitchen where Freddy sat at the table staring numbly out the window, his large work-man's hands gripping a bottle of Powers whiskey. I extended my con-dolences to him and he mumbled something in return. Iris sat down, reached for Freddy's bottle, and took a large swig. Then she returned to the front room and knelt in front of Bridget's body.

"Am I cursed?" she wailed. "Another child lost! Oh, God, save me from myself!"

Why does she need to be saved from herself?

Elizabeth stepped forward in a no-nonsense manner. "God has taken your children to a better place. They're in heavenly hands now."

Impatient with religious platitudes, I turned to snap at Elizabeth, but saw a transformation sweep over Iris' face—my cousin's words had soothed her. Practicing Catholics, Elizabeth and Iris were communi-cating in the code of their faith. The dead needed an Edenic refuge. I, who had been raised in the Presbyterian Church, rejected the Trinity at age twelve, and foundered for years in Unitarianism, found comfort in the power of the universe. I let Elizabeth take over.

When Iris laid her girl on the sofa, the sheet had slipped from Bridget's face. Elizabeth and Iris dropped to their knees to recite the rosary. I moved closer to the dead girl to get a better look. My heart broke. Bridget's dark lashes were fallen against white cheeks, no longer plump with the vigor of youth, but flat and bloodless. One of the earrings Elizabeth and I had given her hung from her left ear.

Her right ear lobe was torn—someone had ripped off the other earring. *The torn balloon.* A tendril of plankton graced her forehead. That detail thrust into my brain the image of the dead child, Baby Doe, whose body had floated in a stream and lodged in a stand of cattails. Feeling the onrush of panic that vision never failed to call up, I steadied myself on the back of a chair.

Not now.

I dragged myself back to the tragedy at hand. Behind me, Iris and Elizabeth were still praying. Steeling myself, I bent to study the wound on Bridget's throat: deep, about a half-inch wide. Bridget had been strangled—a garrote of some type that cut into her skin and sliced through her right carotid artery. *A garrote! An outrageous weapon to use on a defenseless girl.*

I knew I shouldn't touch Bridget, as the medical examiner had not seen her, but I did lift the blanket. Bridget was naked. Her small breasts lay vulnerable and still. I flinched, but continued my gaze downward to her sex, sparsely-haired. No bruising. Perhaps she hadn't been violated. Her hands were fisted. Did she hold a clue to her murder?

"Holy Mother of God," Elizabeth and Iris recited, "pray for us sinners..."

The kitchen chair made a scooting sound as Freddy Vale came in and dropped to his knees to join the women in prayer. Elizabeth and Iris paused to embrace him. No one was watching. I uncurled Bridget's fists and found cuts on the inside of her fingers. She had gripped the garrote at some point, in an effort to pull it away from her throat. *What happened to you, little Bridget? What kind of maniac did this?*

Choking back a sob, I drew the cover over the body. Then something caught my eye—a wild pansy blossom lodged in her hair near her torn ear. *Pansies didn't grow out of the stones near the park docks. Was Bridget killed somewhere else?*

The front door opened. An officer sent me a questioning look. He glanced at Iris, who had risen from her knees to rest in an easy chair.

"Mrs. Vale," the officer said. "We need to take your daughter's body now."

Iris jumped to her feet. "No! You can't have her!"

"We have to determine the cause of death."

"She drowned!" Iris cried. "Why else would she have been found on the rocks?"

I glanced at Iris. She had been spared the sight of the wire marks on Bridget's throat.

"It's necessary, Iris," I said. "The medical examiner will keep her only for a little while. Perhaps Freddy could go with her."

Iris looked at her husband. When he nodded, she stepped back, allowing the officers to take Bridget's body away, and then let out a scream. No one rushed to comfort her, because it wasn't the kind of scream that begged for comfort. When she finished, she said she was sorry for hurting our ears, and turned to me, asking if I wanted to see the dress and shoes she bought to see Bridget crowned.

"Now," she said, "I'll wear them to her funeral."

She took my hand and led me into the bedroom she shared with Freddy. From the closet she brought out a pair of sky-blue pumps and an ivory dress with small blue flowers.

"It's lovely," I said.

She rehung the dress and put the shoes back in the closet before we returned to the kitchen. Elizabeth had made chamomile tea, which Iris spiked with whiskey from a flask kept in her pocket. She was asleep when relations came at midnight from a neighboring village.

As Elizabeth and I prepared to go home, we noticed the crown of white roses Bridget was to have worn as May Queen lying on the sideboard. We walked past the flowers in silence and didn't speak until we reached my cottage.

I opened the front door and Elizabeth went in first. "Who would want to harm that little girl?" she asked.

I drew back the kitchen curtain and stared out in the direction of the sea. Two little girls, I thought. Who would have harmed Bridget? Who would have harmed the nameless infant I found in the creek? I wondered if some thirty years hence, people would be asking who killed poor Bridget, as I still wondered who killed Baby Doe.

CHAPTER TWO

Next day, although a cloud of grief had fallen on the village, the May Day celebration went on as planned. Another girl replaced Bridget as queen, but the maypole revelry was cut short. A few kiosks lined the streets, selling sausage rolls and lemon sodas, but many people stayed home. The Vales mourned at the neighborhood pub, waiting for release of Bridget's body so they could hold the wake.

As part of the May Day celebration, I had been asked to read a poem at the library. Unsure of which one to choose, I had submitted five to librarian Grace Devereaux. She selected the one about migration, titled, "Cork Harbor, Queenstown, 1846-1851," and it began with "Oh, Johnny, you're going away...," showed the sorrow of parting, moved on to a prayer for those who might die at sea, and spat out the six curses:

Curse the government for stealing our fertile land.
Curse the penal codes that forbade us to thrive.
Curse the water mold that turned our potatoes to pulp.
Curse the hunger that sickened and killed and filled our graves.
Curse the churches for not giving aid.
Curse the government for ignoring our plight.
The poem ended with a salute to the Irish spirit:

So, the people sing.
Hear the pipes,
a strong-voiced poet breaking into verse—
hear the fiddle and the flute,
the uilleann pipes transmuting sorrow
into songs of love
plucked from the Irish air.

Attendees were slow to leave.

An old woman in a purple hat approached me. "Sure, and you've got Irish blood in you."

"My grandmother was a Sullivan," I told her.

A man beckoned me close. "Did you know," he said, "there's a mass grave over in Cork where over nine thousand people are buried. Died of starvation or disease in The Great Hunger. Nobody knows who they were. People died, and they put the corpses outside for fear of contamination. The English army came along in wagons, took them away, and threw them into a common grave. Didn't bother to write down their names."

A stout man of sixty or so introduced himself as garda inspector, Dennis Finch. "I was moved by your poem. The famine took most of my ancestors away—either through starvation or emigration."

We fell into conversation. He was fond of Dylan Thomas's poetry and asked if I had studied his "process."

I quoted Thomas: *"Without contraries, there is no progression."*

"He believed in contraries," Finch said, "and also that he was part of the cosmos."

We were enjoying our talk, when his face suddenly sobered. "Ms. Pell, I could discuss poetry with you all day, but I must leave. I'm sure you've learned of Bridget Vale's murder. I have work to do."

"I knew Bridget," I said quickly. "She came with her mother to clean my cottage."

"Did you know her well?"

"Well enough to know that her death is a great loss."

"I'll want to talk to you later," he said, bowing his head and leaving.

I hurried after him. "Inspector Finch, did you find the pansy blossom in Bridget's hair?"

He turned to stare at me. "Pansy blossom?"

"It may have fallen when the body was moved."

"Ms. Pell, where did you see the body?"

"On the sofa at the Vale cottage."

Pale blue eyes narrowed at me through wire-rimmed glasses. "What was her body doing there? I was told it was found by the docks."

"I believe Bridget's mother directed your men to take it to the cottage."

He started to say something, then stopped.

"A grieving mother can be very persuasive," I said, trying to put in a few good words for the officers who had obviously circumvented procedure.

He turned to leave.

"Inspector," I said, "who could have committed this awful crime? Bridget surely had no enemies."

He whirled, gave me an icy look. "We've just begun our investigation. You'd be wise not to meddle. Stick to your lovely verses."

"I'm not meddling," I said. "I was fond of the girl and want to know what happened. Can you tell me what awful thing was used to garotte her?"

He stared at me coldly. Whatever rapport we had gained through a shared interest in verse seemed to vanish. I felt him calculating what advantage he might gain by including me. Though a transient member of the community, I added to the local economy. I paid rent, hired villagers for the upkeep on the cottage, and bought groceries and other sundries at village shops. My money must have spoken—or perhaps it was my poetry—for he shrugged off his irritation and answered my question.

"We haven't identified what was used."

I chanced another question. "When was she killed?"

He lowered his voice. "The medical examiner believes she died the night of April 30."

"She had been to a place where pansies were growing—maybe killed there."

"I'll have my officers check the morgue for the flower." Tipping his hat, he made his way toward the street.

As I returned to the library to fetch my handbag, someone tapped me on the shoulder. Danny Aherne. He was about my height—five-feet-eight—and when I turned, I stared straight into his eyes, which were a sparkling Prussian blue. *Scandinavian roots.*

"Ms. Pell, I wonder if you'd let me set your immigration poem to music."

His hand lingered on my shoulder, which irritated me. I pulled away. "I didn't see you in the audience, Mr. Aherne."

"I was behind a bookshelf."

"Do you have a melody in mind?" I asked.

He began to sing. "*Oh Johnny, you're going away. It's the moment...*"

The annoyance I'd felt left me. I was instantly drawn to his tune.

His tenor voice lifted. "*Before, away was just a word...*"

The heartbreak of parting pulsed in his voice and suddenly I longed to have my words put to his music. I handed him my book of verses. "I'm willing to collaborate."

We exchanged cell phone numbers.

His eyes crinkled. "When I get it right, I'll call you."

When I got home, I told Elizabeth I'd given Danny Aherne permission to use my words in song.

"You shouldn't have done that without checking with your agent," she said peevishly. "You can't let anyone use your work without paying."

I'd been excited by the notion of hearing my words in song and Elizabeth's cautionary response cooled my enthusiasm. She was probably right about the need to contact my agent, but sometimes I tired of her unsolicited advice.

When I arrived in Ireland, I'd planned to be alone. A week later, a knock came at the door and when I opened it, there was Elizabeth, standing on the porch with two bulging suitcases. Her eyes were filled with tears and her little hooked nose was red. She had been fired from her job as director of a small public library for weeding six hundred books from the collection. The library board had been infuriated by the sight of so many empty shelves. Only five feet tall and delicately formed, Elizabeth looked vulnerable and sad.

"They were so old," she said of the books, sipping the tea I served her. "With good conscience, I couldn't keep books with outdated information on the shelves. The history section contained books saying the U.S. had forty-eight states."

"After you weeded the collection, how many books were left?" I asked.

"About three thousand."

I had held my tongue. What was done was done. It wouldn't help to belabor the point.

"I reduced the collection by twenty percent," she said. "Mother is furious that I lost my job."

Only children, Elizabeth and I had lived next door to each other in St. Lucy, a hamlet south of Fennville, Indiana. Our fathers were brothers, and both were tenured professors at Midwestern University. Elizabeth's widowed mother, my Aunt Carol, was sharp-tongued but also forgiving, so I thought their tiff would blow over in time. But five weeks had passed and Elizabeth gave no indication of leaving. The firing had dealt a great blow to her self-esteem.

"I'll contact my agent tomorrow," I said.

But I knew I wouldn't. It seemed such a small matter.

***

As the week wore on, the air was thick with gossip. Bridget was such a good girl. Did she die defending her virtue? Father Malone, a pedophile priest cast out by the church, lived near the docks. Had he killed her? Four days after Bridget's body was found, garda officers learned the ex-priest had been in Belfast for two weeks, visiting his sister. The village found out about his alibi via a leak from the garda office. What about the pack of lads that gathered under the bridge to smoke hashish? Had one or all of them killed the poor lass? Or the band of Travelers that came through the previous week—perhaps one of them had noticed Bridget, in all her nubile loveliness, and come back to rape and kill her.

I sensed Bridget was not killed by a stranger. Her killing seemed up close and personal. I kept my opinion to myself for it likely meant someone in the village had killed her. As the days passed, some people began thinking as I did—that one of their own had committed murder. All sorts of questions were asked: Why was so and so prowling the street at midnight the night little Bridget was killed? What did it mean that so and so came home unexpectedly from university the morning of May 1?

So pervasive did gossip become that six days after Bridget's body was found, Judy Moriarity informed me that Father O'Neill intended to deliver a homily from the Book of James. I surprised Elizabeth by accompanying her to church that Sunday.

"Two Sundays in a row," she said. "I can't believe it. Maybe my example is rubbing off on you."

I had no intention of converting to Catholicism. I *was* interested in the general tenor of the village.

That Sunday, Father O'Neill mounted the pulpit and stared hard at his flock. "Man can tame the vilest creature," he thundered, his round face filled with rage, "*but the tongue can no man tame; it is an unruly evil, full of deadly poison.* If you've been a party to gossip, either to speak ill of your neighbor or to listen to it, you have sinned! Do not defile your neighbor with evil words!"

The most notorious gossip—Judy Moriarity—lived in the priory right under Father O'Neill's nose. With her ready smile, kind blue eyes, and curly gray hair, she appeared benign—that's what protected her. No one thought her words malicious.

Except Iris.

The priest's chastisement worked for a day or two, and then was forgotten. People continued to point fingers.

***

The garda released Bridget's body on Monday. Two days later, her parents held the wake. Elizabeth and I went to the Vale cottage to pay our respects. The cloying scent of carnations overwhelmed us as we walked through the door. I was reminded of Baby Doe's funeral—the first I ever attended.

Iris staggered toward us, a glass of whiskey in her hand, and dragged us to the casket. "Come see my little girl."

Surrounded by urns of pink carnations and roses, a waxen Bridget lay in a white satin-lined coffin. The wound on her throat was undiscernible. Mentally, I commended the mortician for his artistry. Bridget's dark hair flowed over both shoulders onto the white of her dress. In life, she had worn a pony-tail, and I was struck by the effect of her hair worn loose—she looked like a child of six or seven.

Iris clutched the side of the coffin. "My baby!"

Her sister hurried to draw her back into the fold of family gathered on the right side of the room.

"Poor soul," Elizabeth sighed.

We stood for a moment, gazing at Bridget's corpse. Elizabeth made the sign of the cross, sank to the kneeler, and prayed. I remained standing and asked the universe to be merciful to the Vales, sensing Bridget's soul had been absorbed into the ethers.

On our way to chairs at the back of the room, we passed Inspector Finch, who sat between Judy Moriarity and Grace Devereaux, his hat perched precariously on his knees. His lap was too rounded to serve as a table and the hat fell to the floor. I picked it up, handed it to him, and paused for a moment to eavesdrop.

"Do you think one of the girls Bridget beat out for May Queen killed her?" Judy whispered.

Finch glared at Judy through his pale eyes. "Are you referring to one of our young village girls? Certainly not!"

"What was poor Bridget doing in the sea?" Judy persisted. "Maybe the girls chased her off the rocks."

"That's absurd," Finch said.

I burned to talk to Finch, but he'd become impatient with Judy, so I kept quiet. Shifting his paunchy body, he stood up, motioning Elizabeth and me to pass, and then left through the front door. My cousin and I found seats on the couch next to Father O'Neill.

Elizabeth and the priest conversed: "Such a sad day." "So young." "What fate could have befallen the child?" "How will Iris ever recover?" "God is merciful."

I glanced around the room: walls, a mustard shade of yellow; soot marks above the chimney; brown carpet scuffed and threadbare by the door. A large hound lay sleeping on a sheepskin rug near the fireplace. The Vales had little money. Iris cleaned houses and Freddy was a carpenter.

Tessa McMurray, Iris' red-headed niece, passed among the mourners with a bottle of whiskey and a tray of glasses. Elizabeth and I demurred, but several accepted drinks. Iris had quieted in the bosom of her family, mostly sisters, who remained sober, but seemed tolerant of her failing. Now and then, one of the sisters went to the casket, drew out a handkerchief, and wept.

I couldn't weep for little Bridget, who had so carefully weeded my flowerbeds. Coupled with the shock of her death, so many images seared my mind that I felt on fire. When I worked beside her in the garden, we had chatted about her friends and school. I remembered her soft voice, her way of patting the earth after she'd transplanted a seedling, her scent, reminding me of fresh apples. I returned to the casket and reached to touch her hand.

Her face morphed into that of Baby Doe! I cried out, then self-consciously looked to see if anyone had heard. An elderly man, possibly thinking I cried out from grief, offered me his chair and I sat down to collect myself. More images spun off in newsreel fashion: cattails, Father, doll-like corpse, suitcase-sized casket, tiny white dress. Mother thought if I saw Baby Doe in her funeral finery, she could wipe from my memory the sight of the drenched corpse in the cattails. The mortician had painted Baby Doe's face. I recalled wondering if he had used watercolors.

Danny Aherne appeared at my side. "Are you all right, Ms. Pell?"

I brushed my hair from my face. "Yes, yes, I'm fine."

He riveted me with those dark blue eyes. "Would you like a shot of whiskey?"

"Water. Water would help."

He left and came back with a tumbler of water, which I drank. He waited for the empty glass and then took it away. I rejoined Elizabeth. Around four o'clock, we started for home.

Elizabeth stepped around a sleeping cat on the sidewalk in front of the market. "Iris's sister said more relatives are coming from Dublin. While you were talking to Mr. Aherne, I sneaked in the kitchen. The refrigerator is nearly empty. Just bottles of ale. They're going to need food."

I looked at her sharply, annoyed that she'd opened the Vales' refrigerator. Neither of us knew Iris well enough to do that.

"Why don't you organize a food drive?" I asked, trying to keep sarcasm out of my tone. Elizabeth had joined three church women's organizations since she came.

"I'll call the women in my prayer group when I get home," she said. "Oh look, Maria, the market has salmon on sale. Do you feel like salmon croquettes?"

She headed inside the market and needing to break free of her, I went down the stone stairs leading to Innis Bay, a quiet place I'd found. When I reached the bottom of the stairs, I leaned against a boulder the size of a Volkswagen and gazed out at the Irish Sea. The sun warmed my bones, consoled me. Thinking I heard wings fluttering, I looked around for birds, but none were in sight. Then I saw seagulls flying toward the eastward stones.

My annoyance with Elizabeth was minor and I could easily work through it. She wouldn't live with me forever. The only person I'd ever enjoyed living with was Mathieu, and he'd ruined that by being unfaithful.

I tried not to think of Mathieu. Too much pain.

CHAPTER THREE

The mists were thick on the morning of Bridget Vale's funeral. So bowed down with sorrow were the Vales that they could barely trudge up the stone steps of the old church. Iris's sturdy sisters supported her as she made the climb. Freddy lagged behind, as if his feet were stuck in cement. Bridget's young friends, their heads draped in black veils, sat together, their thin shoulders touching.

The sanctuary could not hold all the mourners. Many lined up in the vestibule and on the front steps. Arriving early, Elizabeth and I were able to sit inside. A fragile Margaret Mulligan came on the arm of her son, Pearce. Lina Mulligan, Pearce's Peruvian wife, and a short, dark-haired man walked a few steps behind. As Inspector Finch took a seat in front of us, he turned and nodded. Danny Aherne, dressed in a somber black suit, took a seat next to him. Finch put a comradely hand on his shoulder and released the kneeler.

Sitting in the somber church, a memory came to me: I was mowing the yard with a hand mower as Bridget, kneeling by a flower bed, pulled weeds from the nasturtiums. A large housefly, no doubt tantalized by the scent of my perspiration, landed on my arm, and I stopped mowing to swat it away. Bridget turned to smile at me and that's when I noticed a multi-colored woven bracelet on her arm.

"Bridget," I'd said, "do you have a boyfriend?"

She had blushed. "No, Ms. Pell."

"Your bracelet. Isn't it fastened with a lover's knot?"

"It's a shamrock knot," she said, turning her face away.

I never saw the bracelet again.

Now, sitting in the church sanctuary, I wondered again: did she have a boyfriend? Everyone assumed she didn't because she was so young.

A boyfriend could have lured her from her home. A boyfriend could have killed her.

Iris shrieked and the shrillness reverberated against the stone walls. Someone—I couldn't see who—quieted her and the procession began. Poor Iris. She could not contain her weeping. She wept when her darling's coffin was sprinkled with holy water at the church doors and didn't stop until the final amen.

St. Columba's stone walls had borne vibrations of grief for over five hundred years. I remembered the mournful music rising up from the beaches the night Bridget's body was found. How deep the common sorrow ran when one of the children died.

Could I write a poem about the village's grief?

Later, when Bridget's coffin was lowered into the ground, Iris tried to jump into the grave and would have succeeded if Freddy had not reached out a strong arm to restrain her. She then fell to her knees and hugged the headstone, a white marble plinth on which was carved two lines from William Blake: *Sweet babe in thy face, holy image I can trace.*

When Father O'Neill ended the service with "Go in the peace of Christ," a startling thing happened. A cuckoo perched high on an aspen called to its mate: *Cuckoo. Cuckoo. Cuckoo.* Only a few people gave the response: "Thanks be to God."

Cuckoo, cuckoo, cuckoo. A tall man picked up a stick from the grass and waved it at the bird. The bird stood its ground, uttering one more "cuckoo" before flying a way. A murmur went through the crowd. A woman laughed nervously. Realizing the rite was over, people began to move toward the sidewalk.

A white-faced Judy fell into step with Elizabeth and me. "It's an omen," she hissed. "A cuckoo in the graveyard means someone will die."

"Just superstition," I said, seeing how terrified she was. "The bird was calling to its mate."

Elizabeth broke in. "How beautiful the words of the mass were."

Back to her old self, Judy replied tartly, "If only we could have listened to Father's words without Iris making such a commotion."

"She's very upset," I said. "Her first child died, and now Bridget..."

"It's her own fault," Judy snapped. "Her drinking cost her both her children."

I turned to her. "Judy, you must never say that to Iris. It would destroy her."

It was true that Iris and Freddy had gone to the pub, leaving Bridget alone in the house. Still, the girl was thirteen—old enough to be left alone for a few hours.

But what had Judy meant by saying the drinking had cost her both children?

Though I kicked myself for encouraging Judy's talebearing, I asked. "How did Iris's drinking cause the death of her first child?"

"She's careless when she drinks."

"How did her carelessness result in her first child's death?"

Judy ignored my question. "Did you notice the headstone? Carved in only a few days. Margaret Mulligan paid for it." She gave me a knowing look. "What do you think it cost to have that verse carved on it so quick?"

"I can't guess."

"Margaret paid a pretty penny, you can be sure. Iris had wanted to put up a stone with a picture of Bridget in her May Queen finery, but Margaret talked her out of it. I'm glad she did. I hate to walk through the cemetery and see those headstones with pictures of the dead. It feels spooky with their eyes on you."

We continued up the cobblestoned street leading to the priory. I did not ask again how Iris was responsible for the death of her first child.

Judy put her plump arms around Elizabeth and me to gather us close. "Inspector Finch called on the Father early this morning. You'll never guess what about."

Elizabeth frowned and bit her lip. I waited.

"He wanted to know if Bridget had confessed anything that might give a clue to her death."

"I'm sure Bridget wasn't involved in anything sinful," Elizabeth protested. "She was an innocent young girl."

"Oh, I know she was a saint," Judy said quickly, "but the garda was asking, which must mean they know something..."

"It could also mean the Inspector has no idea who caused her death and is simply asking questions," I said.

"Of course, the Father said he could divulge nothing he'd heard in the confessional, but then the inspector asked if he could reveal such information to her parents, since she was underage."

"What did Father O'Neill say?" Elizabeth asked.

"He said it made no difference who asked him, his lips were sealed."

We had stopped in the middle of the street. A car horn honked and we moved to the sidewalk.

"Then the inspector wanted to know if Father O'Neill thought any of the young girls who were competing for May Queen could have killed Bridget," Judy went on. "Father was firm that they could not have done her harm."

I shivered, remembering an Indiana case in the 1970s, where a twelve-year-old girl was tortured and killed by four other girls. Jealousy was the motive. In asking the question, Finch was covering all bases.

A tall, sparrow-faced woman with wild black hair stepped around us. She was dressed in a long dirndl skirt with a gray shawl thrown over her thin shoulders. I noticed her aura: bright red.

Judy scowled at the woman's back. "Was she at the funeral? That's Deirdre O'Malley. She's the priestess of that terrible Druid sect that meets in the woods."

I looked after Deirdre O'Malley with interest. The name, Deirdre, carried multiple meanings: rage, melancholy, or fear. *Deirdre of the Sorrows* was a mythical tale of a beautiful woman who grieved for a murdered lover.

"Stay away from her," Judy warned. "She casts spells on people. She put one on poor Brendan Calloway."

I looked at her quickly, intending to ask what kind of spell had been cast on my landlord, but she was hurrying up the priory steps. Elizabeth rolled her eyes, telling me that superstition was alive and well in Coomara. We walked on to the cottage.

"Whew!" I said. "Judy has exhausted me. What a font of information. Or misinformation."

Elizabeth was in a huffy mood. "Father O'Neill should remind her that discretion is part of her job."

Surely the priest was aware that Judy spread rumors in the village. He must have known he could not force her to hold her tongue.

I wondered how I might meet Deirdre O'Malley.

Upon returning home, I climbed the stairs to my study, intending to return to an article about the *Leabhar Gabhaile,* or *Book of Invasions*, written by seventh century monks, which combined legends, myths, biblical references, and oral histories of pre-Christian Irish people. According to the holy men, the first Irish were descendants of Noah's son, Japheth.

I'd left the article on my desk and sat down to pick up the story of the Tuatha Dé Danann (tribe of goddess Dana or Danu) when the Gaels came ashore. But then I remembered Bridget's woven bracelet. It could be a vital clue. Should I inform Inspector Finch about the bracelet? It could have been a token of friendship, given to her by another girl. Hadn't she said it was a shamrock knot? I wasn't able to tell what kind of knot it was. Or did she have a boyfriend? Perhaps Iris knew. Still, to disturb her so soon after the burial might be unkind. I debated with myself for a few seconds, then threw caution to the wind and headed for the Vale cottage.

Iris's pretty niece, Tessa, answered the door when I knocked. The family was just sitting down to a meal provided by one of the women's groups. My blue bowl was on the table—Elizabeth had contributed a fruit salad. Iris sat on the sofa in the front room, looking a picture of agony, and I wondered at her thoughts. Two children dead; Judy said both had died because of their mother's carelessness.

As usual, Iris' red hair was disheveled and I could see the top of a flask protruding from her skirt pocket. Her slender arms were wrapped around a framed photograph. I sat down beside her on the couch that had held Bridget's corpse only a few days before. Iris thrust out the photograph for me to see. Posed in front of the cottage, Bridget wore a long-sleeved, virginal white dress, a crown of roses, and the earrings Elizabeth and I gave her. The expression on her face was one of immense pleasure—lips parted in expectation, eyes sparkling. Beneath the long sleeve on her left wrist, the multi-colored bracelet peeped out.

"Bridget was wearing her bracelet," I said quietly.

"One of her friends gave it to her," Iris said. "I said it was too garish for her white dress, but she thought the sleeve would hide it."

"Where is the bracelet now?" I asked.

"I haven't seen it."

"Could Bridget have had a boyfriend?" I asked cautiously.

Iris turned defiant eyes toward me. "No, of course not. She was only thirteen and happy with her da and me. She knew we loved her."

"Never was there a better loved girl," I agreed.

"When me and Freddy went down to Connor's for a pint, I told her to stay home. If only she had minded what I said..."

I looked at her sharply. "Had Bridget asked to go somewhere?"

"She wanted to go out with her chums to see a film, but I was afraid that Tim Hawkins would be hanging around. He's sixteen—too old for Bridget."

"Did you tell this to Inspector Finch?"

"I did. Me and Freddy left about half-past six. Bridget promised to stay home and clean up the dishes in the kitchen."

"And did she do the dishes?"

"Every single dish was washed, wiped, and put back in the cupboard. The lights were off when we got home. Her door was closed and we thought she was in bed asleep."

The lights were off. Did that mean Bridget intentionally left the house and meant to return before her parents got back from the pub?

"When did you notice she was missing?"

"We slept in late the next day, Sunday. Didn't go to mass." Iris made the sign of the cross. "Bridget's door was closed when we got up, and we thought she'd gone off to church. Later, I took laundered clothes to her room and found nothing amiss." Her voice broke. "When she didn't come home after church, I wasn't worried. Oftentimes, she went to a friend's house to listen to music or...or...talk."

She began to cry, and I embraced her. One of Iris's sisters approached, insisting that I sit down and eat, and pulled Iris to the table. I had a bowl of tomato soup and listened as Iris spoke of Bridget's fondness for gardening. From time to time, she turned to me for verification. Wasn't her girl a wonder with the roses? Didn't she get the daffodils to grow when they were sulky? Yes, and yes again. Little Bridget was truly a wonder.

After a while, I took my leave. As I passed through the front room, Tessa McMurray was standing by an end table, holding Bridget's photograph. Her face was blotchy from weeping. I didn't know the girl well enough to put my arm around her, yet hated to pass by without offering some form of comfort.

I put my hand gently on her shoulder. "I'm so sorry, Tessa."

"We were like sisters."

"I see she's wearing a woven bracelet," I said. "Did you give it to her?"

"No," Tessa said curtly.

I sensed she did not approve of the person who gave Bridget the bracelet. Did I dare press her for the name of that person? I looked at the set of her jaw and decided not to. Giving her shoulder a pat, I left.

Inspector Finch needed to know about the bracelet. I hurried home and called him. He was in a receptive mood, saying I had been on his mind. He wanted to know if Bridget had confided anything to me while working in the garden.

"She spoke about what she was studying. A time or two, she mentioned soccer."

"Did she drop any clues about her mates?" he asked.

"She mentioned a couple of girls—Madelyn and her cousin, Tessa."

"We've spoken to them."

"Are you aware that Bridget wore a woven bracelet fastened with a lover's knot?" I asked.

"No," he said, his voice perking up with interest. "Who gave it to her?"

"She wouldn't say, but it was meaningful enough that she was photographed in her May Queen finery, wearing the bracelet."

"I'll ask her mother about it," he said.

"It is possible Iris doesn't know who gave it to Bridget, but I think Tessa McMurray does."

"I'll send someone to question her again."

Finch thanked me and ended the call.

Did the sixteen-year-old boy Iris mentioned gave Bridget the bracelet? What was his name? *Tim Hawkins.*

Elizabeth came into the room, carrying a bouquet of larkspur. "Do you suppose Bridget was mixed up with those teenagers who gather outside the Green Mountain Café?"

"What do you know about the Green Mountain Café?"

"Only what Judy tells me. It's a hangout for teenagers. The garda patrol it for drug dealers." She laid the flowers on the counter. "Still, Bridget was so virtuous, I'm sure she never went near the place. She'd have more sense."

I looked at Elizabeth. "It's hard to say. I hope not, but with teenagers..."

"You never know."

"Maybe I'll take a bicycle ride past the café later this evening."

Elizabeth didn't comment. She went outside to prune the pansies in the flowerbox beneath the kitchen windows.

Pansies.

The pansy blossom in Bridget's hair. I had seen wild pansies growing in profusion in the hills. Where had her killer taken her?

CHAPTER FOUR

After dinner, sufficient daylight remained to bike to the Green Mountain Café. The restaurant sat on the eastern rim of the village in the middle of a row of store fronts. Its sign, shaped like a mountain and inset with candle-shaped lights, resembled a branchless Christmas tree. Riding up, I looked through the front window—the restaurant was filled with patrons, most appearing to be young working people. Fastening my bike to a rack, I went in, took a booth near the window, and inhaled the smell of fried fish. A slender redhead with a catsup-smeared apron tied around her waist approached and handed me a menu. Since I had eaten with Elizabeth an hour earlier, I ordered only a cup of tea and a slice of custard pie.

My order came. The custard was watery, but I forked it down. Outside, teenagers gathered in the glow of the twinkling mountain. Dark clothes. Cigarettes. Lank hair on the girls. Byronic curls on the boys. Not Bridget's crowd, I hoped.

One of the girls was speaking. What was the topic of the moment? Rage at the establishment? Misogyny? Unemployment? Ennui? A tall boy in his mid-teens stepped forward with authority. As he moved into the periphery of the lit mountain, his features came into focus: shaved head, earring, the beginning of a Mephistophelian beard. He wore a red and black Notre Dame jacket. Was he American?

The girl finished speaking and the bearded teen took her place. I drained my tea cup, paid at the counter, and went outside, spending enough time fumbling with my bicycle lock to ascertain that the young man was an American with a Midwestern accent similar to mine.

Spouting a mixture of Allen Ginsberg and Shakespeare, he seemed high on something.

"Who killed the pork chops?" he wailed, flailing his right arm. "Forsooth, foul night-walking cat, he doth but dally while in his holdfast foot the weak mouse panteth..."

As I stifled a giggle, a pretty brunette in a yellow dress moved within his radiance and gazed adoringly at him. On her wrist was a woven bracelet just like Bridget's.

The young man turned to her. "But hark! It's the fucking dawn, I say. It is gyroscoping over yon mountain with the day between its teeth..."

A boy in a gray hoodie called out, "What a bloody blow off."

A titter in the crowd. Someone cried, "Eejit!" A boy carrying a gym bag threw a shoe at the poet. Shrieks, laughter. A male voice: "Go home, Yank! We've got our own poets!"

The American glared at his audience. "I'm not going to waste my time on you fuckers. Fucking, stupid Irish. Why did it take you so long to throw off the Brits?"

Whoever this kid was, he knew how to make enemies. I tensed, wondering if a fight would break out. Fortunately, no. He held out his hand to the pretty girl and she took it. They disappeared into the trees at the far end of the parking lot.

Steadying my bike, I turned to the girl nearest me. "What an interesting poet. Does he have a name?"

She brushed blond hair out of her eyes. "Tim Hawkins. He's from across the pond."

The Tim Hawkins whom Iris Vale had forbidden Bridget to see.

"Does he come here often?" I asked.

"He's here on Saturday nights...sometimes mid-week like now."

I straightened my bike. "Did Bridget Vale come here?"

"The girl who was killed?"

I nodded.

She was about to say more when a youth in a ragged tee shirt nudged her. "No talking to coppers."

I laughed. "Don't mistake me for a policewoman. I'm a teacher."

"Oh yeah? I don't remember seeing you at school."

"I teach in America."

"She was asking about Bridget Vale," the girl told him.

The youth addressed me. "Why are you asking about Bridget Vale if you're not a copper?"

"She was my friend."

He muttered something I couldn't make out. Two older teens, garbed in black jeans and tees, approached. Some of the young people dispersed, but others, including the blonde and her tattered-shirt friend, joined the newcomers. They headed for the trees.

Drugs.

I went inside the cafe and beckoned to the waitress with the soiled apron. "Did Bridget Vale come here?"

Her green eyes gave me a level look. "As I told the garda officer, Bridget came here sometimes—not often."

"Did she hang around Tim Hawkins?"

"I think she had a crush on him, because she would ask if he'd been here. I don't know how he felt about her. I only saw her with him once."

"When was that?"

"About a week before she was killed. Can't be exact."

I thanked the waitress and went back outside. Black clouds were pressing in. I needed to hurry home while there was still visibility. As it was, I could barely see the edge of the road. A hare darted out and nearly sent me tumbling off my bicycle. A garda car passed, going toward the Green Mountain Café. Perhaps someone from the café had called them. I hoped they would catch the drug dealers.

Reaching my cottage, I steered the bicycle inside the gate and sat in a wicker chair on the porch. The village was quiet, the street lights dim in the heavy mist. Seaward, the foghorn sounded, warning vessels away from the rocks. The hum of television voices emanated from inside. Elizabeth would be hooking a rug and watching a BBC detective program.

In time, I told myself, Inspector Finch would solve Bridget's murder. Why did I feel so impatient, so invested? It wasn't only because I had known and loved Bridget—it was also because of Baby Doe. The two deaths seemed linked. I didn't know why.

A man coughed—Brendan Calloway, my scruffy neighbor and landlord. I shrank back against the chair, somehow feeling violated. Had he heard me put away the bicycle and climb the steps to the porch? The fog was so thick I couldn't see him, but I smelled his pipe tobacco—a fruity vanilla aroma. I sat still. He coughed again.

"Fog's a little dense for bike riding," he said. "You might get hit by a car."

I was about to reply that I had reflectors on my bike but checked myself in time. Brendan wanted to converse. I wouldn't encourage him.

"Reflectors are of little use when the fog's so thick," he added.

Was he a mind-reader? If so, I hadn't picked him up on my radar, as I usually did when in the company of fellow sensitives. Regardless, it irritated me that he seemed to sense my thoughts.

What did I know about Brendan Calloway? Tall and craggy like the cliffs, he had shaggy black hair and a brooding expression—rather like Lawrence Olivier as Heathcliff. His clothes hung on him, as if he'd recently lost weight. He kept a silver Viksund motor boat, called the *Dusky Hawk*, moored at the dock below his property. He seldom used it. He had asked me out once, but I said I was too busy for dating.

Brendan was part of the O'Coilean clan on his mother's side, Judy had said, which gave him kinship with patriot Michael Collins and a superiority complex. He'd made his money in real estate—didn't have to go off to work each day as others did.

According to Judy, Deirdre O'Malley had put a curse on him. She hadn't been specific about the nature of the curse—something about stolen sheep and having to wander in the darkness until the curse was lifted.

A thought chilled my brain. Had Brendan spied on Bridget when she labored in the garden? Was he a sexual predator? I went over all the transactions I'd had with him. Had he given any sign of perversion? I couldn't say. He was odd, but so were many people—including myself.

I went inside, letting the door slam.

Why did I let the door slam? Did I want Brendan to know I had been on the porch, but was unwilling to talk to him? Was I trying to erect a barrier he could understand? Belatedly, I realized he might take the door slam as a kind of flirtation.

Elizabeth was engrossed in her television show so I went upstairs to bed.

***

The next day after breakfast, I sat down at my desk and became absorbed in the tale of Fer Fidail, a Druid with supernatural powers. A Celtic chieftain fell in love with a beautiful maiden, who was kept under guard by a group of women. The chieftain sent Fer Fidail to kidnap her, so Fer disguised himself as a woman and entered the bedchamber, staying there for three days. After casting a spell over the maiden, he carried her to a river where he left her sleeping on the bank while he searched for a boat. A wave rushed in and drowned her. The chieftain had Fir Fidail killed as an act of revenge.

A line from an Eavan Boland poem flashed into my mind: *...myth is the wound we leave in the time we have...*

Bridget's death was a wound on the village. I felt a poem spike within me, and picked up my pen, hoping words would follow. Instead, dreadful images rushed at me. Bridget's torn ear. Her bloody throat. Clothes torn from her body. Closing my eyes, I envisaged the Vale door, closed and locked, and Iris and Freddy heading off to the pub. A dark figure watched them leave. Then...then, someone must have persuaded Bridget to come out. Had her killer been in a rage then? The torn ear, the deep cuts to the throat indicated rage. What had Bridget done to provoke such anger? Had she withheld sex?

I went for a walk—not that it helped. Thoughts of Bridget leapt in my brain like sparks in a brush fire. It was mid-afternoon, and there was traffic in the streets. Odor of diesel fuel. Sunshine. Inside a playground, school children played. Only two or three years ago, Bridget had climbed on the monkey bars, swung in the swings, played tag with her friends.

I walked on. An elderly man with a cane exited the library. He dropped a book. I picked it up and handed it to him. He thanked me and offered me a stick of gum, smelling of peppermint. Bridget had favored gum with a fruity smell. I took the gum, thanked the man. Passing two pubs, I gagged at the smell of cigarette smoke. Most evenings, Iris and Freddy Vale habituated the pubs.

At the end of the block, I climbed down the stone steps to Innis Bay. The breath of the sea was invigorating. Waves coiled like frolicking dolphins against the stone islets, and I was reminded of the children on the playground and Bridget. She had walked this sea walk, alone or with her friends. Perhaps Iris and Freddy, her parents, had also walked with her here.

From what I knew of Bridget, she had lived a happy life—although her parents' drinking surely had troubled her—but maybe it was all she had ever known. I had not seen sadness in her face, as I often saw on those of lost teenagers in alleyways, street corners, places they congregated to set themselves apart.

But she had frequented the Green Mountain Café and she had a crush on an American youth who wanted to look like Satan.

Her body was found only a quarter mile from where I stood. Had she rendezvoused with friends on the shore? Or with Tim Hawkins? Was Bridget not the pious girl we all thought she was?

Suddenly, I heard fiddle music—the notes of an old tune buried deep in memory— "She Moves Through the Fair." I looked around, but I was alone. The music was in my head, and I followed each note with the lyrics: A man watched the ghost of the girl he intended to marry walk through the stalls at a fair. She vanished. He could only wonder what happened to her.

Just like Bridget.

The song finished, then started again, louder. The fiddle twanged, screeched, rasped. Sitting on a bench, I put my hands to my ears. The discordant tune went on and on, then stopped. Spirits were speaking to me. Because she was so recently dead, I didn't think Bridget could be among them—she wouldn't know how to break through the ethers to reach me. But I heard the message: spirits were telling me something was dreadfully awry in Coomara.

And they expected me to do something about it.

I went to see Inspector Finch.

***

He was in his office, hunched over a stack of papers.

"Inspector," I said, "I've come to see if you've made any progress on the Vale case."

"How is that any of your business, Ms. Pell?"

I had steeled myself for his curtness. "It wouldn't be if I hadn't known her well."

"This is garda business." He raised his head to peer over the rim of his glasses. "We don't ask private citizens for help unless absolutely necessary."

Sensing an opening, I slid onto the chair beside his desk. "I have special gifts that would help. I'm trained to be observant. Have you found out who gave Bridget the bracelet?"

"No."

"Could it be Tim Hawkins, the boy whom Iris had forbade Bridget to see?"

"We've talked to the Hawkins boy. He says he didn't know Bridget well. He has an alibi for the night of April 30—said he was at home with his aunt. She confirms the alibi."

"The waitress at the Green Mountain Café said she saw Tim and Bridget together about a week before she was murdered. She said Bridget often came in to ask if Tim had been there."

Finch waved a dismissive hand. "Yes, I know. It seems to be a case of a young girl having a crush on an older boy."

"Recently, I saw a girl with Tim. She wore the same type of bracelet."

"Hmm," Finch said. "My granddaughter wears a woven bracelet. She's seven. She didn't get it from Hawkins."

My eyes roved around the room. Tan walls, window looking out onto the street, ivy plant in need of watering.

"Have you worked out what kind of garrote was used?" I asked.

He stared at me. Had I gone too far? Would he tell me to leave?

"I saw the puncture wounds in her throat," I went on. "Something other than a wire garotte was used."

Finch pushed his chair back from the desk and stood. "We're working to identify the murder weapon."

I tried another tack. "Iris said Bridget wanted to go to a film with her friends the night she was killed. I'm sure you questioned her friends..."

"Her friends said they didn't see her that night."

"Perhaps they're not telling the truth. Have you considered that someone might have phoned Bridget to ask her to come out of the house?"

Finch walked around the corner of his desk. "You would be surprised at how efficient we are, Ms. Pell. We checked her phone. No record of such a call."

He was about to usher me out of his office. I pressed my back against the chair. "Was Bridget abused...sexually?"

"It's time for you to go. I understand your interest in the case stems from affection for the victim and her family, but you must leave the police work to us."

I stood. "Was she raped, Inspector? I really need to know."

He paused, then said, "As far as the medical examiner could tell, no."

At least the poor girl had not had to endure rape.

He motioned toward the door. I left.

***

When I got home, I reported to Elizabeth that Bridget had gone to the Green Mountain Café.

"The waitress thought she had a crush on an American named Tim Hawkins," I added.

Elizabeth sat for a long time without moving. "Young people," she said. "It's so hard to keep them safe. I'm glad I never married and had children."

I'd not wanted children either, preferring to chart an academic life path, and I had gotten as far as a few paragraphs on my dissertation, a study of folk poets in mid-America, when my poetry began to receive recognition. The PhD took a backseat. Someday, I hoped to complete it. The university benefitted from having an award-winning poet on the faculty, and encouraged my efforts, understanding it took time and mood to compose poetry.

"I wonder if it will dawn on Iris that she spent too much time at the pub," Elizabeth said.

"Freddy, too."

"I suppose, but it's the mother..."

She didn't finish because she knew my sentiments about men sharing family responsibilities. Elizabeth was old school. Aunt Carol had been a submissive wife who came into her own only after her husband died. My mother had been a feminist from birth and my father had respected her beliefs.

The newspaper lay on the kitchen table. I glanced at the headline: "Sex Trafficking Reaches Dublin." A letter lay beside the newspaper.

"What's this?" I asked.

"Oh, yes," Elizabeth said. "It's from Mathieu. It came in the post today."

I'd never received a letter from Mathieu. He usually communicated via email, texting, or phone. Perhaps he thought I'd soften if he went to the trouble of selecting stationery (cream vellum), penning (rollerball, black ink) his thoughts, and going to the post office (two blocks from his office) to buy an overseas stamp, I'd look upon him with more favor. I slit open the envelope. The first five paragraphs contained declarations of eternal love. My stomach churned. On the second page, he wrote that he was coming to Ireland in a week to participate in an archeological dig near Coomara. Did I have a spare room?

Anger engorged my belly, charged up my esophagus, and reddened my cheeks. *Did I have a spare room!*

"Mathieu's coming to Ireland," I said, trying to keep calm.

Elizabeth didn't know about Mathieu's infidelity and I didn't plan to discuss it with her.

"Would you like me to move to the inn?" she asked.

"He won't stay here. He can go to the inn."

"Shall I make a reservation for him?"

Elizabeth had always favored Mathieu.

"No."

"You'll need to email him the telephone number for the inn."

How had Mathieu wangled a place on an excavation team in Ireland? I read on. His close friend, Drago Zeller, a noted archaeologist, had found room for him on the team when another member had a heart attack.

I went upstairs and took a shower to cool off. Mathieu would stay at the inn and go about his business at the dig. I could keep him from barging into my life. Changing into a nightgown, I got into bed with a five-hundred-page book on Irish myths. Elizabeth tapped on my door.

"Yes," I said.

She came in to show me a pansy she had picked in the garden. "See its little face. Bridget gave us these pansies. She said she dug up the shoots near the old abbey."

Her remarks hung in the air and then stung me like a wasp. "I'm going to the abbey tomorrow," I said.

Perhaps that was where Bridget had been killed.

CHAPTER FIVE

Rising early, I tried not to awaken Elizabeth as I prepared for a visit to the abbey ruins, but in my still-drowsy state, I dropped the hairbrush on the tiled bathroom floor. Soon after, I heard my cousin moving around in her bedroom. Drat! I'd hoped to slip out without waking her.

"Maria," she called out. "Are you going to the abbey to look for the pansies? I'd like to see where Bridget got the shoots."

"Why do you want to do that?" I hadn't told her about the pansy lodged in Bridget's hair.

Elizabeth came to my bathroom door. "I can't explain why. Maybe to feel close to her."

A half-hour later, my cousin and I set off on foot for the abbey ruins, which were a mile away in the foothills of the Wicklow Mountains. The mists were just lifting, leaving a cool dampness against our skin. To our right rose the mountains—purple, against a hazy sky. All around us, life was stirring—forests becoming visible, birds chirping, small animals bustling about.

"A beautiful morning," Elizabeth said.

The sprawling Abbey of St. Columba had been constructed in the eleventh century. Roofless, the gray and tan stone walls still stood, their lancet windows providing a view of the sea. Near the entrance, we encountered a massive Celtic cross that had borne the onslaughts of a thousand storms. To the right of the cloister court were the nave and chapel, and ahead, a stone bridge crossed a placid stream. The abbot's house, great hall, and kitchen were across the bridge. A stone tower stood outside the walls.

"When the monks sighted Norsemen," I said to Elizabeth, "they hid their treasures at the top of the tower."

"Wouldn't the Norsemen climb up and get it?"

"There's room for only one man at the top. Whoever was up there would block the door with something heavy."

"People are inventive," Elizabeth said.

Before entering the abbey, we went around to the back and found a field of wild pansies.

Elizabeth stooped to pick one. "Bridget must have taken the shoots from this patch."

The pansies grew in profusion with other wildflowers. I kept my eyes open for areas that were crushed or torn from a struggle Bridget might have had with her killer, but the plants seemed undisturbed. I noticed tracks of a vehicle that had pulled onto the green and parked. The grass had been wet and the wheels left impressions. Maintenance, I supposed. Someone had to mow.

But maybe not. The killer could have brought Bridget to the abbey in a vehicle and parked it on the grass. Perhaps Bridget had gotten away and her killer had run after her, capturing her in the patch of pansies, and that was how a blossom became lodged in her hair.

Was I standing at her murder site?

Elizabeth's voice broke my concentration. "I want to see the chapel."

We went inside, walked the length of the nave, and entered the small chapel. Immediately, my nerves jangled. Here holy men had bared their consciences to God. What torments of the soul they had endured! I felt their tensions as they had labored to mold themselves into saints.

"Does this place affect you, Elizabeth?"

She glanced at me. "Not particularly. I can see it's old."

"Can you feel the suffering that took place here?"

"No, Maria. Thankfully, you're the one with the sixth sense." She shivered. "I really don't appreciate old sites like you do. They remind me of loss."

So great was the holy men's distress that my heart began to hammer in my chest. I left Elizabeth in the chapel, went to the cloister court, and leaned against a wall to recover my equilibrium. I had just calmed myself when Elizabeth cried out.

"Maria!"

I ran back to the chapel.

Elizabeth was standing near a small stone cross. "Look!"

Wedged on the floor between two stones was Bridget's lost earring. A deafening roar sounded in my ears. *Bridget died in this place.*

Elizabeth knelt to pick up the earring.

"No," I said. "Leave it where it is. I'm calling Inspector Finch."

I dialed the garda number on my cell phone. Finch wasn't in, but I spoke to Sergeant Mary Potts, telling her what Elizabeth had found, and she said she'd come straight away. While we waited in the chapel, I looked for traces of blood and found a large splotch on the wall.

Sergeant Potts and two officers arrived and cordoned off the abbey. Elizabeth and I were not invited to stay.

"Was Bridget killed in the chapel?" Elizabeth asked as we started home.

"I think so."

She bit her lip. "What a dreary place to die."

We trudged through the meadow to the roadway.

***

Upon returning to the cottage, Elizabeth hurried off to a luncheon appointment with women from one of her church groups. I warned her not to tell anyone about finding the earring. She was usually discreet.

My mind fizzed with questions. Why was Bridget killed at the abbey ruins? Had she been a human sacrifice? Was someone spitting in the eye of the Catholic Church by killing a young virgin who was to be honored as May Queen? I looked at my watch. Ten o'clock. Too early to call Inspector Finch and ask if his officers had discovered anything I missed.

My cell phone rang. I answered without looking at caller ID.

"Darling!" Mathieu said. "Did you get my letter?"

His mellifluous voice held the rhythms of Africa. In the beginning, I'd been seduced by his warm tone, which called up the languid rivers of a continent. He had other qualities as well: intelligence, kindness, an amazing physique, long-lashed brown eyes. Women sought his attention in droves.

"I did," I said. "About the matter of where you're lodging, I have no room for you, but there's an inn here in the village."

I gave him the inn's telephone number.

A sigh. "Maria, when are you going to forgive me?"

I didn't respond.

"Maria, are you there?"

"Yes, I'm here. You sound like a broken record—asking the same thing over and over."

"We've never had an honest talk about what happened."

What he said was true.

"Tell me about the dig," I said.

Another sigh. "A farmer turned up some trinkets near a place called Ballygosteen. I'm part of Drago's team, which will examine them."

Ballygosteen was only a half-hour's drive from the village.

"How old are the trinkets?" I asked.

"They're from the Neolithic Period—9000 to 3000 (BCE). Perhaps you'd like to come on the dig. We'd let you hold the artifacts. Your study is about prehistoric Ireland. You might find inspiration for a poem."

"How did you find out about my study?"

"It was announced in the university newsletter. Think of it, Sweetness. You could hold in your hand a Celtic maiden's bone and feel her energy."

It *was* an idea. "We'll see."

"I'll be there the day after tomorrow. Can't wait to see you, Maria."

Day after tomorrow.

I tensed, not eager to explore my feelings for Mathieu. He and I had managed to navigate through his immigration problems and doctoral thesis, not to mention our interracial relationship, but none of the lessons learned from these ordeals kept him from falling for another woman or enabled me to forgive him when he did.

The woman with whom he had strayed—Zara—was still employed at the university but had moved to a different department. She reminded me of Mathieu's ex-wife: statuesque, copper-toned skin, green eyes. If that was the type of woman he was attracted to, what had he ever seen in me? I was five feet eight, weighed one hundred and twenty pounds, and had pale skin that burned when too long in the sun.

"How long will you be in Ireland?" I asked.

"Depends on what we find."

A lull in the conversation. He shared gossip about people we both knew at the university (not mentioning Zara), and spoke of the May weather in central Indiana and the perennials coming up in beds I'd planted in our front yard.

"When I arrive in Coomara, will you have dinner with me?" he asked.

"I don't think so. I'm busy with work."

"You can't keep avoiding me. We need to talk—if for no other reason than to determine what we'll do with the townhouse if we split up permanently. Our furnishings. Our cemetery plots on the banks of the Wabash..."

"We decided against the cemetery plots."

"I bought them anyway," he said. "It's such a beautiful setting."

My head began to ache. Dividing everything seemed like so much work.

"Will I stand out like a jammed thumb in your quaint little village, Maria?"

Mathieu occasionally confused American idioms. Once, I found it charming. Now I suspected he did it to get attention.

"Sore thumb," I corrected. "If you mean are there other blacks here, there are a few immigrants from Africa. I believe they are Nigerian."

"Brothers," he said. "Close to my Togo."

"They go to the Catholic Church."

Mathieu, if he practiced religion, was an animist, believing that creatures, plants, and inanimate objects, like rocks, had souls. He kept a block of Togolese granite the size of a clay brick on his desk at work, claiming it held the spirit of a harvest god.

Having run out of things to talk about, we said goodbye.

***

At noon, I went to the garda station to speak to Inspector Finch, figuring his officers had had sufficient time to investigate what was probably the murder scene and report to him. He was in his office. I rapped on his door and he invited me in.

Removing his glasses, he rubbed the bridge of his nose. "Ah, Ms. Pell. I expected you. What were you and your cousin doing at the abbey?"

I took a seat next to his desk. "Elizabeth remembered Bridget had brought us pansies from the abbey. Since I'd found a pansy blossom in her hair, I wondered if her killer had taken her there."

"We're grateful you found the earring," he said. "It matches the one she was wearing when her body was found."

"Elizabeth and I gave her those earrings for her birthday."

Finch carefully put on his glasses. "St. Bridget's eternal flame."

"We were thinking of her May Day costume."

"I'm sure you saw the blood stain on the chapel wall," he said. "Though with an artery severed, there should have been more blood."

"Bridget's killer might have used a tarp to cover the ground."

"Yes, we've thought of that. We are proceeding on the assumption she was killed there. Do you have an opinion on why her killer took her to the abbey?"

I was only too glad to share my suppositions. "The abbey is out-of-the-way, sure to be empty of tourists at night. He—I'm assuming her killer was male—took her into the chapel, the most sacred part of the abbey. A garotte was used. He wanted to pull her close as he killed her. There's something sexual there."

Finch stared at me with his small eyes. "Something sexual, you say?"

"Perhaps."

"The medical examiner said she wasn't violated."

"There are other ways of violating women besides penetration," I said. "She was nude."

"We didn't find her clothing at the murder site."

"Then she may have been naked when her killer dragged her into the chapel," I said. "Did you find anything besides the blood and the earring?"

"We know a vehicle was parked on the green outside the abbey. We checked with the grounds keeper and he said he never parked there."

"I was also reminded of ritual human sacrifice."

The corners of Finch's mouth twitched. "Our Druids are tame," he said. "Mostly plump little women dancing naked under a full moon."

"Judy Moriarity said Deirdre O'Malley is a Druid priestess."

"She is, but she'd never be a party to violence. Deirdre is a learned woman, speaks seven languages. Sometimes we ask her to interpret."

"Why do you think Bridget's body was moved to the rocks?" I asked.

"Perhaps the killer wanted it found quickly."

"Or perhaps someone didn't want it found in the abbey," I said.

We sat, not speaking. I was thinking of reasons the killer didn't want the body found in the abbey. Perhaps after committing the murder, the killer realized he had profaned a holy place. But then why had he taken her to the abbey in the first place? Had he not meant to kill her?

Finch's right hand lifted and fell on a stack of papers. I realized he had no more time to give me, but I needed to ask a final question before I left.

"Did you ask Tessa McMurray if Tim Hawkins gave Bridget her woven bracelet?"

"Tessa said she didn't know who gave her the bracelet."

I thanked Finch and left. Feeling at a loss about what to do next, I wandered into Miss Molly's Tea Room for lunch. The room was wallpapered in pink roses, which matched the tile on the floor. White eyelet curtains hung at the windows, and the tables, chairs, and booths were all painted springtime green.

I took a booth near the back, looked at the menu, and tried to decide between a hamburger and a fried pike sandwich. The waitress, an older woman wearing a hairnet, came to my table and I ordered the pike, a tomato salad, and a pot of tea.

"We have a lovely butterscotch pie," she said.

Sugar was my downfall. I ordered the pie.

I was reading an email on my cellphone when a voice called my name. I looked up. Pearce Mulligan stood in front of me. He was at least six feet four, with an angular face, drooping eyelids, and a large, ruddy nose—the latter of which I attributed to excessive drink. Parted in the middle, his graying hair swooped down to partially conceal large ears. He reminded me of a shaggy ram I'd seen in Switzerland. I sensed he was a weak, silly man.

"Ms. Pell," he said, raising my hand to his thin lips, "so good to see you. I hear you're doing a study of our Celtic heritage."

I was about to answer when Lina Mulligan sidled over to whisper in her husband's ear.

Mulligan looked at me. "Lina says our table is ready. Someday, I must tell you the history of the O'Maolagain family. My forefathers fought to..."

"Pearce," Lina interrupted. "You mustn't get started on the Mulligans. We have to eat quickly before we leave for London."

"Another time, Ms. Pell." Pearce patted my hand and left with his wife.

As husband and wife walked away, I admired Lina's taut derriere. She had a model's walk, one foot planted in front of the other. With her outrageously high-wedge sandals, she was nearly as tall as her husband. She had to be at least twenty years younger than he. How had they met?

The door burst open and three schoolgirls about Bridget's age came in with backpacks. They were in a jolly mood, smothering giggles behind their hands. Removing their backpacks, they selected a table, and ordered soft drinks. One wore a woven bracelet. She was the dark-haired girl who had gone off with Tim Hawkins at the Green Mountain Café.

The waitress brought my food and I ate slowly, watching the girls. They communicated in whispers, no doubt suspicious of adults in the room. One of the girls addressed the dark-haired girl as Valerie. After finishing their sodas, they heaved their packs onto their backs and prepared to leave. Valerie struggled with a fastener, and a pink notebook slipped from her pack to the pink-tiled floor. She didn't notice.

"Wait for me," she called to her friends, who were already at the door.

The girls waited. Valerie caught up with them. They left.

In a second, I was across the floor scooping up the notebook and transferring it to my purse. As I settled back in my booth, the waitress came with my pie. I thanked her and ate quickly, eager to see inside the notebook.

I paid at the counter, observing Pearce and Lina Mulligan still at their table. Pearce had a nosebleed. Lina foraged in her purse for tissues.

"Oh, Pearce," I heard her say. "You would get a nosebleed just before we are to leave for London. I have an appointment at seven with Stella McCartney."

Pearce mumbled something.

"Go to the men's room," she told him. "There's bound to be paper towels."

I had tissues in my purse and handed them to Pearce as I walked out of the restaurant. Lina thanked me. Pearce grabbed them and hurried to the men's restroom.

Outside, I found a bench in a secluded area and opened Valerie's notebook. Her full name was Valerie June Anderson and she lived at 124 Cheshire Street. The notebook contained class assignments, but in the margins, Valerie had doodled and penned comments. One comment: *Jamie loves Ann.* Another: *Tessa is a sow.* Was she writing about Tessa McMurray, Bridget's cousin? Farther into the notebook, opposite an English assignment, she had written something and then tried to cross it out. After several minutes, I deciphered what she had written: *Sister Augustine chose Bridget. What a stook. Stook* was slang for idiot or fool. Did Valerie mean Bridget was a fool? Or was Sister Augustine the fool for choosing Bridget?

When had Valerie made the notation about Sister Augustine? A page before, she noted that an assignment had to be turned in by April 3. Bridget announced she was to be May Queen around the first week of April. I looked through the remainder of the notebook. Valerie seemed prone to doodling upside-down men—faces that made sense whether you viewed them up or down. Her comments, presumably about her classmates, were acerbic. She was particularly cruel to someone named Ben. Did she have a crush on him? Occasionally she doodled a stick man with unusually short legs and arms. It seemed to be code for something that affected her from time to time. Not her menstrual period. It happened too often for that.

On the last page, she had drawn a picture of a priest. At first, I thought it was Father O'Neill, but this priest was thin and bald. Father O'Neill had a robust build and a thick head of hair. Was it Father Malone, the defrocked priest? He had a slight build and no hair. Valerie had added the words: *What does Miss Priss see in him?* Who was Miss Priss? Did Malone have a girlfriend? I'd heard he liked boys.

I hated to return the notebook to Valerie and wondered what would happen if I kept it. Should I give it to Inspector Finch? Probably not, since I had taken it without Valerie Anderson's consent. I stuck it back in my purse and went home, planning to examine it more closely, especially the part about Sister Augustine being a stook.

CHAPTER SIX

That evening, Danny Aherne called to say he'd set my poem to music, and invited me to his pub to hear him sing what he termed "our song." Since Elizabeth and I had no automobile and his pub, Gaelic Earls, was across the river on the far side of town, I phoned Judy Moriarity, who owned a car, to see if she would take us. In payment, I offered to buy dinner. Judy agreed and the three of us set off for the pub in her old battered silver Volvo.

After crossing the river, we found the pub nested in a stand of aspens, its sign flapping from a pole secured to the front of the brick building. The A was missing from EARLS, which indicated Danny was too busy writing and singing songs to pay attention to details. Judy turned into the pebbled lot and parked near the entrance.

We entered through a wooden door with a loose hinge and found the pub dimly lit. To the right was a long bar and to the left, booths and tables. A sign told us to find our seats. We did, beneath a stuffed owl, and next to an old couple slurping soup. In a corner by one end of the bar, a woman with long auburn hair sat on a stool strumming a zither and singing about larks in a green meadow. She finished her song, went to the bar, ordered a tankard of ale, and eased into a booth.

A waiter came, a youngish man with a beard the color of ripened wheat. We ordered a Guinness each and asked for menus. He brought us a slate, along with the drinks. We had to squint to see what was written.

"Can't go wrong with fish and chips," Elizabeth said.

"The beef and Guinness stew sounds good," I said.

Judy ordered lamb.

Gaelic Earls began to fill up. As the waiter brought our first course, Danny appeared. Dressed in signature black, he took his place on the stool. People applauded. He ran his hand through a mass of dark brown curls and smiled. His blue eyes were unusually bright. For several minutes, he bantered with the audience about the weather, and made a few benign political remarks.

"My first song is about the Great Hunger," he said. "You may know the tale. A young husband steals corn from an Englishman's field to feed his family. He's arrested and sent to Australia on a prison ship, never seeing his loved ones again. Lend an ear to 'The Fields of Athenry.'"

His tenor soared and we were pulled back into one of Ireland's greatest sorrows. The potato fields had suffered a blight in the mid-1800s, and as a result, many starved to death or emigrated to other countries. As Judy listened, tears flowed from her eyes.

"My gran told me stories," she said softly.

A sob quivered in my throat. Elizabeth remained oddly stoic.

When Danny finished, there was complete silence, and then cheers erupted. "Cheers, Danny boy!" "We love you!" "God blessed you with an angel voice!"

"Thank you, thank you," he said. "I have a new song. The words were written by Maria Pell, a visiting poet. Please stand up, Ms. Pell."

I stood. People clapped their hands. I sat down and waited to hear the song.

"This is 'Cork Harbor, Queenstown,'" Danny said.

He sang my poem with enormous depth of feeling. He had set "Cork Harbor" to music in both major and minor keys. I heard the partings in my soul. I heard the anger against forces that refused to help a desperate people. In the final stanza, which depicted the indomitable spirit of the Irish, Danny reached a crescendo of joyful sound. Tears of gratitude streamed down my face.

When he finished, I cried, "Bravo, Mr. Aherne!"

He bowed to me. "Thank you for your beautiful words."

"Did you contact your agent?" Elizabeth hissed.

I ignored her. Danny launched into another song.

"Well, Maria," Judy said, "I can't remember the last time Danny showed an interest in a woman."

I stared at her. "Surely, you don't mean..."

"I think he's smitten," Elizabeth teased.

"He was married to Iris Vale, you know," Judy said.

My eyes opened wide. "He and Iris were married?"

I don't know why the information surprised me. Perhaps it was due to the fact that the divorce rate in Ireland was among the lowest in European countries.

"I know Iris lost another child," I said, "but assumed Freddy Vale was the father. Was it Danny's?"

"Perhaps. The boy was born six months after Iris and Danny married. He claimed it was his, but I always wondered..."

The waiter stopped to ask if our drinks needed refilling. We said no.

Judy resumed her story about the Aherne child. "Right after the birth, Iris took the baby and left. The little tyke was poorly and went missing before his first birthday."

Elizabeth's ears perked up. So did mine. "Went missing?" we said in unison.

Judy shook her head sadly. "No one knows what happened. His blanket was found on the cliff, and Iris was nearby, drunk, and saying all manner of craziness. The garda thought he'd crawled off the cliff. It was a sheer drop to the sea."

"When did this happen?" I asked.

"Maybe 2000—about the time I had my gall bladder removed. There was a fuss about baptismal papers or something. I remember having difficulty climbing the stairs to find them. No, that was for the custody battle...maybe the little tyke left us in 2001...or was it 2000?"

"There was a custody battle?" I said.

"Yes, but that was earlier, of course. It will come to me when it all happened. Because Iris was a practicing Catholic and Danny was a heathen, the court gave the boy to her."

"Haven't I seen Danny at church?" I asked.

"Only for funerals," Judy said.

I looked at Danny Aherne with renewed interest. No wonder he could sing Ireland's sad songs—he'd known tremendous personal grief.

Danny finished the set and vanished through double doors behind the bar.

"I've remembered," Judy said. "The baby vanished in 2000. It was the same year that Danny's mother died. Two funerals in the same family only weeks apart. Little Alain's casket was empty, of course."

"How awful," Elizabeth said.

"Were the deaths related?" I asked.

Judy gave me an assessing look. "His mother went first. It was said her heart gave out worrying about little Alain."

"Alain was the child's name?" Elizabeth asked.

Judy nodded. "It means *stone*. Danny wrote a song for him called 'Little Man Stone.' I doubt he'll sing it tonight. He seems to be in a good mood. He sings it when he's down."

We ordered dessert. Crème brulee all around. Danny returned and favored us with more songs. Then he introduced the woman with the zither and she sang about finding mushrooms in the valley, a silly song with a bouncy air. When we finished, I called for the check. Soon after, the set ended and Elizabeth complained of headache. I had hoped to thank Danny again for putting music to my verse, but he had disappeared through the double doors again.

"He sings his heart out," Judy said. "He goes to his office to decompress."

Elizabeth said, "Or to get another snort of cocaine."

I turned to her. "What a nasty thing to say, Elizabeth."

"Didn't you see his eyes?"

"His eyes are an unusual shade of blue," I said. "Scandinavian blood must run through his veins."

Elizabeth shrugged. "If you say so."

A young couple preceded us out the door. Once in the parking lot, they turned left and we turned right. Then I heard a bell—a jingle bell.

Someone screamed. A young girl in shorts and a white T-shirt ran toward the couple.

"Help me!" she cried. "I've been kidnapped."

Behind her was a woman of medium height in a black dress. "Mary!" she yelled. "You g-g-get back here!"

The woman was an American. She had a stammer.

A man pulled up in a dark automobile. The woman grabbed the girl, exchanged a few words with the couple, and pushed the girl into the car. The bell, tied to her ankle, jingled furiously. The car sped off.

I ran to the couple. "What happened?"

"The woman said the girl was her daughter and she was bi-polar," the man said. "She'd gone off her meds."

An alarm went off in my head. Hadn't I read that the garda was investigating sex trafficking in Dublin? Had this young girl been kidnapped by sex traffickers right before my eyes? I phoned the garda station and described what I'd witnessed in the parking lot of Gaelic Earls. The young couple didn't want to get involved, but I explained that they already were and advised them to stay until the officers arrived.

"You can provide a description of the girl," I said. "I didn't see her face."

Reluctantly, they remained until the officers came. After taking our statements, the officers took the couple to the station to look at photographs of missing girls.

"We did our civic duty," Judy said, as we got into her Volvo.

I looked out the window into the darkness, suddenly wishing for Mathieu. I can't say why, except I felt someone step on my grave.

After Judy dropped us off at home, I stayed up. The incident in the parking lot had set my nerves on edge. Had the girl really been kidnapped? Had I missed a chance to rescue her before she was taken to some godawful place and abused, or even worse? If she was kidnapped, why had her captors pulled into the parking lot? Had they stopped for food on the way to Dublin?

Why had I wished for Mathieu?

My cell phone dinged—a text message from my dean, asking how I was progressing in my research. I had to think for a moment about where I was on my study outline. A fourth of the way into it? Definitely I needed to get back to it. I took a sleeping pill and went to bed, determined to break open the books and read more about the ancient Celts in the morning.

***

I awoke to birds chattering in the garden, saw the sun break over the sea, and crawled out of bed focused on learning more about Celtic myths. After breakfasting alone—Elizabeth slept in—I called Inspector Finch, hoping to speak to him about the girl who claimed to be kidnapped. An officer said he wasn't in but offered to tell him I called. Uneasy about the girl, I tried to settle down with my books.

Except for the old stones, myths were the only key to Ireland's prehistory. I had marked several myths to read and set to doing it. Nearly all depicted acts of revenge. One story told of a Leinster king's son who asked a poet for food. The poet refused so the prince burned down his house and killed his child (Hardly an eye for an eye!). The poet then satirized Leinster in a poem and put a curse on its crops. With the people weakened from hunger, another king invaded and conquered the kingdom. The prince wrested himself from capture and killed the poet. The victorious king banished the prince from the kingdom. Later, the prince killed the conqueror.

Many acts of revenge in that story.

My mind wandered to the nature of revenge. Taking a psychology book down from the shelf, I found the appropriate section. The Hebrew god set up the first act of revenge when he preferred Abel's offering to Cain's. Cain killed Abel in a fit of jealousy. In Roman and Greek myths, Juno and Hera punished mortal maidens for tempting their husband-gods. Odysseus slaughtered Penelope's suitors. Hamlet slew his uncle. Literature was filled with vengeful themes. The need for payback seemed to be a human condition. In a way, revenge restored the order, which had been disturbed by the original bad act. It also allowed the avenger to rid himself of feelings of resentment, to undergo catharsis.

I had faults, but fortunately the need to avenge was left out of my DNA. If someone cut me off in traffic, it irritated me, but I did not want to run the driver off the road. Slights hurt, but the pain was fleeting. I didn't let grievances fester.

Or did I? I thought of Mathieu. He claimed I wouldn't forgive him because I wanted to punish him. Was that true? I didn't trust him to not betray me again. Wasn't that why I kept away from him? He would be coming to Coomara soon. I already felt him invading my space.

But not yet. He was still in the States.

Returning to the theme of revenge, I thought of Elizabeth. She readily confessed to acts of vengeance, finding nothing ignoble about them. Take her firing—I suspected excessive weeding was not the only reason she lost her job at the library. Months before the weeding project, Elizabeth had told me about a board member named Dolly Tate, who had been opposed to her hiring. Mrs. Tate had supported another candidate and closely questioned Elizabeth's qualifications. A few weeks after her hiring, Elizabeth surreptitiously keyed the passenger side of Mrs. Tate's brand-new Lexus. When Elizabeth told me this, I was shocked.

"What on earth made you do such a thing, Elizabeth?"

"Dolly Tate caused me untold pain and humiliation."

"And keying her car made you feel better?"

"It evened things out...and she never found out who did it."

I wondered about that.

Elizabeth also told of accusing her neighbors of throwing loud parties and calling the police—though her bedroom was well-insulated and on the far side of the house. She had been upset because she wasn't invited to the parties. To get back at her mother for refusing to grant loans, she hid her glasses and favorite tea cup. How depressing it was to think of Aunt Carol, now in her seventies, fumbling around in her house, trying to find items Elizabeth had hidden.

Elizabeth could be a vengeful creature.

I closed my books and texted the dean, telling her I was well into my study and planned to spend time in the countryside to begin my verses.

Afterward, I called Inspector Finch to find out if the young couple was able to identify the girl from the photographs of missing girls.

"No," he said. "They couldn't identify her. Did you see the girl?"

"Only from a distance."

"Come down and look at the pictures. You might have noticed something."

I went downstairs to tell Elizabeth I was headed to the garda station, but she was gone. On the kitchen table was a note, saying she had gone to a meeting to plan St. Kevin's Festival. St. Kevin, I had learned, was a monk who founded the abbey at Glendalough. He had lived in a cave and communed with birds and small animals. Another St. Francis of Assisi.

As I rolled out my bicycle, Brendan Calloway loomed from behind a hedge.

"Mr. Calloway!" I said curtly. "You startled me."

He tried to look contrite. "I'm sorry, Ms. Pell. I was wondering if you'd like to drive to Glendalough with me tomorrow. The meadows are filled with wildflowers."

"No, thank you. I'm behind on my research and have no time for frivolity."

He moved to block my gate. "Perhaps the meadows would give you inspiration."

"I'd need to be alone for that."

"I'm sorry to hear that."

"Now please get out of my way. I must be somewhere."

He moved, so I could get through with the bicycle. "Perhaps another time?"

I didn't answer. What was it about the man that annoyed me so? I thought it must be his habit of lurking. He lurked. I thought again of Bridget working in the garden. Had he watched her as he did me?

***

By the time I reached the garda office, I had worked myself into a fury about Brendan. My mood was still showing when I knocked on Finch's door.

"What's happened, Ms. Pell?" Finch asked.

"Brendan Calloway is always popping up when I think I'm alone."

"He's a queer duck, but harmless."

Finch took me to a room where photographs of missing teen-aged girls were pinned to the wall.

"I don't think I can be much help," I said. "It was dark. The girl was several feet away."

Standing in front of the photos, I carefully examined each picture. All the pictures had been taken in happier times and presumably supplied by parents. The eyes of the girls haunted me.

"Just take your time," Finch said. "Perhaps it would be helpful if you tried to mentally revisit the incident."

He indicated a leather chair, so I sat down, closed my eyes, and took a deep breath. Last night's incident was still fresh in my mind, but I was reaching beyond the obvious for details. I had been distracted because of fear for the girl. Images flashed into my mind—young couple silhouetted in darkness, girl running from the parking lot, the woman in black, the car pulling up. What else?

"The woman was an American," I said, after a few moments. "She had a slight stammer and may have been from one of the southern border states like Tennessee or Kentucky and was shorter than I, perhaps about five-feet-five. The girl was no taller than five feet. She was fine boned. Her ankles were small. She had short hair, probably brown."

"Her accent?"

"English."

I opened my eyes. "They had tied a bell on her ankle so they knew where she was."

Finch muttered an oath. "Like an animal."

I looked at the photographs again. On the end was a picture of a girl with a short haircut with a pixie face. Her sparkling blue eyes laughed at the world. Another girl, toward the middle, had short dark hair and delicate bone structure.

Turning to Finch, I said, "It could be either of these girls, or it could be neither."

"What about the woman?"

"I didn't get a good look at her."

He showed me some mug shots of women, but I didn't find the woman's picture.

"Can you describe the car?" Finch asked.

"It was a large car. It was a dark color—maybe black or dark blue. Oh...the interior light went on when the man opened the door. The upholstery was red."

"The seats were red?"

I nodded. "That's unusual, isn't it?"

I hadn't been much help. I told Finch goodbye and went home.

***

Elizabeth was in the kitchen making scones with cheddar cheese and onion. I told her I had gone to the garda office to answer questions about the girl with the jingle bell on her ankle.

"I didn't help the inspector much," I added.

She leveled off a cup of flour. "Everything happened so quickly."

"The situation troubles me," I said. "I wish I'd had my wits about me."

"Maybe the police will find the girl before she's..."

I stared at Elizabeth. I don't know what she was thinking, but I was remembering articles I'd read about European and Asian whorehouses where young white virgins were repeatedly raped. Most never saw their families again.

"Maybe the police will find her," I said.

The telephone rang. I answered.

Iris Vale.

"Oh, Maria, my niece, Tessa, is missing!" she cried. "We can't find her anywhere!"

An image flooded my mind: sweet, innocent, blue-eyed Tessa with red hair the color of sunsets. "Tell me what happened."

But Iris had hung up.

CHAPTER SEVEN

The phone rang again.

"Iris?" I said, hoping she'd called back.

"This is Judy, Maria. Tessa McMurray set off for her granny's with fresh-baked gingerbread about two o'clock and never arrived."

I looked at the clock. "It's only four. Could she have stopped off at a friend's?"

"She wanted her gran to have the gingerbread while it was still warm. Search parties are gathering at the church. I knew you'd want to know."

"Thank you, Judy."

I ended the call and told Elizabeth what was happening. We changed into jeans, sweatshirts, and sneakers and hurried off to St. Columba's. Fog was drifting in from the sea, which would make the search more difficult.

Tessa's father, Declan McMurray, had just come back from his mother's cottage, walking the same path Tessa would have taken. "Found neither hide nor hair of my girl," he said, shaking his head.

I felt his fear. I patted him on the back. He thanked me.

Two parties had already gone off to search the seashore. Judy, who seemed to be organizing the searches, placed Elizabeth and me in Pearce Mulligan's group. He was dressed as if he were going on a fox hunt, in a red coat and shiny black boots. At least, we could keep track of him in the fog.

"Declan says Tessa was wearing blue corduroy pants and a pink sweater," Pearce told us.

"What kind of shoes was she wearing?" I asked.

He drew a scrap of paper from his jacket pocket. "Trainers, I believe...yes, pink trainers."

"Any jewelry?" I asked, remembering Bridget's woven bracelet.

He consulted the list again. "There's nothing here about jewelry. If anyone finds Tessa or something that belongs to her, we've agreed to come back here and ring the church bell." Brandishing his walking stick like a sword, he narrowed his eyes and shouted, "Come! We are off!"

We headed toward the forest, most of which covered part of the Mulligan estate. Elizabeth and I tramped over uneven ground, parted thickets of bracken, and ducked under low-hanging willow branches looking for signs of Tessa McMurray. A stream ran through the trees and we kept to its bank because the undergrowth was sparser.

As we went deeper into the woods, the Douglas firs stretched skyward, capturing a few rays of sun. We surprised two red deer at the edge of a stream and they immediately bolted. Around eight o'clock, the setting sun blasted through the heavy mist and we were treated to a mystical glow that illuminated dark spaces. I kept my eyes peeled for snatches of pink yarn, for small, narrow footprints in the damp earth.

Then the church bell rang.

Mulligan shouted and led us back to the village. We ran through the thicket, several of us tripping over exposed roots, but when we got to the churchyard, we learned Tessa was still missing. A search party had found one of her trainers along the rocky shore. Declan McMurray burst into tears—his wife had died from ovarian cancer two years before and now it looked as if something dire had happened to Tessa.

"She shouldn't have been near the sea," he wept. "That's nowhere near where her gran lives."

I caught Finch's eye. The sea, we were both thinking. Sex traffickers might be anchored in one or more of the pretty yachts visible on the horizon. Coomara's pure, beautiful girls were in jeopardy.

Yesterday's newspaper had reported that each year an estimated eight hundred thousand women and girls were trafficked across international borders to become slaves in the commercial sex industry.

Shuttled from one country to another, they became disoriented—everything was strange and most importantly, no one spoke their languages. Deprived of food and sleep, they lived in captivity. Some serviced up to thirty men a day. Organized crime was mostly responsible. My stomach turned as I thought of the innocent village girls, stolen from loving families, turned into sex slaves.

"It's like the old days," an old man muttered. "It's like the Vikings came and took our girls."

***

The next morning, while most of Coomara was at church, I went down to the beach where thirteen-year-old Tessa's shoe was found. Had she kicked it off to let us know what had happened to her? I remained by the sea, trying to get an impression of her last moments on shore. Inviting the tumult that the girl must have suffered, I felt a jolt of fear. My heart thundered in my rib cage and I bent over, as if kicked in the solar plexus. Druid spirits closed around me. They began to chant, faintly at first, then stridently. I felt their impatience. I had the power of prescience and they expected me to stop the kidnappings.

"Tell me what to do!" I cried.

A cold hand touched my arm. I screamed.

"Ms. Pell," Brendan Calloway said, "you are clearly agitated. Come away from the water."

I jerked away. "Get away from me."

"The sky is clouding up. It's going to rain. Are you walking or riding your bicycle?"

"I said get away!"

"Why do you hate me?"

"I don't hate you. You are...too persistent."

"You enchant me," he said. "Don't run away."

In my haste to get away from him, I fell and he pulled me upright. I yanked away and ran up the stone steps. He was close behind. When I reached the common walk, I fell in step with a group of schoolchildren. Brendan slowed his pace, stayed behind.

I was relieved.

At the corner, I turned toward my cottage, and of course, he turned too, because his cottage was next to mine. I was breathless when I opened my front door, glad to finally get away from him.

"What happened?" Elizabeth asked.

"Brendan."

"Oh dear," she said. "What happened this time?"

"He's stalking me. I wonder if he had anything to do with Bridget's death and Tessa's disappearance."

Elizabeth frowned. "He does live next door. Bridget was here a lot helping Iris. Did he have a connection to Tessa?"

"I don't know."

"Perhaps you should mention his behavior to Inspector Finch."

"I did. Finch said he was harmless."

Someone knocked. Thinking it was Brendan, I marched to the door, prepared to tear into him.

I threw open the door. Mathieu. Resplendent in a bespoke tan suit and polished broughams. I choked on the words I'd had ready for Brendan.

"Villagers will think you're a film star," I said.

He smiled. "May I come in?"

I stood aside. He entered and admired his reflection in the hall mirror. "Too much, do you think?"

"You'd be better off wearing casual clothes. That is, if you're trying to fit in."

"Mathieu!" Elizabeth hurried across the room to embrace him. "It's been ages."

"You're looking well," he told her, then turned to me. "So are you, Maria."

"It's the moist weather," Elizabeth said. "So good for the complexion."

"You seem surprised to see me, Maria," he said.

I rubbed the back of my neck. "I knew, of course, when you were coming. It's just that...that so much has been happening here..."

"Coomara's girls are being kidnapped and murdered," Elizabeth said.

"Maria!" A woman's cry from the porch.

Grace Devereaux, the librarian, burst through the open door. "We're having a meeting at the community hall. Inspector Finch has devised a plan to help protect our girls. Can you come?"

I introduced Mathieu to Grace. Since he had a rental car outside, we all got in and drove to the community hall, which was on the opposite side of the river from Gaelic Earls. I counted forty people at the hall and twenty-six more arrived after we got there. Most people were still in their Sunday clothes, so Mathieu's attire was not overly conspicuous.

The mood was bleak. The auras were all muddy green.

Inspector Finch took the podium, began with mild pleasantries, and then launched into directives to keep children safe. "Parents must be extra vigilant where daughters are concerned," he said sternly. "Children should not walk alone, especially in the evenings. They should not be left by themselves while you go to the pub. Always, one parent must stay in the house with the child."

Iris Vale bowed her head. She sat in the row ahead of me and I touched her shoulder.

"During the day when children go to and from school, they must walk in groups. An adult must accompany them."

Pearce Mulligan entered with his poet mother, Margaret. A murmur went through the crowd. Margaret Mulligan rarely left Ravensclaw. Dressed in black, she looked smaller than she actually was, and used a cane. A man and woman seated on the aisle got up and found other seats so the Mulligans could sit near the front.

Margaret Mulligan owned the largest estate in the county and was treated like royalty.

Finch continued: "Every block must have a safe house where a frightened child can seek refuge. We'll tie a red bow on the gate. Who will offer their houses?"

Hands went up, Elizabeth's among them. Thus, my cottage became a refuge.

"I'm increasing street patrols with cars and officers," Finch said, "but the children's safety depends on all of us. We must work together to keep the children safe."

"Who do you think took Tessa McMurray?" a woman asked.

"Sex traffickers may be behind it," Finch replied. "We know they are operating in Dublin. Recently, there was a suspicious incident here in Coomara. It is possible that traffickers are kidnapping the girls and transferring them to a vessel anchored in the sea. We've set up patrols to make sure no one but people we know come ashore."

"Can we find the vessel?" Declan McMurray asked. "Can we rescue my Tessa?"

"We've enlisted the help of the Irish Naval Service," Finch said. "We'll do our best to get her back, Declan."

The crowd murmured approvingly. Something positive was being done.

"What about Bridget Vale?" a young woman, holding a baby, asked. "Was she killed by sex traffickers?"

"We're treating that as a separate matter," Finch answered, "though there may be a connection."

Mathieu stood up. "Inspector!"

He was asking to speak. *What on earth does he have to say?* I shrank inside myself, not wanting to hear.

"Yes," Finch said. "Please identify yourself."

"I'm Dr. Mathieu Broussard and I'm with a group of archaeologists working at the site at Ballygosteen. I may have insight into what is happening."

"Please, Dr. Broussard. We need all the help we can get."

"I know something of strangers raiding villages and taking children," Mathieu continued. "Not many generations ago, my grandfather was stolen as a boy from his Togolese village. He was forced to go on forays to steal other children and learned the ways of the thieves. They often paid members of a tribe to point out the homes of the strongest boys, and then they would steal the children when they found them alone. My grandfather was able to escape and return to his home. To keep your children safe, they must never be alone."

A thick-set man stood up. "Are you saying someone in the village may be fingering the girls?"

Mathieu shrugged. "Evil is everywhere. It happened in my village. It could be happening in yours."

The crowd, which had been quietly attentive, now began to grumble. Mathieu sat down. Finch thanked him, but I noticed his tone was perfunctory: Mathieu had sown seeds of distrust in the village. I wondered if that was wise.

Margaret Mulligan raised her hand.

"Mrs. Mulligan," the inspector said.

She rose slowly to her feet. "The taking of our girls is unacceptable. Dr. Broussard raises an important point. Tessa McMurray may have been selected for kidnapping. Perhaps her cousin, Bridget Vale, was also selected, but something went wrong, and she was murdered. Both girls were athletic, beautiful, and devout. Our very best. I find it unlikely that kidnappers came to Coomara and randomly selected both girls. They had to be targeted."

She sat down. Her last five words reverberated in the room. For several seconds, no one spoke. Then Father O'Neill asked to be recognized.

"Evil, we are taught, is the result of human choice," he said. "Not even Satan can force us to sin. To quote poet Leon Bloy, *Whoever does not pray to God, prays to the devil.* Do not forget the price Jesus Christ paid for your salvation. The doors of the confessional are always open."

The priest's words startled me. Through the confessional, Father O'Neill knew the secrets of Coomara's villagers. Perhaps he knew who was working with the kidnappers. Perhaps he knew who killed Bridget.

Finch also seemed shaken by the possibility that someone he knew might have been betraying community trust. He swept his eyes over the crowd. I did the same. Then Finch gathered his wits and asked Father O'Neill to close the meeting with a prayer.

As we stood to leave, a reporter for the local paper approached and asked the spelling of Mathieu's name. Finch came over to ask where Mathieu was staying.

"At the inn here in town," Mathieu said. "I haven't checked in yet."

"I take it you're a friend of the two Ms. Pells."

I held my breath. *Will he reveal that he was my partner?*

Mathieu beamed a smile at me. "I've known them both for several years. Maria teaches at Midwestern University in the United States, as do I."

He chose wisely. I did not know how race played out in this quaint Irish town, but I wasn't ready to defend a bi-racial relationship that was uncertain, to say the least.

We stood near the door. I felt eyes boring a hole in my back and turned to see Brendan Calloway. I reached to touch Mathieu's sleeve. Brendan hurried down the stairs, out of sight.

"What is it?" Mathieu asked.

"Nothing...I...."

"You're trembling. What is it, Maria?"

He looked toward the stairway, but Brendan was gone.

Grace Devereaux walked up with Deirdre O'Malley. "Dr. Broussard," she said, "I'd like you to meet my friend, Deirdre O'Malley."

For the first time, I saw Deirdre up close. She was a tall, ill-formed woman. Her arms were too long and so were her legs. Always drawn to a person's eyes, I saw that hers were unexpectedly dreamy—a tawny shade that nearly blended with her skin. Romany, I suspected. Her raven-black hair was drawn up in what fashion commentators called a "messy bun." She had a protruding chin and I guessed she was stubborn. She was dressed in a magenta midi-skirt, patterned with white tigers. A black shawl was drawn over her narrow shoulders.

"May I compliment you on your skirt?" Mathieu asked. "It is gorgeous."

"It's from Russia," she said. "I'm interested in the dig at Ballygosteen, Dr. Broussard. Old artifacts fascinate me. I was fortunate to help Professor Abramowitz at a site in Gaza."

"Which one?" Mathieu asked.

For several moments, the two conversed about excavations they'd participated in and sites they had visited. I heard words like "Endor," "Book of Joshua," "St. Hilarian," "Ceide Fields." It was clear they could talk archaeology forever.

Grace interrupted. "Perhaps we could all adjourn to a pub."

"Not me," I said. "I have work to do. Drop me off at home."

"Me, too," Elizabeth said. "I have to prepare for a meeting tomorrow. We're planning activities for St. Kevin's Festival."

Mathieu shot me a dark look. The last thing he had planned was to spend his evening with the town librarian and the resident Druid priestess.

After he dropped Elizabeth and me at the cottage, we shared a laugh.

"Poor Mathieu," Elizabeth said. "That awful Druid person..."

"She's an educated woman," I said. "Inspector Finch says she speaks seven languages."

"Oh, my," Elizabeth said. "But then all these European countries are so close together."

Entering the house, I found a hammer and nail, and brought them outside so Elizabeth could attach her red bow to the gate.

"I wonder if anyone will use our house as a safe house," she said.

We went inside. Elizabeth puttered around the kitchen for a while. I went upstairs. As I prepared for bed, an unpleasant thought went through my head: Mathieu, only a few hours in town, had managed to make himself the center of attention—such was the force of his personality. Actually, he had added a new dimension to solving Tessa's disappearance. It made sense that someone in Coomara was cooperating with the kidnappers.

Who?

CHAPTER EIGHT

Gurgling water. Spotted leaves furled like funeral boats. Mossy stones. A red-eyed baby stuck in the cattails. I swung an arm to keep from falling in the creek and knocked over a table lamp. I sat up, pressed my fingers against my temples. The nightmares had plagued me when I lived with Mathieu, and he would reach out a strong brown arm to pull me close. That's all I'd needed to get through the rest of the night.

He wasn't here to help me now.

Thirty years ago. That's when I found the baby. For weeks after, I suffered from night terrors, screaming, vomiting. My psychiatrist believed I had assumed the persona of Baby Doe, and feared that I, like she, would end up in a sluggish stream. My parents were diligent in loving and supporting me, and by my fifteenth birthday, the bad dreams were less frequent.

But Baby Doe remained anchored in my mind, and now she'd become entangled with the fates of Bridget and perhaps, Tessa. Was my subconscious heaving something up—something I should pay attention to? How could there be a connection between a death in Indiana in the mid-1980s and another in Ireland, thirty years later? I had no answers, but I felt the presence of that long-ago dead baby.

I got out of bed and went downstairs. I would have gone out on the back porch to breathe the sea air but didn't want Brendan to see me in my nightgown. Instead, I brewed a cup of tea and sat down at the kitchen table.

A blue-lined notepad lay on the table. I jotted down similarities: Baby Doe and Bridget Vale. Dead girls. Dark hair. White faces. Plankton curling on their foreheads. Water. Death. Weeds. That day, so many years ago, my father had taken Baby Doe from the water. Mother, upon seeing him with the dead child in his arms, asked, "Whose child can she be?" Father looked toward his brother's house. "Where is Robert?" he had asked.

Why had my father wondered about his brother's whereabouts?

My parents were discreet people. Certain things were not for the ears of young children. I know now they used a kind of shorthand speech familiar to two people who communicated often and well. What was unsaid that day when my father stood with Baby Doe in his arms? How had Mother sounded when she asked that question: *Whose child can she be?* Was a baby girl missing? What did Uncle Robert have to do with it?

Someone tapped on the front door, snapping me back to the present. I hurried to answer, lest the noise awaken Elizabeth. Looking out the peephole, I saw it was Mathieu and opened the door. He'd seen me naked. He wouldn't find a cotton nightgown alluring.

Dressed in jeans and a plaid cotton shirt, he held a sack of doughnuts. "Breakfast."

"I'm not inviting you in, Mathieu."

"That's okay. You can still have the doughnuts."

We looked at each other. He was wanting to smile. I turned away. Then I heard Brendan's front door open.

I changed my mind. "Come in, Mathieu."

He stepped into the cottage and I went to the kitchen to put on the kettle for tea. We had just settled at the kitchen table to eat the doughnuts and strawberries I'd found in the refrigerator when Elizabeth came downstairs.

"Mathieu," she said, "I thought I heard your voice."

"He brought doughnuts," I said.

She joined us at the table and took a doughnut from the sack. "How was your evening with Grace and Deirdre?"

Mathieu smiled. "Deirdre is an interesting woman. Seven languages she speaks. I understand she is also a Druid."

"Did she talk about Druidism?" I asked.

"A bit. She invited me to attend a ceremony in a meadow."

"Are you going?" I asked.

Before he could answer, Elizabeth cried out and swatted my blue notepad onto the floor.

"Why did you do that?" I asked her.

"Why do you keep harping about Baby Doe? That was thirty years ago, Maria. Can't you forget about her?"

"I don't harp about Baby Doe," I said indignantly. "When was the last time I discussed her with you?"

"I suppose not for a long time, but I hear you moaning in your bedroom. Sometimes you cry out and say her name."

"I never knew her name."

"Well, Baby Doe. You call her Baby Doe."

I picked up the notepad from the floor. "You should remember that day, too. You were eight years old. You were playing dolls on your porch with Caroline Benner."

"How can you remember with such precision? It's so long ago. I could have been upstairs in my room or in the kitchen with Mother."

She pushed back from the table and ran upstairs.

Mathieu touched my arm. "Are you still dreaming about that child, Maria?"

I brushed his hand away. "It's not your concern."

"Okay." He got up from the table and left.

Hurrying to the door, I watched him drive away. I'd hurt his feelings. *Good! Now he knows what rejection feels like.* I turned, flinching from my reflection in the mirror. I looked mean, vengeful, filled with hatred. That was not me. Immediately, I was remorseful.

I went upstairs to dress, passing Elizabeth's bedroom door, and heard her moving around. I had little patience. The nightmare had robbed me of a restful sleep. Elizabeth said she had a meeting today and I hoped she would leave the house soon.

As I was making my bed, I heard the downstairs door close. Elizabeth was leaving. I went to the window to check the weather. Slate gray sky. Fog rising from the sea, limiting visibility. Was a storm coming? A flock of terns batted their wings and headed for a clump of cypresses. I grew sad, thinking of Bridget and Tessa.

Glass shattered.

I jumped.

Someone had broken into the house! Seizing a wooden coat hanger, I crept down the stairs. Hearing activity from the sitting room, I pressed my back against the wall, not knowing whether to run back upstairs and call the police or peer around the corner. Something thudded to the floor. It sounded like a stack of books I'd piled on the coffee table. I ran back upstairs, locked my bedroom door, and called the garda on my cell. The intruder came pounding up the stairs. Heavy footfalls. A man. He was outside my door, breathing hard.

Was it Brendan?

"Brendan!" I yelled. "Is that you?"

A siren sounded. The man thundered down the stairs. The backdoor slammed and I ran downstairs. Two officers, Sergeant Potts and Sergeant Gowdy, hurried in through the open front door.

"He went out the back door!" I cried.

We ran through the cottage and out onto the back porch in time to see Brendan Calloway throw one long leg on top of his fence. Sergeant Gowdy, a short muscular man, grabbed him by the shirt collar and jerked him backward.

"Are you all right, Ms. Pell?" Sergeant Potts asked.

I answered that I was and focused on Brendan, who was standing, shoulders hunched, head down.

"What do you mean by breaking into the cottage?" I demanded. "You scared me to death."

Brendan burst into tears, making a strange honking sound. The officer led him into my cottage and told him to sit down on a kitchen chair.

"Do you intend to file charges?" Sergeant Potts asked me.

"Of course, I do."

"I believe he owns this cottage," she said.

"He may own it, but I'm paying rent. According to the lease, as long as I pay the rent, this cottage is my home."

"This is confusing," Potts said. "Miss Pell, could you please come down to the station?"

The officers took Brendan away in their patrol car. Fuming that they were treating the situation like a domestic feud, I refused to get in the front seat and followed on my bicycle. When I arrived at the station, Inspector Finch was talking to Brendan.

"Ms. Pell," Finch said, "Brendan says a witch put him under a spell."

"Not a witch," Brendan said. "Deirdre O'Malley."

"What spell?" I demanded.

"She said I would fall in love with a woman from across the sea and must marry her or end up in an early grave. You are the woman."

"Since he thinks he's under a spell, do you want to press charges?" Finch said.

I looked at the inspector incredulously. "Of course, I do. He can't just break into my cottage when the mood strikes him."

Finch looked thoughtfully at Brendan. "Ms. Pell has a point."

"I won't break into the cottage again," Brendan said, "and I'll get the door repaired straightaway."

"Why did Deirdre O'Malley put a curse on you?" I asked.

"There was a matter of stolen sheep," Finch said. "Deirdre thought Brendan took them. It was never proven that he did."

"Did you steal her sheep?" I asked Brendan.

"On my mother's grave, I did not."

Though I was skeptical about the curse, the home invasion, and Finch's compassionate treatment of the perpetrator, I agreed not to file charges if Brendan promised to stop stalking me. He solemnly promised—again on his mother's grave—and also offered the use of his motor boat as a further apology. I had noticed the boat moored at his private dock, a shiny silver Viksund.

"It has plenty of petrol," he added.

I knew how to pilot a boat. Taking the proffered boat key, I left garda headquarters, wondering where Deirdre O'Malley lived. I had not gone one block when I encountered Judy Moriarity.

"I hear Brendan Calloway broke into your cottage," she said breathlessly. "Are you all right?"

I got off my bicycle. "I'm fine. Where does Deirdre O'Malley live?"

"Why do you ask?"

"I'm in a hurry and will tell you later."

A look of disappointment flitted across Judy's face, but she rallied and gave me precise directions on how to find Deirdre's farm, which was south of the village.

"She raises sheep," Judy added. "A year ago, someone rustled all her animals. Inspector Finch never found out who did it. While she was off to some Druid convention in Glasgow, she left a neighbor boy in charge of the sheep. Someone brought in a truck by night and made off with them. She has a new flock now."

A drop of rain fell on my forehead. Though I wanted to search out Deirdre's farm, I had left my raincoat at the cottage. More drops. I thanked Judy, bicycled home, and got out of my damp clothing.

Elizabeth was home. "What happened to the door?"

I related the story of Brendan's break-in and his promises, which included replacing the door. Elizabeth apologized for her rudeness earlier in the day and sympathized with my ordeal. She even brought me a cup of tea. We settled down to watch the news. Then I went upstairs to read about the Milesians, a Gaelic race that may have arrived in Ireland from Spain before recorded history. Thomas Moore had written a poem about them: "The Coming of the Milesians."

They came from a land beyond the sea,
And now o'er the western main
Set sail in their good ships, gallantly,
From the sunny lands of Spain...

Toward evening, the rain stopped and a man appeared on our porch with a new door and installed it.

***

The next morning, the sun was shining, and after a breakfast of waffles and strawberries, I mounted my bicycle and went in search of Deirdre O'Malley's farm. As I paused for highway traffic, I saw Albert Malone, the pedophile priest, emerge from a grocery store. He *did* look like the drawing in Valerie Anderson's notebook. He was slight, bent, and his bald head glowed like a pink Easter egg. I wondered again who Miss Priss was.

I crossed the highway and following Judy's directions, took a paved road south until I came to a side road marked Glenrose Lane. Deirdre's farm was a half mile west. The sun grew brighter and so did my mood. Hopeful that I would no longer need to look over my shoulder to see if Brendan was stalking me, I felt a buoyancy I had not felt in days.

The lane to Deirdre's farmhouse was concealed by thick hedges and puddled with rainwater. Midway, I laid my bicycle on the soggy grass and continued on foot. Apple trees in bloom flanked the lane on both sides and their fragrance filled the air. As I stopped to break off a blossom, a small black car came thundering past, headed for Glenrose Lane. Deirdre was behind the wheel. She slammed on the brakes, splashing muddy water on me. Throwing the car in reverse, she stopped.

"I nearly ran you down, Ms. Pell," she said. "Look at you. What a mess. Come into the house and get cleaned up."

I started to get into her car.

"No, no," she said. "You'll dirty my car. You'll have to walk."

She backed up the lane. I followed. When I reached her cottage, I started to explain who I was, but she shushed me.

"I know you're the American poet. I heard you read at the library a few weeks ago. Good stuff, you write. You commune with the spirits. I can feel it in you."

I also sensed Deirdre's otherworldliness.

As she opened her door, two afghan hounds barked in greeting. I walked into a vestibule painted the same shade of green as the hedges. Photos of red deer hung on the walls. On the floor was a dark purple carpet.

"Come in, come in," she said impatiently, motioning me through the sitting room into her bedroom.

She rummaged in her closet and found a black velour robe bordered in gold. It smelled of oranges.

"Here," she said, "take a shower and put this on. I'll put your clothes in the washer."

Soaked to the skin, I began to strip out of my clothing. She left the room. I undressed and went into the shower. When I finished bathing, my clothes were gone. I put on the fantastical robe and went to the sitting room. Deirdre was in the kitchen, cleaning mud off my shoes.

The sitting room had black walls stamped with star decals, metallic silver drapes, a couch covered in inky velvet, purple wing-back chairs facing the fireplace, and a green throw rug for the hounds. An entire wall of built-in bookcases prompted me to look at the titles. Several volumes were dedicated to Druidism and other religious practices, as might be expected, but also Shakespeare, Locke, Camus, and Keats—a mixture of philosophy and literature.

Finished with the shoes, Deirdre brought them to me, along with a cup of hot tea.

"Your clothes are in the washer," she said, sitting on the couch. "What brought you to my farm?"

I told her about my skirmish with Brendan Calloway the previous day.

She threw back her head and laughed. "What a lecher! Never did I cast a spell on him. He made up the story so the garda wouldn't put him in jail."

"There was something about stolen sheep..."

"My sheep *were* stolen, but I never thought Brendan took them. That old clatterfart Moriarity—she's probably behind the falsehood that Calloway took my beasts—and the so-called curse."

Sadness swept over me. Though I had her pegged as a gossip, I'd assumed Judy was a fairly reliable narrator of village comings and goings.

"Do you know who took the sheep?" I asked.

"I do. I had only to follow the tire treads through the meadow to Pearce Mulligan's property to know his men did it. I went to the livestock sale at Ballygosteen the next day. At the sight of me, my sheepies came bawling. I confronted Doyle, Pearce's estate manager. He treated the whole thing like it was a prank and brought my beasties home."

Deirdre smiled. The smile transformed her avian face and I began to feel more comfortable. She asked about my academic background and I told her I'd received my undergraduate degree from a northeastern college, and my MFA from Columbia. She shared that she had a degree in Philosophy from Trinity College in Dublin and had intended to pursue a PhD at Oxford.

"My partner committed suicide and I returned to Coomara sunk in grief and guilt," she said. "Then the sacred spirits pulled me into their embrace and I realized my true calling was to remain here where the very soil resounds from the tramping of their feet."

I had not yet spoken with the spirits at the cove. "Do you speak with them?"

"Sometimes," she said, "but not often. Ancient Druids are silent spirits, rarely moved to speech."

She got up to put my clothes in the dryer and came back with a fresh cup of tea.

"There is much evil here," she said. "Our girls—one dead, one missing."

"I knew Bridget Vale well," I said. "Her mother cleans my house. Bridget often came with her."

"Poor Iris," she said. "She's lost both her children. There was..."

She stopped. I wondered what she intended to say and why she changed her mind. She went to look out the window.

"Oh, look," she said, beckoning me to the window. "There's a grey partridge near the shed."

"What were you about to say about Iris losing both her children?"

"Hurry," she said. "Come see the partridge. We don't see them much anymore."

I got up to view the partridge, which pecked at the ground and fluttered off into the brush. Deirdre's hand grazed my breast. I drew away.

"Your clothes must be dry," she said, as if nothing had transpired between us. "Let me get them."

Why did people hesitate to say what happened to Iris's first child? Judy had hinted that Iris was drunk and let the child fall off a cliff. Was that really what happened?

Deirdre disappeared into the kitchen and returned with my clothing. I went into the bedroom and changed. As I left, I thanked her for her hospitality. She offered to drive me home, but I declined.

"Friends and I are worshipping at the thorn tree in Mulligan's pasture at midnight on Saturday," she said. "I invited Dr. Broussard. He said he might come. I'd be glad to pick you up."

Mathieu had said he was invited. I wondered if he would go.

Deirdre didn't press me to answer, perhaps intuiting that I needed to think over the invitation. We exchanged telephone numbers. I went outside into the mists, found my bicycle, and went home.

At my cottage, I found Elizabeth at the kitchen table with three women who were on her committee for the feast of St. Kevin.

"Where have you been?" my cousin asked.

"I went to see Deirdre O'Malley."

A woman wearing a green cap cried, "Deirdre O'Malley! Stay away from her. She's a witch."

"Why do you say that?" I asked.

"She hates us villagers. Whenever there's a death, look to Deirdre O'Malley, for she has surely cursed the deceased."

"Do you think she put a curse on Bridget Vale?" I asked.

"She must have. Otherwise, the little darling would still be alive."

A redheaded woman chimed in. "It all goes back more than a hundred and fifty years ago when famine swept the country. Deirdre's great-great-great grandfather plotted to rob a granary in Dublin to feed the village and was betrayed by local men who feared retaliation. Peter O'Malley was executed. Since that time, generations of O'Malleys have despised people of the village."

"Deirdre's hatred is especially potent," the green-capped woman said. "She's in league with the devil."

The third woman, wearing a large crucifix around her neck, said, "She's the high priestess. She hates the church. Judy says she spits every time she passes by St. Columba's."

Judy, again. Did Deirdre really spit as she passed the church?

Elizabeth's committee disbanded around four o'clock. I sat in the living room and read Seamus Heaney's Nobel lecture. We were contemplating what we would have for dinner when I realized I had not replied to Deirdre's invitation. Excusing myself from Elizabeth's watchful eyes, I went outside and called her.

"I'd like to come to the ceremony," I said.

"Wonderful," Deirdre said. "I'll pick you up Saturday night around eleven-thirty."

For a moment, I thought about the story Elizabeth's red-headed friend told about Deirdre's ancestor. I didn't believe Deirdre would exact retribution on the town for betraying her great-great-great grandfather.

Then I remembered the revenge myths I'd been reading.

CHAPTER NINE

As I unlocked my bicycle Thursday morning, Finch's car went past the cottage with Mathieu in the passenger seat. I had planned to go to the garda station to see if there was any news from Dublin about the girl who asked for help. Now Finch was headed out of town with Mathieu.

Damn Mathieu! Why isn't he at his dig in Ballygosteen? He made a spectacle of himself at the community meeting sharing stories of his Togolese grandfather. Now he and Finch are best friends! Well, Finch can have him. Mathieu doesn't have a prescient bone in his body.

I rolled the bicycle into its niche by the porch and went back inside. The thought went through my head that I was jealous of Mathieu. It was an unpleasant thought, substantiated by the many times I had watched his career at the university overtake mine—he had a PhD and I did not. Knowing all these thoughts were unworthy of me, I paced the floor. Elizabeth came downstairs.

"What on earth is the matter with you?" she asked.

I didn't know what to say.

My gaze fell on the key to Brendan's speed boat. "I think I'll take the boat out."

"Do you know how to steer a boat?"

"Of course." I had piloted speedboats in lakes and once or twice in the Atlantic.

I climbed down the steps to the dock where the *Dusky Hawk* was moored and checked the fuel gauge. Full tank, just as Brendan promised. I started the motor and maneuvered the *Hawk* down the inlet, heading out. Sea and sky were one color—a pallid blue with hints of gray. Steering along the coast, I scanned the craggy cliffs. The Milesians had come in rude boats all the way from Spain. They would have landed on the island farther south, but the terrain was much the same. What did they say when this landmass emerged from the fog? What language had they spoken? What was their culture?

I searched the horizon for craft that might belong to sex traffickers and saw none. A pod of dolphins cavorted in the east, causing silver ripples in the water. The dolphins seemed interested in me and soared through the air, following the *Hawk* for several minutes. I was sorry when they swam out to sea.

As I passed the Mulligan dock, Lina Mulligan was sunbathing topless on a patch of beach. She was alone. Then a dot appeared on the horizon. Another speedboat. It seemed to be heading for the dock. I continued down the coast, then circled back in time to see the boat moored at the dock and a dark-haired man talking to Lina. I'd seen him before at Bridget's funeral. Who was he? Judy would know.

My cellphone rang. I looked at the number. Elizabeth. I decided not to answer. Steering the boat farther out, I navigated a group of misted islets, a remainder of extinct volcanoes that had erupted several million years ago. Fog stole in, leaving trails like gossamer scarves. I felt dampness on my face and arms, and knew I should head for home.

Then the sound of another motor startled me. On my starboard side, a gray and white yacht appeared, then powered off in a northern direction. *Does the yacht belong to sex traffickers?* I slowed, reached for a pair of binoculars I'd noticed near the helm, and watched the boat's stern vanish in the haze. Grabbing my cell phone, I called garda headquarters and reported seeing the yacht. The officer I spoke to said he would notify the sea patrol.

I had been within yards of the yacht. The man whom I'd seen with Lina Mulligan had come from the same direction. Had he rendezvoused with the yacht? More importantly, had he transferred Tessa McMurray to sex traffickers? Opening the *Hawk's* throttle, I chased after the larger boat, hoping to see where it was headed. Then fog closed around me. I strained my eyes, trying to see, but the haze was impenetrable. I turned around. Soon light appeared in the distance and I followed it to the coast, marking familiar rock formations as I returned to Brendan's pier.

Someone stood on the dock—a man with broad shoulders, baggy clothes, as if he were hiding a brace of pheasants, and holding a pipe. Brendan. I tossed the line to him.

He tied the line around a cleat. "Glad you came in, the island's covered with fog."

"It fell all at once."

"It's good to see someone using the boat. I don't take it out much anymore."

He and I were holding a civil conversation—a welcome change from the cat-and-mouse game we'd been playing. Had his skirmish with the police caused him to rethink the so-called curse? I fervently hoped so.

I smiled. "Have a pleasant afternoon, Brendan."

"Yes," he replied. "You, too."

I climbed the steps to my back yard and went inside the cottage.

Mathieu and Elizabeth were sitting at the kitchen table eating bacon and tomato sandwiches on wheat toast. They stopped chewing long enough to tell me hello.

"Glad you're back," Mathieu said. "That fog is thick as stew."

"Pea soup," I corrected.

"We were worried about you," Elizabeth said. "I tried to call you."

I sat down at the table. "Did you fry enough bacon for me?"

"Of course," Elizabeth said.

She got up from the table and made another sandwich. I took it and thanked her. As we ate, I told them about the yacht and the man talking to Lina Mulligan. I did not add that I'd tried to chase after the yacht.

"I called the garda station," I said. "The officer is sending the sea patrol."

"The man you're referring to is probably Lina Mulligan's brother," Elizabeth said. "Judy said his name was Hector Perez-Conti."

Somehow, I'd thought Hector Perez-Conti was more to Lena Mulligan than a brother. I'd not had a brother. Does one sunbathe topless in the presence of a brother?

"Is he visiting Ravensclaw?" I asked.

"Judy thinks he lives there."

"Ravensclaw is an unattractive name," Mathieu commented.

"The original name was Mulros," I said. "Mul for Mulligan and ros for promontory."

"Lina changed it to Ravensclaw," Elizabeth said. "Judy said Margaret Mulligan refused to allow a legal change. She still gets her mail addressed to Mulros."

Though old and fragile, Margaret Mulligan was a force of iron. I had heard—Judy, again—that Margaret strongly disapproved of her daughter-in-law.

"Mathieu," I said, "why aren't you in Ballygosteen?"

"We excavate tomorrow morning. The crew from France will be here then."

"What interests you about these Neolithic artifacts?"

"Any new dig interests me. Some of the stones have carvings on them—an early attempt to express language. Why don't you come over Saturday? I can pick you up."

"I'd like to go too," Elizabeth said.

I glanced at my cousin. "I thought you hated ruins."

"I do, but I'd still like to see the site."

It was settled. On Saturday, Elizabeth and I would go to Ballygosteen with Mathieu. After he left, I called Inspector Finch to find out if the sea patrol had caught up with the yacht I'd seen in the islets. He said the fog had been too thick.

I retired to my study to work on a poem about the Milesians and was deep in thought when someone knocked on the door downstairs. Elizabeth answered it and called me to come down. Seated on our sofa was a girl of about twelve with a tear-stained face.

"This is Nora," Elizabeth told me. "She was frightened by a man who honked at her from his truck."

I ran outside to look for the trucker. He was out of sight.

"Could he have been one of the kidnappers?" Nora asked.

"Perhaps," I said. "You did right in coming here."

"I saw the red bow on your gate," the girl said.

Elizabeth served her cookies and milk while I took her name and called the garda station. Within a half hour, an officer came to hear the girl's story and take her home.

"The system works well," I said to Elizabeth.

"Have you noticed the patrols on the street? Volunteers have come from Dublin."

"Let's hope the town is safe now," I said, thinking of the mysterious yacht that had disappeared into the fog.

***

The next morning, I went to see Inspector Finch, who was eating breakfast at his desk—a cranberry scone, an apple and a pear.

"I see you're having a Cezanne morning," I quipped.

"A what?"

"Paul Cezanne, his paintings of fruit bowls."

He smiled. "Oh yes. Rightly so."

He told me he'd had no word from Dublin on the stuttering woman or the girl who had cried for help. There had been no sign of Tessa McMurray.

"I hope she wasn't put on that yacht," I said, shivering. "What do you know about Hector Perez-Conti, Lina Mulligan's brother?"

"That's an impertinent question, Ms. Pell," he said, cutting his scone into fourths, "but I will answer. I know nothing about him. He hasn't committed a crime, nor is he a person of interest."

I sat down in the chair beside his desk.

"Have you eaten, Ms. Pell? Would you like a bit of scone? Perhaps the pear?"

"No, thank you. I had breakfast." I averted my eyes as he chewed. "Do you have a sister,Inspector Finch?"

"As a matter of fact, I have seven sisters. Why do you ask?"

"Would any of them sunbathe topless in your presence?"

Finch turned the same shade of red as his apple peel. "Of course not!" Then he recovered himself. "I take it you saw someone doing so."

"Lina Mulligan. I think that's odd."

"She is South American—Peruvian, I think. Perhaps they do things like that there."

"Peru is not the Riviera," I reminded him.

We sat in silence. The sun broke through the slats in the window blinds. I looked at the ivy plant. Someone had watered it. I was getting ready to leave when an officer burst through the door.

"A Bingham man called the garda, saying he'd seen a girl who looked like Tessa McMurray," he said. "They're still in a restaurant. The Bingham garda is headed there now."

Despite his girth, Finch moved quickly. He grabbed his hat and ran out the door. I followed, hoping he would take me with him, but he did not. He jumped in the passenger side as an officer drove up with his car and sped away.

I asked Mary Potts, who was at her desk, how far it was to Bingham.

"At least seventy kilometers."

I could go home and wait, or I could talk to Judy Moriarity, and wrest information about Lina Mulligan from her. Hoping she was available for lunch, I called her. As it turned out, she was free, and we arranged to meet at a small tearoom not far from the priory. As I walked there, I noted three uniformed officers standing on street corners.

The tearoom was called Tea for Two and run by a mouse-like woman with long brown hair. She had painted the walls pale lavender, hung white ruffled curtains, and added lavender wooden tables and chairs. She usually sat behind the counter, ringing up checks.

Opening the door, I nodded to the woman and asked if Judy was there.

"Over by the window."

I greeted Judy and sat down at the table.

"I'm so glad you called," she said. "I'm worried sick about poor Tessa McMurray."

I didn't tell her about the call from the Bingham officers, but sympathized with her and asked what she'd like to order.

She scanned the blackboard menu. "Fresh tuna sounds good."

I agreed and that's what we ordered, along with lemon tea.

The waitress brought our tuna sandwiches. After swallowing a mouthful, Judy commented that she'd been thinking about Pearce Mulligan; his house, built on a promontory, was the perfect spot to watch the sea.

"A person could stand there with binoculars and see almost to Wales. Think how easy it would be to signal with mirrors to a ship at sea."

"Are you suggesting Pearce is involved in the girls' kidnapping?"

"Not necessarily Pearce himself, but have you given an eye to the men who work for him? A rough lot, all of them."

"But why, with all his money, would he resort to criminal activities?"

"Who says he has so much money? The money belongs to Margaret. Her father was in shipping. He made a fortune during the war. Some say..."

I interrupted. "But Pearce is her only heir. He wouldn't need to resort to shady dealings. Besides, his mother would never be a party to kidnapping village girls."

"That's so. Margaret Mulligan is a candidate for sainthood, if ever there was one. Pearce was never interested in managing the estate. He was a wild one until Margaret laid down the law. As a young man, he chased after village girls like a stag in rut."

Pearce Mulligan? It was hard for me to imagine him as a Lothario.

Judy lowered her head. "I still wonder about that pedophile Father Malone. Of course, I shouldn't call him *Father*—he was defrocked when it came out he'd molested those boys at the school in Dublin."

I'd seen the old priest occasionally in the park. He kept away from people.

"Do you think he took Tessa?"

"No, but if it was a boy gone missing..."

Danny Aherne walked past the window. He turned his head to peer inside but didn't slow his pace. I remembered Elizabeth's suspicion that he took drugs.

"I wonder where Danny's off to," Judy said. "He's a strange one. Hardly ever comes to mass. Never got over the death of his boy. At least that's one thing about Albert Malone. Never misses a Sunday. Confesses regularly, too. The Father has a soft heart for him."

I was about to inquire about Danny's boy but the tea room door opened and Grace Devereaux entered. Behind her was Lina Mulligan and her brother, who took a table near the door. Lina, wearing a Stella McCartney dress that she must have picked up in London, threw a bright blue shawl over the back of an empty chair. Her brother carefully folded the shawl and replaced it. For the first time, I was seeing him up close. He had black hair, dark eyes, and a pencil-thin mustache. The two of them were laughing, which startled me—I hadn't heard laughter in days.

What was so hilarious when village children were in peril?

"There's that Hector bloke," Judy whispered. "We have only Pearce's word that he's Lina's brother."

I looked at her sharply—she had the same suspicions I did. Smiling like a cat with cream on its whiskers, Judy tapped her lips with her fingertips. I wasn't sure of her meaning. Mum's the word, perhaps?

We ordered slices of blueberry pie. Conversation turned to St. Kevin's feast. We chatted on as I watched Lina and Hector from the corner of my eye. They *did* seem unusually close—touching hands, gazing into each other's eyes, laughing with sparkling white teeth. They didn't resemble each other at all. Both were dark, but she had fine features and a delicate complexion, while he was tanned and looked more like an actor...perhaps Javier Bardem.

"Tell me about Danny Aherne's boy's death," I said to Judy.

"A terrible tragedy. It breaks my heart to remember."

Grace Devereaux touched my shoulder. "Hello, Maria. I'm having a poetry program at the library in July? Would you read some of your verses?"

"Yes, of course. I'd be delighted."

"Grace," Judy said, "I heard your nephew was a friend of poor Bridget Vale."

Grace stiffened. "Tim knew her slightly."

"Some say he was with Bridget the night she died."

"He was home. I can vouch for that."

"Is Tim Hawkins your nephew?" I asked Grace.

"Yes, have you met him?"

"I heard him reciting poetry at the Green Mountain Café."

Grace seemed to relax. "What did you think of his poetry?"

"It is certainly exuberant," I said. "I detected the influence of Allen Ginsberg."

"I'll tell him. He'll be pleased that you heard Ginsberg in his work."

The restaurant door opened and Deirdre O'Malley walked in, wearing a purple sheath with a bright green blazer.

"Oh, there's Deirdre," Grace said. "I'm supposed to help her search for information on the Carrickfergus witch trial in County Antrim in the early 1700s." She bent close to me. "A nest of Presbyterians had settled there, wouldn't you know."

Grace went out the door with Deirdre. Judy said she must return to the priory to do the accounts. I parted from her, paid our bill, and left the tea room. On the way home, I realized Grace Devereaux had interrupted before Judy could tell me about Danny Aherne's son's death.

When I reached our cottage, Elizabeth was asleep on the sofa. With a pang, I realized her resemblance to Baby Doe. Same dark hair, same nose and lashes. I had never noticed it before, and for some inexplicable reason, it calmed me.

Mathieu called as I was setting the table for dinner.

"Tomorrow is Saturday," he said. "I'll pick you and Elizabeth up at eight. Be sure to wear sturdy shoes."

I caught a whiff of excitement. Would the stones at Ballygosteen hold a message for me?

CHAPTER TEN

At Ballygosteen, the stones lay in a circle to the right of a capstone balanced on two portal stones. I knelt, pressing my ear to one of the circle stones. Closing my eyes, I shut out birdsong, the rush of river water, and the chatter of workers as they dug shallow trenches. I heard an ancient life force, which sounded like beating hearts.

Hands had placed these stones with great care. People would have been smaller than I, but they would have been strong, existing on a healthy diet of fish, pig, fowl, and berries found in the woods. It had all been woods then. Evidence of great forests was buried deep in the bogs. I placed my palms on the stones, feeling their warmth.

Mathieu's American crew was working in a tent set up to evaluate the artifacts. The French crew—two archaeologists and four university students—squatted in a shallow ditch, probing for buried objects.

Mathieu came over and put his ear to the stone. "This is the papa one. He is the recorder of time."

I pointed to a smaller stone. "And this one?"

He laid hands on it. "Life-giver."

Earlier, he had taken Elizabeth and me inside the passage tomb, showing us wedge chambers, and now she was sitting on a canvas chair practicing her French with one of the students from Lyon. Mathieu and I remained at the circle, speculating on the positions of the stones.

"These people were sky-worshippers," he said. "They found deep meaning in the moon, sun, and stars. These stones are aligned with the stars—that would be my guess. The portal stone is positioned to catch the sunrise."

"The sky must have given solace," I said. "A cover, always there."

His hand rested on the mother stone and so did mine. There was comfort in the moment, discussing stones with him. With a start I realized that if I moved my hand a half inch, I would touch his. His long-fingered brown hand that had brought me so much pleasure....

I moved my hand away.

"Dr. Broussard!" a young man called. "Come see what Jack has uncovered!"

Mathieu hurried into the tent. "Maria!" he cried. "Come and see."

I went after him. The student named Jack had scraped mud from a stone carving with four faces that appeared to be feminine. The noses were delicate.

"Does she represent the four seasons?" I asked.

"We usually see things in threes," Jack said.

The sacred three—male genitalia.

Mathieu bent close to the carving. "She represents a goddess. The stone is so smooth, she must have spent millions of years in the water."

"You could call her Dea, which means river goddess," I suggested.

"Dea, she is," he replied. "At least for the time being."

I smiled at him. We had given new life to a Neolithic goddess. That was satisfying to me. Jack removed the final layer of mud from Dea and I asked to touch her. I traced her four noses with my fingertips. Had a prehistoric woman been the model for this carving? Or had she carved it herself? It frustrated me to know so little about the people who had lived when the earth was young. Elizabeth loaned me her camera and I took pictures of Dea.

"How long can you keep her?" I asked Mathieu.

"A week or two. You'll have plenty of time to visit her before we send her to the museum in Dublin."

When we returned to Coomara mid-afternoon, people were gathered in the church courtyard. Had another girl been kidnapped? Mathieu parked the car at the curb and with dread in our hearts, we joined the townspeople to see what had happened.

The kidnappers had struck again. They had taken two more girls. The Hardesty sisters, aged twelve and fourteen, had been kidnapped from a neighboring village. Just before noon, Katelyn Scanlon, a fifteen-year-old Coomara girl, got the scare of her life. She had been home, watching television with her little brother, Mikey, when the doorbell rang. Though she had been instructed not to open the door, she did. A man reached in and tried to drag her out. Mikey kicked the man in the shins and tore off his leather glove. Katelyn slammed and locked the door, and immediately called the garda, but the perpetrator got away.

Father O'Neill stood on the church steps. Mathieu left to speak with him.

Iris Vale ran toward me and gripped my hands. "Isn't it terrible, Maria? More girls gone, and the devils nearly got our Katelyn."

She was trembling. I took her hand.

"At night, I hear my Bridget singing," she cried. "It is such a sad song, missing us all."

"Does it happen in a dream?" I asked, instantly alert, for I knew the dead could communicate with the living.

"I'm not sure. I wake up and feel her presence. Her song lingers in the air like the scent of lilacs."

Was Bridget trying to tell her mother what happened to her?

"What is her song about?" I asked.

Freddy Vale rushed to his wife's side. "There is no song," he said. "I lay beside Iris all night. There's nothing to hear but her snoring."

Iris laughed, a hideous strangled sound of grief, drunkenness, and amusement. I bowed my head, unable to respond in any other way. Elizabeth and I embraced the couple, and they walked away, heading toward their cottage.

"Are you still going to the Druid ceremony tonight, Maria?" Elizabeth asked. "I'd think with all the terrible things that are happening, you'd want to stay home."

I stared at her wild-eyed, for I was thinking hard about what Iris had shared: Bridget's spirit could be sufficiently restless to speak from the ethers. She had sung to her mother in a dream.

"What did you say?" I asked.

"The Druid ceremony. Are you going?"

"I'd forgotten," I said. "Thank you for reminding me."

I glanced at Mathieu, who was still speaking with the priest. As I walked over to them, Father O'Neill clamped a brotherly hand on Mathieu's shoulder.

"Mathieu has offered to teach our girls self-defense," the priest said. "I'll make the announcement tomorrow. Classes can be held at St. Columba's primary school."

"Mathieu," I said, "when did you learn self-defense?"

"After you left, I took karate classes and earned a brown sash, Maria. That's two levels down from the black belt."

During our time together, Mathieu and I had worked out at the gym twice a week, but I had never heard him express a desire to learn karate.

"What about the older girls?" I asked.

Ireland's primary schools included children four to thirteen.

"We'll release them from classes early so they can attend," Father O'Neill said.

"Did you think of this yourself?" I asked Mathieu. "Was it really your idea to offer karate lessons?"

Mathieu regarded me with bemusement. Was he thinking how little I knew him?

"It's a terrific idea," I said quietly.

It actually was, but something about Mathieu teaching karate to the village girls bothered me. Was I jealous that he'd found a way to do something positive for the village in its time of trouble, and I hadn't?

I competed with him. I couldn't deny it.

***

That evening, Elizabeth tried to talk me out of attending the Druid ceremony. "You don't know what might happen, Maria! How big is the coven?"

"You're thinking of Wiccans," I said. "A group of Druids is called a grove."

"How disgusting. Father O'Neill despises Druid worshippers."

"That strikes me as odd," I said. "He seems an enlightened priest. Did Judy tell you he hated them? I'll bet some members of the grove are practicing Catholics."

Elizabeth didn't reply. I had upset her. She was, after all, a devout Catholic. She did not get up to help with the evening meal.

"Do you feel like eating grilled cheese sandwiches?" I called to her.

She didn't respond. I knew then that I had more than upset her: I had offended her—maybe even worried her about the condition of my soul.

I ate my meal, washed the dishes, and went upstairs to shower and change into clean clothes. When I came down, Elizabeth was in the kitchen. I smelled salmon baking in the oven. I read for a while and put down my book when Deirdre knocked on the front door at eleven-thirty. Elizabeth had gone to bed, so I had no opportunity to introduce the women. Deirdre handed me a brown robe with a hood. I slid it over my clothes.

She put on her robe. "Some of our members pull the hoods over their faces. They go to Father O'Neill's church and don't want to be recognized."

Did I want to cover my face? I decided not to. I had no employer monitoring my activities, nor colleagues here to spread gossip. I was deliciously free of such constraints.

"Is Dr. Broussard coming?" She fastened her seat belt and put the car in gear.

"I don't know," I said. "We went to the dig this morning but didn't discuss it. When we returned, we found out about the Hardesty girls and that Katelyn Scanlon had a scare."

"We have to unmask these devils," Deirdre said fiercely.

"You've heard Mathieu's theory, that someone here in the village is fingering the girls."

"He's right. Someone who knows them. The Hardesty girls were taken from their aunt's house. They had spent the night there. Whoever took them knew their routine."

Could someone at the schools be monitoring the girls and passing information to the kidnappers? I made a mental note to discuss the possibility with Finch.

"What is the ceremony like?" I asked.

"The moon is in its waning phase. It is a time for deep divination. We'll pray for our intuitive senses to be heightened. We hope that one or all of us will be struck with insight into who is taking the girls."

Deirdre drove to the edge of town and turned onto a rutted road that appeared to be someone's meadow. Hadn't she said the thorn tree belonged to the Mulligans? Several cars were parked near the stone fence. I looked for Mathieu's rental car but didn't see it. Deirdre also parked by the fence, and using a flashlight, guided our way through rows of corn for a quarter of a mile or so. There, surrounded by a circle of stones, was a twisted thorn tree. Strategically placed torches lit up the area. Members of the grove gathered around the ancient tree. All were hooded.

"The thorn tree is also called the *faerie tree*," Deirdre explained. "Some believe it could be a faerie and to cut it down would bring calamity. Pearce Mulligan chooses to plant around it."

"Superstition?" I asked.

Her tawny eyes flashed with amusement. "Perhaps. Perhaps not."

Deirdre lowered her hood and walked toward her fellow worshippers. I bowed my head so my hood fell halfway over my face and followed. Deirdre pulled me into the circle that had formed, then loosened her hand so she could walk freely. She began to pray:

May there be peace in the east,
peace in the south,
peace in the west,
and peace in the north.

She repeated the prayer and we joined in, moving swiftly around the tree. Torches flared in the midnight breeze. Suddenly I felt hands touching me—my head, my back, breasts, groin, legs, and feet. It was not Deirdre's friends who were stroking me, but unseen hands. Inside my skull, my brain awakened. The grove addressed an unnamed goddess, asking for wisdom. An image of the stone goddess, Dea, flashed in my mind. Perhaps her four faces represented the past, the present, the future, and the unknowable. I prayed to each of her faces to protect Ireland's girls from the kidnappers. I prayed for justice for Bridget.

You have the answers.

The words came from within my subconscious, but I had no idea what they meant. *How can I have the answers? What do I know that will unlock the identity of Bridget's killer? What do I know that will save the girls from sex traffickers?*

The worshippers loudly invoked the name of the garda, asking that the police be blessed with creative thinking so they could solve the crimes that had devastated the village. A woman read off the names of the dead and missing. The chanting became frenzied, incomprehensible, and then I realized they were speaking in Gaelic, which I only partially understood.

I watched from under my hood. One small person—a woman—slowly broke away from the circle and approached the thorn tree. She knelt and prayed, and when she got up, she nearly fell and cried out. An older woman's voice. Then a man—I assumed it was a man by his musculature and height—did a one-footed dance and moaned. A young woman with slim ankles raced around the tree as if she were chased by banshees. Others broke from the group and assumed postures of penitence. A tall man loped to the thorn tree to raise his hands. The chanting intensified, and then Deirdre broke free and walked around the tree, sowing seeds. Upon completing the circle, she threw up her hands and addressed the waning moon.

"Invest us with wisdom," she cried. "Give us love."

Then it was over. People walked down the planted rows toward the cars. Deirdre turned on her flashlight. We didn't speak. When we got in the car, we fastened our seatbelts and drove home.

"I wonder how many felt the goddess' blessing," she said.

I didn't answer, having no way of knowing. I did know, however, that my own mind and body felt unusually energized. I also felt the weight of the words: *You have the answers.*

"You're quiet," Deirdre observed.

"It isn't every day I attend a Druid ceremony."

"What did you think of it?"

"Ask me another day," I said, "when I've had time to reflect."

"Fair enough," she said.

She dropped me off at my cottage. On the kitchen table was Elizabeth's list of activities planned for St. Kevin's Festival, which was two weeks away. Scanning it, I saw members of Mathieu's karate class would demonstrate their skills in the parade.

So soon?

As I went upstairs, Elizabeth cried out, and I opened her bedroom door. She was asleep. She turned over and clearly exclaimed, "No! Don't torment me. It's over!"

I wondered if I should wake her, but she immediately calmed. What on earth had she been dreaming? Undressing, I got into bed and fell asleep.

***

At breakfast the next morning, Elizabeth questioned me about my experience in the meadow.

"It was quite energizing," I said.

"What was energizing about it?"

"I had to exercise my brain—find access to parts I don't normally use."

"What do you mean by that?"

"I prayed for justice for Bridget and for protection for the girls. Then I heard the words: 'You have the answers.'"

"What did you take that to mean?"

"That I have enough information to identify Bridget's killer and to stop the kidnapping ring."

Elizabeth curled her lip. "Hocus-pocus."

I instantly regretted sharing my experience with my cousin—not because she sought to shame me for participating in the Druid event, but because if it were known among the villagers, many of whom believed in the supernatural, that I knew who killed Bridget and who was taking the girls, the perpetrators could come after me.

I glanced at Elizabeth, who was slicing her breakfast pear. "Please don't share what I told you. If the killer thought I knew who he or she was, I would be in danger."

"I'm not an idiot, Maria. I won't tell anyone."

I had offended her again. To make amends, I asked her to tell me the origin of St. Kevin's Festival.

Elizabeth was glad to comply. "His feast day is June third, the day he died in 618. He founded the monastery at Glendalough and was known to love animals, like St. Francis. The village considers him a patron saint and holds an annual festival to celebrate his life."

"Seamus Heaney wrote a poem about him," I said. "'St. Kevin and the Blackbird'."

"That's right." Elizabeth rinsed her bowl in the sink. "Today, after Mass, I'm meeting with Father O'Neill and Judy. There's talk of calling off the trip to St. Kevin's Bed because of Bridget's murder and the kidnappings."

I knew about the pilgrimage to St. Kevin's Bed—a cave at Glendalough, a few miles away. The saint had lived there as a hermit for seven years. Each year on June third, a caravan of cars lined the road to Glendalough so villagers could fall to their knees and pray within sight of the bed, perched on the side of a mountain.

"That would be too bad," I said. "People need something to take their minds off the missing girls and Bridget's murder."

"And to feel God's blessing."

She went to the mirror, placed her little straw hat on her head, and said goodbye, heading to the church. Her tone was short. I had committed multiple offenses: apostasy, the Druid ceremony, giving credence to the message I received there, and not trusting her to keep her mouth shut.

I turned on my computer, hoping to research a Neolithic temple at Newgrange. Ancient people were deeply absorbed in worship to explain the unknown. Did they feel love for each other? What would *family* mean in 3200 (BCE)? Would *family* include the entire tribe? I began to jot down a few words, hoping they would inspire a poem. When my mind wandered to the disappearance of the village girls, I wrenched it back to my study.

I worked into late afternoon. A concept had begun to form in my mind. My poems for the Lewison project would depict the lives of prehistoric women, which would have been attuned to nature. What was it like to see the sunrise? The moon? I hunkered down over my notebook, writing down words that would convey a sense of wonder.

Elizabeth returned around five.

My telephone rang soon after. Inspector Finch.

"I wanted to tell you, Ms. Pell, that the girl at Bingham turned out not to be Tessa McMurray."

"What a shame. Thank you for telling me. Has anything turned up to identify Bridget's killer?"

"Not a thing. The trail has grown cold."

He ended the call and I tried to return to my work, but the words, *you have the answers*, dinned in my ears.

What did I know?

CHAPTER ELEVEN

I decided to write down every fact in my possession. It seemed best to separate Bridget's murder from the kidnappings. So far, nothing linked the crimes, except the age and gender of the victims. Bridget was lured out of her cottage. But wait—I didn't know she was lured. She could have freely walked out of the cottage. To say she was lured was logical, considering her reputation for piety and good behavior, however....

Where had I put Valerie Anderson's pink notebook? Rummaging through my desk drawers, I found it beneath a folder of half-born poems and paged through to Valerie's notation that Bridget was undeserving of being chosen May Queen. Either Valerie was showing spitefulness or Bridget had led a secret life. I bit my knuckle, wishing I could show Finch the notebook, but didn't dare because I had, in effect, stolen it.

The only other evidence I had that Bridget led a secret life was that she had inquired more than once about Tim Hawkins at the Green Mountain Café, a known hangout for drug dealers. The waitress had seen her with Tim on one occasion.

Though Iris thought she held a tight rein on Bridget, the truth was that Iris and Freddy spent their leisure hours at the pub. At night, Bridget led an unsupervised life. I dialed Finch's number. He answered immediately.

"Inspector," I said, "what if Bridget Vale had a secret life?"

"What do you mean?"

"What if she wasn't the pious girl we all thought she was?"

"Impossible. I talked to the sisters at the school. She was a model student."

"But if she deceived everyone..."

"Ms. Pell, why would you want to besmirch a dead girl's reputation?"

If it turned out that Bridget was involved in something disreputable, her reputation would be ruined. Iris would have yet another reason to drink herself to death.

"I wouldn't want to," I said, choosing my words carefully. "If we find out something unfavorable to Bridget, I would hope we could keep it under wraps."

He heaved a sigh. "Do you have a theory?"

"If we accept that Bridget led a secret life, which would have been possible, considering she was largely unsupervised, she could have hung out with bad associates. She went to the Green Mountain Café, where drug sales occur. She had a crush on Tim Hawkins, who seems to be a radicalized teenager with too much money and too much idle time."

"We've questioned the Hawkins boy. As far as we know, he isn't connected with the drug trade."

"What if Bridget saw something she shouldn't have seen? That would be a reason to kill her."

"How do you propose to uncover this secret life of Bridget's?" Finch asked.

"I don't know."

I wished I could show Valerie's notebook to Finch.

"You're on the wrong track, Miss Pell."

After ending the call, I sat staring at Valerie Anderson's notebook. Her address was on the first page: 124 Cheshire Street. I turned off the computer and ran down the stairs.

Elizabeth was back from Mass. "Where are you going, Maria?"

"I'll be back in a little while."

Taking my bicycle out of its niche, I rolled it onto the sidewalk and rode off in the direction of Cheshire Street. I had no idea what I would say to Valerie Anderson. She wouldn't want her parents to see the notebook. Could I use that to advantage?

The Anderson cottage was painted blue with white shutters. The patch of green in front was well tended. Pink geraniums bloomed from window boxes and a small blue tricycle was parked on the porch. I knocked on the door. A tall man answered. I assumed he was Valerie's father.

"I'm Maria Pell," I told him. "I live in the pink cottage by the cliffs. Several days ago, I was in Miss Molly's Tearoom and found a notebook on the floor belonging to Valerie Anderson. I've come to return it."

He reached out his hand. "I'll give it to her."

"I must speak to her first. Is she at home?"

He frowned, as I expected he would, but went to the hallway and called Valerie. She came from another room, carrying a toddler, and I removed the notebook from my purse so she could see it. Her eyes widened.

"Here, Da." She passed the toddler to her father, hurried over to me, and maneuvered both of us out on the porch.

She moved close to me. "Where did you find my notebook?"

"On the floor of Miss Molly's Tearoom."

She began twisting a lock of dark hair. "I haven't been in there for nearly...two weeks."

"It's taken me a while to figure out whether I should return it to you."

She cast her eyes downward. "You looked inside."

I nodded. "Why did you think Sister Augustine was a fool for choosing Bridget to be May Queen?"

"I don't know."

"Wasn't Bridget the sweet, good girl everyone thought she was?"

"She was all right."

"I'm thinking of turning the notebook over to the garda."

She raised her head. "No, don't do that! They'll give it to Da."

"Then tell me why Bridget didn't deserve to be May Queen."

"She sold drugs," Valerie whispered.

"How do you know?"

"I saw her in the woods selling to some boys from Flyn."

Inside the cottage, a woman called the family to Sunday dinner. Valerie's father replied. I heard heavy footfalls heading toward the door.

"Who is the stick man you've drawn?" I asked quickly.

"I don't know his name."

"What does he do?"

"He brings drugs to Coomara."

"Who is Miss Priss, Valerie?"

"Bridget."

The door creaked open. I handed Valerie her notebook and left.

Bridget Vale was Miss Priss? She had dealings with Albert Malone? Had the fallen priest corrupted her as he had the boys in his care in Dublin?

Was Valerie Anderson truthful? Was she biased?

On my way home, I saw Finch's car parked outside the garda station, got off my bicycle, and went in. The front desk was unattended, so I went down the hallway toward the inspector's office. A sergeant was talking to Finch. I eavesdropped. They were talking about someone named Milton.

"I sent Katelyn Scanlon's assailant's glove to Dublin," the officer was saying. "They were able to get fingerprints off the leather and found a match in the Interpol database. He's Franco Milton and he has several aliases. He's been in prison for armed robbery."

"Do you know where Milton is from?" Finch asked.

"He has several addresses, mostly on the continent. Nothing in Ireland."

"Put out an alert for him."

The officer got up to leave. I hurried back to the entrance, acting as if I'd just come through the door.

"Inspector Finch is in his office, Ms. Pell," the officer said.

I hurried down the hall.

"Inspector," I said, "I have a new theory for you to think about. What if I were to tell you that a young girl said Bridget was selling drugs? And that the supplier was a stick man with short arms and legs?"

He looked up from a document on his desk. "I would think you were daft."

I looked him straight in the eye. "Did you search Bridget's room after her body was found?"

"Of course. Nothing was found."

"You should go back and look again."

He bent over the document, not replying. Feeling I'd overstayed my welcome, I left. Riding home, I was struck by a thunderbolt of thought. If Bridget were involved with the drug trade, her killer could have been the man with short arms and legs. He could have garroted her.

That led me to another thought. Had Tessa known something about the murder? Were we wrong to think she had been kidnapped by sex traffickers? Was Tessa lying garroted somewhere, just like her cousin?

Cousin.

The girls were blood relatives. Did that mean anything?

When I reached home, Elizabeth was taking a meatloaf from the oven. I didn't share with her my new theory of Bridget's murder. She had gotten over her huffiness and was filled with enthusiasm for her festival committee work.

"I thought of inviting Mathieu to dinner," Elizabeth said, "but knew I should check with you first."

"You can invite Mathieu," I said. "He'd enjoy a homecooked meal."

"Maybe in a day or two," she replied.

Before bedtime, Mathieu called, asking if I'd like to go out to dinner the following night. I opened my mouth to say no, then changed my mind. I could test my theory about Bridget on him.

***

We dined at a restaurant on the river, called the Wicklow, for the mountain range visible from the windows. It was a Monday and there were few diners. The décor was understated—ivory walls, moss-green drapes at floor-to-ceiling windows, mauve carpeting on the floors. I ordered white wine and Mathieu asked for a martini.

My gaze flicked over him. Handsome Mathieu. He had dressed in brown trousers and a tan jacket. He looked great, whatever he wore.

He smiled. "I was surprised you accepted my invitation. You usually say no."

"You shouldn't have been surprised. After all, we're old friends."

He bristled. "Is that what we are now—old friends?"

A fashionably-dressed African woman walked past our table, accompanied by a dark-skinned man. She swept hate-filled eyes over me.

Mathieu looked uneasily at me.

I shrugged.

As a bi-racial couple, we'd experienced our share of negative attention from both blacks and whites. I'd thought we were taking it in our stride, but a year or so into our relationship, I intuited that Mathieu was sensitive to gestures from women of his race indicating resentment that he'd chosen a white mate. I knew he felt he'd betrayed his black sisters. Was his attraction to Zara an attempt to atone?

"It doesn't offend me," I said, referring to the woman's glare.

"It's because you're white," he said. "You have an inborn sense of superiority."

I considered what he said. "'Superiority' is the wrong word. 'Confidence' would be more accurate."

I had come into the world as a white child, grown up with loving and educated parents, and set off on a path that had presented few obstacles.

"Your race gives you confidence," he said.

I didn't argue.

The waiter came for our order. I ordered monkfish. Mathieu chose venison with sweet potato.

"I admire your confidence, Maria," Mathieu said. "Certainly, it helped me over rough spots when I worked toward my doctorate."

"Yes, I suppose. Let's talk about what you've dug up at Ballygosteen. Have you found other artifacts?"

"Nothing as spectacular as our four-faced goddess," he said. "Parts of an axe, a tool that was probably used to skin animals."

"I'm interested in prehistorical family relations, particularly women's roles."

"People lived in tribes. Everything was communal. Women would have done lighter work because they lacked the physical strength of men."

"Do you think men and women had tender feelings for one another?"

"It's hard to say."

Until our meals came, we discussed various findings and theories of the division of labor in prehistoric communities. After our salads—wonderful creations of lettuces, artichokes, and blueberries—without revealing Valerie Anderson as my source, I presented my supposition that Bridget Vale had been connected to the drug trade. Mathieu listened attentively, rarely speaking. When I finished, he told me I was barking up the wrong bush.

"Tree," I said. "Why do you say that?"

"From everything I've heard about Bridget, she was a good Catholic girl. It would be morally wrong to destroy her good name."

I felt wounded. He had the same objection as Finch.

"But she could have inadvertently become involved with the drug trade," I insisted. "She was naïve—she could have been pulled in by Tim Hawkins."

"According to Dennis, she was either in school, attending mass, or conducting herself as a respectable young person."

Dennis! He was on a first name basis with Finch!

"Her murder had nothing to do with the way she led her life," Mathieu went on. "Her murderer was settling a score."

"He could have been a drug dealer. He..."

"The score was personal," Mathieu insisted. "Whoever killed her wanted her dead for personal reasons."

"And you're saying this because...?

"Because of the way she was killed. She was garroted. Her killer wanted her close to him when she died. He wanted to feel her suffer."

I had thought that, too, until I learned Bridget might be leading a secret life.

The waiter appeared with our orders. As he set the monkfish in front of me, I cast a resentful look at Mathieu—he was refusing to even consider my theory about Bridget.

He picked up his knife and fork. "The venison looks delicious."

I couldn't leave the matter alone. "I spoke to Bridget's classmate. She claimed Bridget spoke to the defrocked priest."

"Perhaps she offered him compassion, Maria."

The dinner date wasn't turning out as I expected. I thought Mathieu would give some credence to the idea of Bridget having a secret life. I was miffed. My monkfish no longer appealed to me. I watched as Mathieu cut into his venison with apparent relish and ate.

"Concealing Bridget's shortcomings won't solve her murder," I said.

"You have only the word of a teenage girl, who may have envied Bridget."

We were back at square one—the integrity of Valerie Anderson's accusation. I toyed with my asparagus. Would Finch send someone to search Bridget's room, as I suggested?

Mathieu finished his meal and asked the waiter for the dessert menu. I shook my head, wanting the evening to end, but Mathieu ordered a slice of chocolate cake.

"Want a taste?" he asked, waving his fork at me.

"No, thank you."

***

He returned me to the cottage. Elizabeth was in the kitchen, working on a green plastic banner for St. Kevin's Day. I went upstairs and turned on the computer but couldn't concentrate. Was it morally wrong to reveal Bridget's hidden life—if she had one?

Who was Mathieu to speak of moral wrongs? Look what he had done to me! Two years ago, I assumed we were in a monogamous relationship. We had a standing lunch date on Wednesdays. I went to his office, opened the door, and found him copulating on top of his desk with that Amazonian Zara. Right next to the granite block he claimed held the spirit of a fertility god!

Knowing Mathieu, who was as punctual as the tide, he had not forgotten our date. He had wanted me to know he needed the woman. What had I missed? Had I become an unenthusiastic lover? Until that moment, I had loved him, body and soul.

Hadn't I?

Blast Mathieu!

For a long time, Mathieu and Zara were minted on my cerebral cortex as surely as faces on a coin. I conjured up the image again. To my amazement, I did not feel the wrench in my gut I always had felt.

Was the incident blurring with the passage of time?

CHAPTER TWELVE

Bong! Bong! Bong! The church bell was frenzied. Elizabeth was already up, but I had lain in bed, festering over the outcome of my dinner with Mathieu. By the second peal, I was into my underclothes. By the sixth, I had swiped my underarms with deodorant, thrown a knee-length tee dress over my head, and velcroed my feet into sandals. As I ran down the stairs, Elizabeth rushed out the front door ahead of me.

"Hurry," she cried. "Another girl must have been taken."

Stepping into the brilliant sunrise, I scanned the street before continuing on to the church. I didn't know why. Was I afraid for myself? The bell rang again. My heart twisted with fear for the child who had been taken. Nearly out of breath, I reached the church steps where a grim-faced Inspector Finch stood, holding a megaphone.

Beside him stood Seamus Scanlon, Katelyn's father.

The kidnappers had come back for her.

People gathered, some holding mugs of tea. A young woman, dressed in a green shift, held a squalling baby. Judy Moriarity ran out of the priory in a pink chenille robe. I looked around for Mathieu, wondering if he had heard the bell. No sign of him.

Finch raised the megaphone. "Katelyn Scanlon was kidnapped on her way to school this morning. A van pulled up and a man yanked her into the back. Her brother, Mikey, was with her and the assailant knocked him unconscious."

Anger roared through the crowd.

"Harmin' our kids!" a man yelled. "Get the fuckers!"

A woman's voice. "How is Mikey?"

"Mikey's fine," Inspector Finch said. "He's a tough little lad. The men were masked. Mikey thinks there were three of them. He said the van was dark blue and the license plate contained a T and a B. Now we know there are four kidnappers, one of them a known criminal named Franco Milton. We've put out an alert for the van."

Actually, we knew of five kidnappers—possibly six—the stuttering woman who had pulled the girl into the car in Danny Aherne's parking lot. If the man driving the car was not Milton or one of Katelyn's kidnappers, then we knew of six.

Mathieu approached from the street, stood at the edge of the crowd listening, and then walked over to Elizabeth and me.

He lowered his voice. "How sophisticated are the garda's interrogation methods, Maria?"

"What do you mean?"

"Would they know how to question a little boy? How old is the child?"

"Seven or eight," Elizabeth said.

"Then he can identify smells and sounds," Mathieu said. "Why don't you ask to speak to the boy, Maria? As a poet, you deal with the senses. Mikey might know more than he told the garda officers."

"The garda will have questioned Mikey thoroughly," I said.

"Just a thought," Mathieu said. "I'm on my way to Ballygosteen. I'll be back this evening. Be careful."

He pecked me on the cheek, which made me jump and the villagers gawk, and hurried to the rental car he'd parked on the street.

Judy Moriarity hustled over. "Isn't it terrible about poor Katelyn? Father's gone to comfort the mother. I'm going to make scones to take to the house."

Elizabeth said she would make a casserole.

"I'll take it to the Scanlons," I said, rethinking Mathieu's suggestion that I speak with Mikey.

"Is Dr. Broussard a Muslim like the Iraqis that work at the fishery?" Judy asked. "Father is always curious about what strangers in the village believe."

I doubted that. It was Judy, who was curious.

"I don't know if he's Muslim," I said.

Of course, I did know. Mathieu believed that having souls just wasn't a human prerogative, but that rocks, dogs, ants, mountains, and rivers also had them. Judy would be shocked by Mathieu's religious beliefs.

She looked at me with shrewd eyes. "You must know Dr. Broussard well."

She was referring to the kiss on the cheek.

"Fairly well," I said.

Elizabeth touched my arm. "If I'm to make a casserole for the Scanlons' dinner, we should stop at the market."

We told Judy goodbye and headed down the street. At the market, Elizabeth purchased sausage, noodles, and fennel, and when we got home, she added Parmesan cheese and turned the ingredients into a fine supper casserole. Around two o'clock, I took it to the Scanlon home.

Father O'Neill was just taking his leave from the Scanlons. A short, broad-chested man, he walked with his head down, seemingly deep in thought. He nodded distractedly.

I knocked on the door and was admitted by Seamus Scanlon. His wife, Gertie, was seated amid a group of neighbors, who were doing their best to console her. Her anguish took my breath away. Too often these days, villagers were weeping in the arms of friends over missing or dead children.

There was a ray of hope: the Irish Naval Service boats might have prevented the kidnappers from transferring the girls to a seagoing vessel. The girls might be held captive somewhere near—in a farmer's barn or a neighbor's cottage. In that case, someone local was surely collaborating with the kidnappers. I stared into the faces of the people who had gathered to comfort Gertie and Seamus Scanlon. Had any of them conspired to take their daughter from them?

I went into the kitchen. The table was piled high with cakes, salads, and homemade breads. On the stove was a pot of lamb stew. I set Elizabeth's casserole on an oven mat near the stove.

Around the corner was the stairwell. A ball bounced down the steps, rolled onto the linoleum, ricocheted off a table leg, and came to a stop near my right foot. I picked it up, looked up the stairs, and saw a young boy with dark hair sitting on the top step, a bandage on his forehead. He was far enough away from the sitting room that no one would bother him but was close enough to hear what was going on.

Thinking the sight of me might be unnerving, I slid onto the bottom step with my back to him, holding the ball in my hands. I sighed, wanting him to think I was so weary I had to sit down. He remained where he was.

What to say? I could tell him how brave he was, but as the little brother who had once saved his sister only to fail the next time, he might not want to hear that. He was probably feeling anxious and sad. Maybe even hopeless.

I put the ball on the step beside me. "Solving a crime," I said softly, "requires keeping a clear head and putting facts together. We already know who one of the kidnappers is."

He moved down three steps.

"We have a description of the van," I went on. "At least four men are involved."

Another step.

"They're taking the prettiest girls," he said.

"That means someone is picking them out."

"Maybe someone at the school."

The psalmist wrote: *Out of the mouths of babes and sucklings hast thou ordained strength.* He had Mikey Scanlon in mind.

The little boy moved to the step behind me. I shifted my position to face him and introduced myself. He had alert brown eyes, plump cheeks, a small pink mouth.

A spark of recognition appeared in his eyes. "You're the lady who read the poem about the elephant."

Soon after arriving in Ireland, I had participated in a library program. The elephant poem had been a protest against ivory poaching.

"That's right," I said. "Did you like the poem?"

He nodded his head.

"Mikey, do you remember any particular smells on the men who took your sister?"

"Pickles."

Had the men stopped at a fast-food restaurant before taking Katelyn?

"What did the men sound like? Did either of them speak?"

"One yelled at me to let go of Katelyn. He sounded like a frog."

"Do you mean he spoke with a croaking sound?"

"I think so."

"Did you tell Inspector Finch about the pickle smell and the frog sound?"

Mikey nodded. "But I forgot to tell him the man who smelled like pickles called Katie by her name."

A revelation.

I took Mikey's hand. "You should tell Inspector Finch about the man saying Katie's name. Can you describe the man who hit you?"

"He wasn't tall like Da. He had a ring on his finger—one with a red stone. I told the garda."

Now we would all be looking at men's hands.

As I patted his cheek, I felt afraid for the boy. What if the kidnapper came back for him? I wrote my telephone number on a scrap of paper, handed it to him, and told him to call if anything made him feel afraid. Retrieving the ball, he scampered to the top of the stairs. I went to the sitting room to pay my respects to his parents. Seamus Scanlon had joined his wife on the settee.

"I'm so sorry about your daughter," I said. "If I can be of help, please let me know."

The Scanlons murmured something in reply and I was about to leave when Gertie suddenly said, "This morning, Katelyn went to school early to practice a song with the music instructor. She was going to sing at St. Kevin's Festival."

"That's why she was up and about so early," Seamus added. "Otherwise, she would have been in bed."

Katelyn's schedule had changed on the morning she was taken.

"Who knew she would be going to school early?" I asked.

"The music teacher," Seamus answered.

"Manfred Fitzgerald, the custodian," Gertie said, "He needed to let her and Mikey inside before the doors were unlocked."

"Why was Mikey with her?" I asked.

"He plays the harmonica and accompanies her."

Eerily, Mikey began to play his harmonica from his perch on the stairs. Conversation stopped. A few people wept. I tried to identify the sad melody but couldn't. The boy finished playing. Silence, as a prayer, was offered up.

I excused myself and went to see Finch.

***

When I stepped onto the sidewalk in front of the garda station, the door opened and the inspector hurried out.

"Inspector Finch," I called out. "I need to see you."

"Not now. I'm busy."

I fell into step behind him. "Have you found Katelyn?"

"No. Some sheepherder found the van abandoned in a meadow. I'm on my way there now."

"Let me come," I begged.

He stopped beside his car. "I told you, Ms. Pell. This is none of your business."

"But it is. Today, I spoke with Mikey Scanlon. He forgot to tell you that one of the men called Katelyn, Katie. He knew her name."

Finch glared at me. "Were you questioning that little boy?"

"Not really. He just...he just told me. It spilled out of him. I took over a casserole and he was sitting on the stairs and..."

Though I hated doing it, sometimes it worked best when dealing with men to play the addlepated female. It was a shortcut I'd learned in transactions with college administrators, most of whom were male. He shot me a suspicious look and told me to get in the car.

"Did you know that Katelyn went to school early to practice a song for St. Kevin's Festival?" I asked.

"Yes, we know all that."

"The kidnappers must have known…"

"And they may not have known. If they were watching the house, they would have seen her come out."

That was so. Still, I wondered about the music teacher and the school custodian, Manfred Fitzgerald. Could one of them be the villager who was identifying Coomara's prettiest girls? Was someone else connected to the school aware of the Scanlon children's early morning activities?

After racing through the streets to the edge of town, Finch torqued onto a gravel road heading up the hill, wound around several bends, and then plummeted downward, ending up at a sheepherder's shed set among gnarly trees. Two garda cars were parked by the trees. Protruding from the open shed door was the rear end of a dark blue van. The license plate read 405 WTB.

"WTB," Finch said. "Liverpool. Undoubtedly stolen."

Officers examined tire treads in the dark soil. "Looks like a truck picked them up," one said. "They took off across the meadow and must have gotten back on the main road."

I got out of the car and peered through the van's side windows. Strewn over the back seat were Styrofoam boxes and crumpled napkins. One box held a half-eaten hamburger in a bun and a few desiccated French fries. An odd morning meal. If the food was from the night before, the men might have traveled some distance to Coomara.

"Get the Crime Scene Unit out here to go over the car," Finch said to his officers. "Find out who this meadow belongs to."

"Belongs to Pearce Mulligan," an officer said. "My cousin used to herd his sheep."

The inspector motioned me back into the car, got in himself, and drove back onto the road.

"There should be a lot of fingerprint evidence," I ventured.

He didn't speak until we reached the edge of town. "Mikey said one of the men spoke Katelyn's name?"

"Yes. He called her Katie."

"He said one of the men sounded like a frog," Finch said. "As a poet, what do you make of that?"

I had been thinking about Mikey's simile. Frogs made different sounds. "Maybe the man had a cold and was hoarse, or..."

"Maybe he had a bass voice," Finch said.

We rode to the station in silence. I thanked the inspector for allowing me to accompany him. He went into the building. I wandered off, wondering how long it would take for the CSU to sift through the evidence in the car.

What to do? My left brain, with its sense of order, had been activated. I wanted clues to follow but had none at the moment. Surely Finch would look into the school custodian and music teacher. To think of Bridget, sweet and virginal, in the hands of rough men who took her life made me furious. I was enraged for Bridget, for the missing girls, for all women who suffered at the hands of men.

Innis Cove might serve to orient my thinking. I had sensed Druid spirits there. Climbing down the path leading to the cove, I sat in my accustomed place against the large boulder. Soon I heard a rustling of robes and felt the spirits come. Five, this time.

Taking seats on the rocks, they nodded to each other. Waves splashed against the rocks. I smelled salt in the air. Dark clouds raced across the pale sky, propelled by the west wind. Gulls paced quietly, pecking the sand for food. I sat, trying to find peace. My mind was not in a reflective mood—it was thoroughly activated.

Had Finch sent officers to search Bridget's room?

I dialed his number.

"What now?" he asked in an irritable tone.

"I'm wondering if you sent officers to search Bridget's room."

He didn't reply right away. I heard papers shuffling.

"I haven't time to talk to you right now, Ms. Pell."

He hung up.

***

That evening, Elizabeth and I went to the corner pub. Out of uniform, Sergeant Potts was sitting at the bar with a handsome man whom she introduced as Neville. I sat next to her. After ordering a glass of stout, I turned to her, remarking that I'd spoken to Inspector Finch earlier in the day.

"He said he'd sent officers to search Bridget Vale's room again," I lied.

"Good thing we went," she said. "We found two hundred and fifty euros hidden in a winter jacket pocket. Keep it under your hat."

Two hundred and fifty euros. That was roughly three hundred dollars.

"Did Iris know where Bridget got the money?" I asked.

"Her mum was surprised she had so much."

"Bridget helped me with gardening," I said. "I paid her. She may have earned the money through odd jobs."

Potts' companion spoke to her and she turned to him. I sipped from my glass. What had Bridget gotten herself into?

CHAPTER THIRTEEN

The *Tarbhfhess* referred to the "bull-sleep" or "bull-feast." I was reading from a book on Druidic prophecy. A bull was killed and its meat eaten by a prophet who then slept while four priests chanted. In the sleeper's dreams, the next king of Tara would be revealed. I wished I could eat a sacred meal and dream the identity of the monsters who were tormenting the people of Coomara. Perhaps I could concoct a pudding of stardust or a pie made from the breath of elves. Perhaps that was the start of a poem....

It was morning. I had breakfasted and was curled up on the sofa, taking notes on the rites of prophets and prophetesses. The telephone rang. No caller ID.

A child's terrified voice. Mikey Scanlon.

He sounded out of breath. "I saw one of the men who took Katie at the petrol station when I was there with my mum."

My nerves tensed. "Where are you, Mikey?"

The phone went dead.

I rang the garda station. Finch was out. I reported Mikey's call to the officer who answered the phone.

"There was no caller ID," I added.

"Where was he calling from?" the officer asked.

"I asked, but he didn't say."

"I'll send someone to the Scanlon house to see if he's safe."

"Will you call me back?" I asked.

He said he would. Elizabeth came downstairs. An hour passed. She and I fixed a light meal. She never ate much and I was worried about

Mikey. In the middle of lunch, we heard a knock at the door. I ran to open it.

Inspector Finch.

"Mikey Scanlon is gone from his home," he said. "Tell me all you can about his telephone call."

"There's not much to tell. He called about an hour ago, saying he saw one of the men who kidnapped his sister at the petrol station. He sounded scared and breathless."

"Had he been running, do you think?"

"He could have been."

Finch scowled at me. "Did you hear background noises?"

"No. Only silence."

"The Scanlons say Mikey doesn't have a cell phone. Where could he have been calling from?"

"I don't know."

"Mrs. Scanlon was at the station an hour ago. Mikey was with her. They went home, she went to the kitchen to prepare lunch, and when she called Mikey, he didn't answer. We've searched the Scanlon home and grounds."

I began to pace. I hadn't been in Mikey Scanlon's life long enough to know his habits.

"Mrs. Scanlon called the parents of his chums," the inspector went on. "He isn't with them."

"Maybe the parents don't know, but the children do."

"I thought of that and sent officers to question them. Why did Mikey call you?"

"I gave him my phone number when we talked on the Scanlon stairs."

"Didn't you think that would be meddling in police affairs?"

I stared at him. "That didn't cross my mind. I was afraid for him because he had seen the kidnappers."

"He might have called us if you hadn't interfered."

I looked away, feeling ashamed. Perhaps Mikey would have had more courage to stay on the phone if he'd called the garda.

Finch's tone softened. "I don't mind telling you, Ms. Pell, that I'm nearly at my wits' end. We have one girl murdered, two missing from Flyn, and two gone from Coomara. Now Mikey..."

"Rather than exclude me, it seems you'd be wise to let me help."

"We're dealing with dangerous people. My officers are trained in self-defense."

"I could keep a low profile."

He gave me a skeptical look. "You've become identified with the case. You've questioned people. The village is like a party line."

"I accept responsibility for my actions," I said.

He shook his head. "It isn't that simple. There is liability."

"You have benefited from my observations and discoveries," I argued. "For example, the pansy in Bridget's hair, which led Elizabeth and me to the place where the poor girl was murdered. And it was through my conversation with Mikey Scanlon that we learned the kidnappers called Katelyn, Katie, which gave weight to Mathieu's suggestion that someone in the village is collaborating with the kidnappers."

"Those things are true, Ms. Pell. But still..."

"At least, let me know what you've discovered so far," I said. "Do you have the DNA results from the trash in the kidnapper's van?"

"We learned very little. Franco Milton was not in the van. We haven't identified the three men who were. The lab is carrying out additional tests, which takes time."

"Deirdre O'Malley said Pearce Mulligan's estate manger stole her sheep," I said. "Could he have abducted the children?"

"No doubt, Danny Doyle took Deirdre's sheep to harass her. She's unpopular because of her beliefs. He would never kidnap children. He has ten of his own."

His cellphone rang. He spoke a few words into it, looked unhappy, and turned to me.

"Mikey Scanlon's chums shed no light on the situation. We are organizing search parties for the boy. If you want to help, join the search. The parties are forming at St. Columba's."

He left and I alerted Elizabeth. We changed into trainers and hurried to the church.

***

The bell ringer pulled hard on the ropes. Father O'Neill stood at the top of the steps and offered a prayer that we might find the young boy before the night chill. Gertie Scanlon collapsed in her husband Seamus's arms. Judy Moriarity rushed down the steps to help carry her into the priory.

Mathieu appeared. "What's this? Another child missing?"

He swore when I told him about Mikey. "Who is behind this?"

Anger was building inside me, as well. Nearly three weeks had passed since Bridget's body was found. So far, there seemed to be no connection between her death and the girls' disappearances. No progress had been made in either case, regarding the perpetrators. Mathieu grabbed my hand and we joined a group led by one of Elizabeth's friends. Mathieu said little. His brow was furrowed, his jaw set.

We searched through the day, covering the same territory we had for Tessa McMurray, and stopped to eat when staff from the two tearooms brought sack lunches and bottled water. Two groups went through the streets of the villages, knocking on doors, tramping through gardens. My group moved to the ruins surrounding the town—the abbey, castle, and old bell tower. Elizabeth stumbled over a tree root, fell into a stream, and went home to put on dry clothes. I didn't see her return.

At half-past four, we heard the church bell. A villager phoned Mathieu, saying Mikey's jacket had been found at a playground. By the time we got to the playground, another child had claimed the jacket.

Exhausted, we sat on the grass to rest. Then someone thought of a cave near Innis Bay, which was separated by sea water from the mainland. We hurried to the bay. The tide was high. Someone supplied a boat and Mathieu and two men rowed out to the cave.

"Can Mikey swim?" I asked.

No one in our search party knew.

The men returned two hours later.

"The cave is small," Mathieu reported, "and the opening is above sea level. No sign of Mikey."

With heavy hearts, we made our way home. Mathieu went back to his room at the inn, but I invited him to the cottage for breakfast the next morning.

***

He came at nine. Elizabeth remained in bed. She was suffering from a cold, undoubtedly caused by falling into the stream. I made bacon and scrambled eggs. Mathieu manned the toaster. When we lived together, we had shared meal preparation and moved within the confines of the small kitchen with familiar syncopation. I found myself forgetting we were estranged.

"I love you, Maria," he said, as he took the jam from the refrigerator.

I didn't reply.

"Tell me you still have feelings for me," he said.

I scraped the eggs from the skillet. "Something remains. I'm not sure what it is."

He didn't press me, which was unusual. We sat at the table, ate breakfast, and when finished, took our mugs of tea into the sitting room.

"How would you describe the people your grandfather said sold out the children?" I asked.

"They were often the most trusted people in the village."

I made a face. "Here that would be Father O'Neill and Inspector Finch. We can be fairly sure they aren't betraying the children. It's not in their natures, nor do they have any incentive."

"What do you mean by incentive?"

"The need for money...or the drive to exact revenge."

I thought of Deirdre O'Malley's ancestor's story. He had tried to save a starving village by robbing a granary. Someone in Coomara betrayed him and he'd been executed, perhaps leaving Deirdre with a grudge. How many more villagers had grievances that stemmed from the past?

"Has Dennis found a connection among the families whose children were taken?" Mathieu asked.

"I must ask him. How helpful you are, Mathieu!"

I leaned over and kissed him, the first time I'd done so in nearly two years. He made no move to pull me into his arms, and for a moment, I regretted that he didn't. But if he had, I probably would have objected.

I called Finch and asked if he'd have time to see me.

"Yes, Ms. Pell," he said. "I'll send a patrol car for you. I want you to look at the security film from the petrol station. You've had contact with Mikey Scanlon. You may pick up on something in his behavior that we've missed."

I ended the call with Finch and told Mathieu I was going to the garda station to look at the tape. "He's sending a car. Do you want to come, too?'

"I'm needed at the dig. I'll be back late this afternoon."

Mathieu embraced me lightly and left. I wrote a note to Elizabeth and went outside to get into the garda car, which had just pulled to the curb. As I hurried down the steps, my muscles tensed. Birds stopped chirping, moisture hung heavy in the air. From the corner of my eye, I saw a black car crawling down the street, a glint of metal—

I threw myself on the grass.

A shot rang out.

My cheekbone thudded against the corner of the wooden step.

The officer ran toward me. "Ms. Pell!"

"I'm all right," I yelled.

He raced back to his squad car and gave chase to the car.

I lay in the grass, feeling its damp blades against my skin. *Thank you, goddess of the universe.* How precious life was! I took a deep breath and marveled at how quickly my lungs filled with air. A breath of life. I tested my limbs and moved my head from side to side. Elizabeth came through the door in her robe. A robin flew off the roof. The smell of forsythia drifted over from Brendan Calloway's yard.

"Was that a shot?" Elizabeth cried. "Maria, have you been shot?"

"He missed."

She ran toward me, cradled my head in her lap. "Can you get up?"

I sat up slowly, afraid that quick movement would make me light-headed. Elizabeth pulled me to a standing position. Leaning against her, I dragged my feet up the porch steps, then lowered my body into a wicker chair.

"Look at your face. You're going to have a terrible bruise."

Elizabeth ran into the cottage and came back with a plastic bag filled with ice cubes. "Thank you." I took the bag from her to hold against my cheekbone.

"Who shot at you?"

"I couldn't see."

"You could have been killed! I'm calling Mathieu."

"What can he do? The shooter drove off. The officer went after him."

"I'm calling him anyway."

My cheek had begun to throb with pain and I was thankful for the ice-bag. Holding it against my face, I got up, walked to the wooden column supporting the porch roof, and found a bullet hole at eye level. It had not gone through the column.

Brendan ran through my front gate, buttoning his shirt. "I heard a shot. Is everyone all right?"

"Mathieu," I heard Elizabeth say, "you must come back at once. Someone shot at Maria."

"Are you hurt?" Brendan asked.

"Someone shot at me," I told him. "I threw myself on the grass and hit my cheekbone on the step."

I bent to pick up the casing.

"No," Brendan said. "Leave it there for the police."

"Yes, of course."

Brendan looked down the street. "We've never had a drive-by shooting in Coomara."

A wailing siren throbbed in the distance. Soon Finch and two officers pulled up in a squad car.

"Ms. Pell," Finch called out, "are you hurt?"

"I'm fine."

He stared at me. "You should have medical care."

"It's just a bruise," I said. "Did the officer catch the person who shot at me?"

Finch shook his head. "He lost him on the coastal road. Some cattle had gotten out and were blocking traffic."

I watched as the officers picked up the casing and dug the slug out of the column.

"This is exactly what I was afraid of," Finch said.

"People think you're too involved," Elizabeth put in.

"Why do you say that?" I asked.

"When I told my friends that you came back from that Druid gathering all fired up because a spirit said you had the information needed to solve the crimes...well...you can imagine their reaction."

I stared at Elizabeth with near-hatred, and almost told her to pack her bags and go home. "I told you that in confidence, Elizabeth. You put me in danger by sharing it."

A look of realization spread across her face. "I didn't think...we were just laughing about the Druids dancing around their faerie trees and..."

"You thought it would be amusing to share that I had been energized by the ceremony."

"Look. I get that you're ultra-sensitive and feel other people's grief and..."

Finch addressed Elizabeth. "Ms. Pell, give me the name of the people who were present when you shared information about your cousin."

"Well, there was Rose Fitzgerald, Judy Moriarity, Vida Crain, and Bea Ford."

Finch wrote down the names in his notebook. I committed them to memory. Was Rose related to Manfred Fitzgerald, the school custodian? Had he supplied information to the kidnappers about Katelyn Scanlon's schedule change?

Then I remembered that before the shooting, Finch had said he wanted me to look at a video from the petrol station. "What did you want me to see this morning?" I asked.

"We have the security video from the station where Mrs. Scanlon bought petrol. I want you to have a look at it."

"Let's go now," I said, wanting to get away from my cousin.

"Are you sure you feel well enough?" he asked.

"Yes, yes, I'm fine."

"But you can't leave," Elizabeth said. "Mathieu's coming."

"Tell him I'll be back." I walked toward Finch's patrol car and got in the passenger side.

***

At garda headquarters, Sergeant Gowdy led me to a small room to see the security video. "It's about fifteen minutes long," he said.

I sat in a padded chair. "What was Mrs. Scanlon driving?"

"A white Kia Sportage."

On the screen, people entered the petrol station and left. Some I recognized but didn't know personally. The defrocked priest, Albert Malone, drove up in a small, dark car. Two trucks pulled in, going past the station to an area reserved for them. Tim Hawkins pulled up to a pump in a small sports car. He looked in both directions, then went into the station. Cautious Tim. I was sure he had something to hide. A dark Porsche parked in front of the station, and the frail figure of Margaret Mulligan got out from the passenger side and went in.

Mrs. Scanlon pulled up to the pump in her Kia. From the passenger window, Mikey looked out at the station entrance. Margaret Mulligan exited with a package a few seconds later. Her driver, who wore an Australian bush hat pulled low over his face, got out of the car, took the package with gloved hands, and put it in the trunk.

It was the last of May and I thought it odd he was wearing gloves, but perhaps he had been called from farm work to drive Margaret into town. He turned and faced Mikey. The boy's hand went to his mouth. His gesture could have indicated he was suppressing a cough, but it was also possible he had stifled an outburst. Margaret and the man got in the car and drove off.

"Who is the man with Margaret Mulligan?" I asked.

"One of the farm workers at Ravensclaw, I suppose. Mulligan hires people from Eastern European countries—Hungarians, Poles..."

I watched the car pull away again. Though I had not noticed before, another car had been parked on the other side of the Porsche.

"What kind of car is that?" I asked.

"That's a BMW."

As the BMW's driver drove away, he ducked his head to look toward the Scanlon car. He could have come out of the station at the same time Mikey's hand went to his mouth.

"Sergeant," I said, "do you know who's driving that blue BMW?"

"No, nor do I know the car. It's a new model. The driver must have been passing through."

Finch came to the room.

"When Franco Milton was identified, did you go to Ravensclaw to see if he was there?" I asked.

"We did," he said. "We showed his picture. Pearce didn't know him."

"Does he know all the men who work on his estate?"

"My guess is he does. He'd want to know the backgrounds of people working there."

"I'd heard Pearce wasn't interested in managing the estate."

Finch nodded. "He leaves much of the managing to Danny Doyle. Ravensclaw covers over two hundred and fifty hectares. That's about six hundred acres. The Mulligans plant corn and wheat, and graze sheep and dairy cows. It's a big operation."

Hadn't Judy suggested it would be easy to signal out to sea from Ravensclaw? I wished for more information about the Mulligans. They kept to themselves most of the time. Margaret had a stellar reputation, but what about the other members of her family?

"Inspector," I said, "A few days ago, I wondered if Bridget Vale and the missing girls were related."

"Bridget was Tessa's first cousin, as you know," Finch replied. "I think the Hardesty girls are related on Iris's side. As far as I know, Katelyn Scanlon is not related to the Vales." He gave me a riveting look. "I suppose you're thinking their selection has something to do with blood ties."

"It crossed my mind."

I picked up my purse from the table, indicating I was ready to leave. Sergeant Potts drove me home. Elizabeth had slunk off somewhere, without leaving a note saying where she had gone. I sat down at the kitchen table and wept. If not for my premonition of danger, I would undoubtedly be dead.

How thin the fabric between life and death.

CHAPTER FOURTEEN

I remembered Elizabeth had called Mathieu. He would soon be at the cottage. With effort, I climbed the stairs to my bathroom and washed my face. The swelling on my cheekbone had gone down, but a dark blue blot was forming beneath my eye and spreading toward my ear. It resembled the map of Pennsylvania.

Tires squealed, a car door slammed, someone pounded on the front door. Mathieu had arrived.

"I got here as quickly as I could," he said. "Elizabeth said someone shot at you. Are you okay? Why is your faced bruised?"

"I'm fine. Just shaken."

He spied a flank steak on the counter that Elizabeth was thawing for dinner. "Here, let's use this as a compress."

"Meat is not the most effective treatment for bruises," I said. "Ice packs are."

He refreshed my icepack. For an hour, he lectured me about letting the police investigate crimes. Three times he went to the porch and examined the bullet hole. Then he checked the locks on the front and back doors, and the windows.

"You've antagonized drug dealers, Maria! Drug dealers! They have no scruples. They're the scum of the planet. They kill everyone who gets in their way."

Throughout his ravings, I listened politely, comprehended his fear, and half-promised to devote all my energy to writing poetry.

"Where's Elizabeth?" he asked. "You shouldn't be alone."

"I don't know." I didn't tell him of Elizabeth's possible role in leading the shooter to me.

"I have to go back to Ballygosteen for a staff meeting. Come with me."

"That's not necessary, Mathieu. I'll be safe here. I want to rest."

"I'll be back as soon as I can. Be sure to lock the door when I leave. I've locked the other door and the windows."

He hugged me tenderly. I sensed his reluctance to go, but despite someone shooting at me, we had to carry on with our lives.

When he left, I locked the door, went upstairs, and lay down, but my mind was too chaotic for sleep. I decided to conduct an internet search for Margaret Mulligan. Finding she was born Margrit Hess on October 31, 1935 in Dusseldorf, Germany surprised me. I'd thought she was descended from an ancient Celtic family. Reading on, I learned she had a twin sister named Anna, who drowned at age fifteen. I pulled up a photograph of Margrit and Anna. They were identical twins.

Margrit—later known as Margaret—started school in Germany. When her father, Klaus, a shipping executive, was transferred to Belfast in 1942, he enrolled the twins at an Episcopal school. In 1950, Anna was killed in a boating accident off the Dublin coast. A speedboat slammed into a sailboat on which Anna and Margrit were passengers. Anna fell overboard and drowned. The speedboat roared away; its pilot never apprehended.

Margaret attended Trinity College in Dublin for a time, then married Terrence Mulligan in 1965. Pearce was born two years later— which would make him around forty-nine years old. It was Terrence Mulligan who had the Irish ancestry. He was descended from a sept, or clan, located in present-day County Donegal.

What had Klaus Hess done during the Second World War? Though Ireland had remained neutral, some Irishmen had colluded with the Germans. I tried to research Hess, but found little information, other than he had died in a hunting accident in Scotland. An article included a newspaper clipping from *The Glasgow Herald*:

*June 5, 1953: Klaus Hess of Belfast was shot dead
in a hunting accident near Edinburgh last Tuesday.
Police conducted an investigation confirming that
Mr. Hess was standing at the edge of the forest
when a hail of bullets meant for quail came from
the trees. Members of the other hunting party
were questioned. No one knew Mr. Hess. The
shooting was ruled accidental.*

How thoroughly had the police investigated the shooting? Klaus Hess was German. Perhaps he had committed war crimes while running his shipping business from Belfast. Someone in the other hunting party might have been paid to shoot him. Turning off the computer, I sat thinking for several minutes.

Then I called Finch.

"Margaret Mulligan?" he said. "Why on earth are you looking into her background? She's known all over Ireland for her good works."

"Her father could have been working with the Germans during the war and made enemies. In 1953, he was shot in a hunting accident in Scotland. The police didn't identify the shooter, but merely questioned everyone in the hunting party and let them go. I wonder who those hunters were."

"How are you connecting the hunting party with Bridget's death?"

"The people whose children were taken may have been connected to participants in the hunting party, and Mrs. Mulligan or her son are seeking retribution."

"Utter nonsense. Just like your theory about Bridget Vale selling drugs."

"I heard your officers found two-hundred-and-fifty euros in Bridget's bedroom."

He was quiet, then asked. "Who told you that?"

"Wasn't it you who said the village was like a party line?"

"I suppose it's worth having a look at those names. I'll get them from Scotland. I'm sure I don't have to tell you to keep quiet about this."

"And there's the matter of Margaret's twin, Anna, who drowned in a boating accident. She fell overboard when a speedboat rammed the sailboat she was on."

"When did this happen?" Finch asked.

"Around 1950."

"Was the pilot of the speedboat drunk?'

"He wasn't caught."

Finch heaved a sigh. "Your theory is that the pilot had something to do with Coomara and Margaret is wreaking havoc on the village to avenge her sister's death."

"Stranger things have happened."

He withheld comment. "If that's all you have to tell me, I need to get back to work. Stay inside. Don't tempt someone to shoot at you again."

"You don't have to tell me," I said.

Someone knocked on the front door. I went downstairs to answer. Elizabeth. She had not taken her key and I had locked her out.

She was contrite. "I'm sorry, Maria. I don't usually indulge in gossip. I'll never betray you again."

She looked so small and pitiful that I forgave her. It wouldn't do to forget.

Elizabeth went upstairs to rest, and I made myself a cup of tea and took it to the garden, which seemed fairly secure as the backyard was fenced on two sides, bordered by the cottage on the third, and protected by a drop down to the sea on the fourth. In addition, Brendan Calloway was perched on his porch and could see in any direction. I waved to him. He waved back. What a relief he no longer pursued me as a potential mate!

Bridget's pansies were blooming, their gorgeous petals every color of the spectrum. A house wren trilled a rapid song and I turned to see it thrust its head toward the sun. I tried to clear my mind so that I could reorder my day, but how does one do that after being shot at?

I needed to be more careful. I had to be more discreet. I had to lock my doors. I couldn't ride around on my bicycle any more.

If I can't ride my bicycle, how will I get around?

"Brendan!" I called out. "Can you take me to the car rental agency?"

He consented. An hour later, I was driving a gray 2006 Mazda. Mikey was foremost on my mind. First stop: the Scanlon cottage.

***

When I rang the Scanlon doorbell, no one answered, so I went around the house and entered the fenced yard through a side gate. Theorizing that Mikey had run out the back door, I looked for avenues open to him. He could have run around the cottage to the street; he could have climbed fences into his neighbors' side yards, or he could have gone through a small green gate into a plum orchard surrounded by hedges. If I were running away, I'd choose the plum orchard.

Garda officers had undoubtedly searched the orchard, but I went through it again, row by row, tree by tree. They might have missed something—a scrap of cloth, a candy wrapper, a....

I saw it then. At the far end, the hedge was disturbed where someone had parted the twigs and gone through. Mikey would not have required much room. Enlarging the aperture, I crawled through. On the other side was a rutted lane, running north and south. Northward was the coast and southward, the lane ran into the village. A forest lay to the east. Thinking little boys must love the enclosure of trees, I headed for the forest. Or did he head toward the coast?

I stood, much in a quandary, when I was seized by a sense of desperation. My chest tightened, much as Mikey's must have.

Oh Mikey, where did you go from here?

Though not yet noon, the sky darkened. Hoping rain would hold off, I hurried toward a grove of willows.

Was that laughter?

Voices. A man and a woman. Keeping my head low, I made my way forward, then heard the swish of dry weeds. Completely naked, Lina Mulligan darted past. Behind her was Hector Perez-Conti, also nude. He captured her in a stand of toadflax, and I watched the purple blossoms thrash, as if caught in a hurricane. If Hector was Lina's brother, I was a billy goat.

Then I spied a dark blue BMW parked at the edge of a sandy road and froze. Was that the car I saw on the security video? Had Hector been behind the wheel? I crept past the car and turned toward the Scanlon cottage, nearly missing a soggy white bandage with blood-stains lying at the side of the road. It had to be Mikey's.

I called Finch. Within fifteen minutes, he and two officers were at the site.

He frowned. "I told you to stay in your house. What are you doing out here?"

"Looking for Mikey."

An officer picked up the bandage and placed it in an evidence bag. The second officer found a spot farther down where the gorse was crushed.

"The boy might have been taken here," he said.

"Or he might have been hiding," Finch said. "Where could he have gone next?"

No one spoke.

Finch noticed the BMW. "That car is identical to the one in the video."

"It belongs to Pearce Mulligan's brother-in-law," I said. "I last saw him in the toadflax."

He turned to an officer. "Go see what he's doing."

I waited with interest for the officer to return. A few minutes later, he did. With reddened face, he called Finch aside to whisper in his ear. They both glanced at me and I looked away.

"Yes, well," the inspector said. "We'll return to Coomara and get this bandage looked at."

I hitched a ride back to my car with the inspector. Turning onto a street with pastel painted cottages, we saw a pay phone. Finch pulled up beside it. He got out, inspected the phone booth and its environs, and made a call to the station.

"Mikey may have called from there. We'll dust the booth for finger-prints."

We continued on to the Scanlon residence.

"I'll keep you informed of our progress," Finch said, as I got into my rented Mazda, "but you must do your sleuthing from home. I don't want you out and about where you can get shot at again."

"I understand." I did understand, but knew I'd find the walls of the cottage too confining.

I drove home, worrying over where Mikey had tucked himself and how he was getting food.

***

Elizabeth was running the vacuum cleaner in the sitting room. I went to the kitchen and fixed a salad for lunch. She came through the kitchen to return the vacuum to the utility closet. She didn't speak. I suspected she had rethought blabbing about my experience at the Druid ceremony and had convinced herself she was innocent of any wrong-doing.

As a child, Elizabeth never admitted culpability. In memory, I saw her slap her friend, Caroline, for marring a hopscotch diagram on the sidewalk. Caroline had cried. When Elizabeth's mother came out to see what was wrong, Elizabeth said Caroline had fallen and that's what had caused the red splotch on her face. Caroline, afraid of being slapped again, did not protest.

Elizabeth walked past me with a dust cloth.

"We need to talk about what happened," I said.

She ignored me.

"You're a guest in my home," I said. "You have to talk to me."

"Or you'll do what? Throw me out?"

"Don't tempt me."

She sat down at the table. "None of my friends tried to kill you."

"I'm sure that's true, but they have husbands, brothers, friends."

"I'm having trouble with this." She bit her lip and left the table.

I finished lunch and called Finch to find out if the bandage was Mikey's. It was. I had a strong feeling the child was safe, and the bandage had fallen off as he rushed through the gorse. An hour later, Finch called to say that a woman stopped by, saying someone had taken a winter cabbage from her garden. She wondered if it might have been

Mikey. Finch sent an officer to check out the woman's garden and he returned to say the cabbage head had been wrenched from the ground, roots and all. A phone call to Mikey's mother revealed he was not allowed to carry a knife.

I thanked Finch for calling, then went upstairs, turned on the computer, and researched Lina Mulligan, nee Arizmendi. Born in Iquitos in northern Peru, she was a beauty queen who had caught the eye of Pearce Mulligan before he embarked on a trip into the jungle. They married three weeks later, in October, 2011. Pearce was forty-four; Lina was twenty-three. I could find nothing about Hector Perez-Conti and wondered if he was using an alias.

Judy Moriarity phoned. "Oh, Maria, the Father went to St. Olaf's Cove. A fisherman found a man's body there. He was shot at close range through the heart."

"How did you find out?"

"The fisherman's wife called the Father. He's gone to bless the body."

"How long had the man been dead?" I asked.

"I don't know," she said, "but it may be Milton, the kidnapper who was after little Mikey. If the child knew, he could come home now."

I thanked Judy. Actually, the death of Milton did not ensure Mikey's safety. He may have been frightened by Hector Perez-Conti, who was very much alive. As I brooded about Mikey, someone knocked on the door. Elizabeth went to answer it.

Mathieu walked in. "Whose Mazda is that outside?"

"Brendan took me to the car rental agency," I said. "I realized it was too dangerous to ride my bike."

He gave me a severe look. "Maybe you should go home where you'll be safe." He meant the United States.

"You know I can't do that. Nor can I stay in the cottage all the time."

He didn't comment, then said, "Elizabeth tells me Mikey Scanlon is still missing."

I brought him up to date on the investigation.

"I heard the garda found the body of one of the kidnappers. Franco Milton. Was that the man who was after Mikey?" Mathieu asked.

"It's not clear that Milton was stalking Mikey," I said. "We don't even know if he was at the petrol station. However, there *was* a driver at the station who might have scared the child."

"You didn't tell me that," Elizabeth said.

No, I hadn't.

Elizabeth slid her eyes at me. "Who was it?"

"We're unsure," I lied.

Mathieu stayed for dinner. We had spaghetti with tomato and olive sauce, and afterward, sat in the living room to watch TV. I accompanied Mathieu outside when he left.

"Come no farther than the gate," Mathieu cautioned.

The hedge separating Brendan Calloway's yard from the street began quivering. Thinking a small animal was trapped in the network of twigs, Mathieu went to free it. He parted the twigs.

Mikey Scanlon.

The boy crawled out on all fours, his dark curls tangled with leaves. His clothes were muddied and torn, and he was hoarse from thirst. Mathieu carried him into the cottage and called Finch while I bathed the child's face in warm water. Elizabeth fed him vegetable soup.

When Mikey had eaten, he looked at me. "You've got a black eye."

I tried to wrap him in a blanket but he was the old Mikey, feisty and energetic, and chose to sit on the floor near Mathieu. Though I ached to question him about why he ran away, it didn't seem wise with blabbermouth Elizabeth in the room.

Mathieu said, "Why did you run away, Mikey?"

Uh oh.

"I saw one of the men who took Katie. He followed Mum and me home, and parked at the end of our street."

I felt a chill. How could Finch protect the little boy?

I hadn't told Mathieu about Elizabeth's indiscretion with her friends and shook my head slightly as a signal to stop questioning, but he either ignored me or didn't get my meaning.

"What did the man look like?" Mathieu asked.

"He has black hair and a mustache. He's the one who had the ring with the red stone."

"Why, that sounds like Pearce Mulligan's brother-in-law," Elizabeth said. "I noticed his ring at the tea room. It was a large ruby. Very costly."

Finch arrived and took Mikey to his parents. I hoped he would go next to Ravensclaw and arrest Hector Perez-Conti.

***

Later that night, people met at O'Grady's Pub to celebrate Mikey's homecoming. My black eye was a topic of concern. I felt the village warm to me. I had involved myself in one of the village's worst troubles (excepting the Great Hunger), and they expressed appreciation for my efforts. I felt the protective cover of the village.

Bathed, combed, and dressed in flannel pajamas, Mikey Scanlon fell asleep against his mother in one of the brown leather booths. His father, Seamus, raised the first of many toasts to Mathieu for finding Mikey.

Mathieu beamed. He loved to be appreciated. I was pleased for him.

A band played an Irish jig and villagers flocked to the dance floor. Mathieu swept me up in his arms and we, too, danced, although it was more of a polka than a jig. Elizabeth, who had learned to jig in the States, flew around the dance floor on the arm of a burly red-bearded man. We were all filled with joy at Mikey's safe return.

But the plight of his missing sister and the other girls weighed heavily on my mind, and as the festivities came to a close, I went out into the black of night, my heart despairing.

CHAPTER FIFTEEN

Hector Perez-Conti had left the country. Finch called the next morning to say Lina Mulligan told his officers that Hector had flown to Venezuela. Finch checked the Dublin flights and confirmed her story. Lina said she didn't know when he would return.

"No extradition treaty with Venezuela," Finch said.

A dead end, at least for now.

You have the answers.

I went upstairs and meditated, hoping to evoke some clue to the girls' disappearance in the stillness of my mind. Achieving a state of calmness, images of Celtic crosses and tombstones drifted into my subconscious, then phrases...*old stories, past griefs, secrets....*

The hum of a speedboat motor broke the silence and I got up to look out the window in time to see Brendan taking out the *Hawk*. It was raining slightly.

The gods are weeping for the girls of Coomara.

I thought of Bridget, lying in her coffin, of Tessa, Katelyn, and the Hardesty girls. I thought of the girl in Danny Aherne's parking lot trying to break free of her captors, and the attempt on my life. The calmness I'd achieved through meditation was replaced by a rampaging fury. I felt as if my head would explode.

To hell with the risk, I'm going outside.

Throwing my rain jacket over my shoulders, I left the cottage via the back gate, which was partially concealed by vines. Meditation had set me in a cemetery, and I headed to the one behind St. Columba's. I'd been there before, looking at headstones, but had had no purpose in mind. This time, I was there for a reason—Coomara's dead and missing girls.

I walked along Coomara's main artery, stepping over puddles while periodically looking behind for potential assassins. Few people were on the street. I went past Tea for Two, the library, and the garda station. St. Columba's lay directly ahead. I entered the cemetery.

Euripides called death the *debt we all must pay*. Here lay those who were now debt free—some granted a fulsome time, and some, like Bridget, shortened lives. The tombstones, wet with rain, stretched before me in uneven rows. I remembered the cuckoo from Bridget's funeral, squawking in the aspen tree, bringing the fear of death to Judy Moriarity's heart.

In the distance was a man holding an umbrella. He was walking in the direction of the church. Was it Albert Malone, the defrocked priest? What was he doing out in the rain?

As I approached Bridget Vale's headstone, I saw that someone had left a vase of pansies on her grave. *Pansies!* I looked again for the man with the umbrella. He was gone. Bridget had been killed near a field of pansies. Had her killer placed the vase on her grave? A shudder went through me. Should I tell Finch and have him dust the vase for fingerprints? Did rain wash off fingerprints? I didn't think so. Ducking under a cypress, I phoned Finch. He listened, then said he'd send someone to get the vase.

"What are you doing in the cemetery?" he demanded. "I told you to stay in your cottage."

"I can't do that."

I ended the call. Picking my way on the wet sod between the graves, I wondered why my subconscious had called me to the cemetery. Was it to find the pansies? Then I came to a small headstone, whose inscription read: Alain Aherne, born September 10, 1999, died June 3, 2000. This was the empty grave of the baby born to Danny Aherne and Iris Vale. He had vanished on St. Kevin's Day sixteen years ago. Taking out my notebook, I wrote down the child's birth date and presumed death date.

Did his disappearance on the saint's day have any significance? Something tugged at my memory—something that had been said or left unsaid about the infant Alain Aherne. I headed back to the street. Near the church entrance, I encountered Father O'Neill.

"You're drenched, Ms. Pell," he said. "Come in and dry out. I'll put on the tea kettle."

I went inside. The priest took my dripping rain jacket into a downstairs bathroom, then invited me into the kitchen where I sat down in a small alcove. He filled a kettle with water and placed it on the gas burner. Where was Judy?

"What were you doing in the cemetery?" he asked.

"Looking for answers."

He looked at me keenly. "Did you find any?"

"I don't know. May I ask you about Alain Aherne?"

The priest winced. "Ah, yes. You would get around to that poor little tyke." He leaned forward. "I know, Maria Pell, that you have a sixth sense, but I also believe you use it only for good."

"I try to."

"About little Alain, I will tell you that some children come into the world to the wrong people. Iris Vale was too young for marriage and too young for motherhood."

"Can you tell me what happened to the baby?"

"I cannot, and maybe it is just as well that I cannot."

"Is it that you won't tell me or can't tell me?"

"Both."

Not for the first time did I wonder at Father O'Neill's role in hearing the sins of the villagers. Not only did he serve as confessor, he also granted absolution and gave counsel. I thought of the sin-eaters of Welsh tradition. The deceased's family prepared food, metaphorically containing his or her sins. For a fee, the sin-eater gobbled up the food.

Whose sins had Father O'Neill gobbled up?

The tea kettle whistled and the priest got up to brew the tea. I took a moment to glance around the kitchen, which was Judy's domain. Cabinets lined one pale green wall. Pressed against another were a gas range and sink, with a counter to the right of the sink. A modest-sized refrigerator stood between the counter and the wall of cabinets. A white cookie jar shaped like a lamb, and flour and sugar cannisters set on the counter. Above the cookie jar was a white clock. A crucifix hung near the breakfast alcove. Judy had laid a yellow and white checked tablecloth on the table. Windows looked out onto the garden.

The priest brought a teapot and mugs to the table, then went to the cookie jar and took out two sugar cookies, which he placed on a plate.

"Judy's specialty," he said. "The recipe was her mother's."

As we drank, we talked of the festival, which would take place a week from Saturday. Father O'Neill was explaining the ceremony at St. Kevin's Bed when Judy burst through the door, her eyes moist and red.

Father O'Neill jumped up. "What is it, Judy?"

"Maria, I'm so glad you're here. I've just come from the garda station. Inspector Finch questioned Rose, Vida, Bea, and me about who might have passed on what Elizabeth said at our meeting—about you worshipping in the pasture with the Druids and getting a message that you knew who the killer and kidnappers were. We all swore we told no one."

Finch's thoroughness surprised me. "I'm sure that's true," I lied.

"I'm so sorry someone tried to shoot you." She wrung her hands. "Not for the world would I say anything that would cause you harm."

"There, there, Judy," the priest said. "You're the soul of discretion. We all know that."

I stared incredulously at the priest. *Doesn't he know Judy is the town crier?*

She ran upstairs to her bedroom.

"Poor Judy," the priest said. "She suffers from nerves. She's led a sad life."

My ears perked up. Judy had not shared much about her life. I knew she was widowed and had been with Father O'Neill for twenty-five years, but that's all I knew.

"She wouldn't mind me telling you that she's originally from Northern Ireland," he said. "Her young husband, a member of the IRA, was killed in a skirmish with the British Army during The Troubles."

"I didn't know."

"They'd been married only two months."

The Troubles occurred in the early 1970s. Judy could have been no more than twenty.

"Thank you for telling me," I said.

"It helps to explain."

His comment struck me as odd. Maybe he *did* know Judy was a gossip. A flash of intuition—perhaps Judy invested herself in the lives of others, not wanting to remember her own losses. I envisioned her, a girl of nineteen or twenty...a husband whom she loved...expectations of the life they would live together. Then he was gone. Knowing her story did help to explain Judy.

I finished my tea, thanked Father O'Neill for his kindness, and left. Before going home, I returned to Bridget Vale's grave to see if a garda officer had come for the vase of flowers. He or she must have—the vase was gone.

I went home, still wondering about Alain Aherne's disappearance. Was it possible someone found the baby crawling toward the edge of the cliff, saved him, and kept him?

***

Hanging my wet jacket in the shower stall, I remembered it was Deirdre O'Malley, who had started to say something about the Aherne child. I called her, but the message on her answering machine said she'd gone to Scotland and wouldn't be back until the thirtieth of May. That was five days away. I'd have to wait.

Danny Aherne stayed in my mind. Did he wear black to mourn his son? I wondered if he still sang my song about Cork Harbor.

The phone rang—it was Mathieu calling to say he was in Coomara to teach his karate class. He asked if I'd like to observe his female warriors. I said yes.

"Afterward, I'd like to go to a pub near the river," I said. "It's called Gaelic Earls. We can have an early dinner there."

"Does this have something to do with finding the girls?"

"I don't know."

"Do I need to bring my brass knuckles?"

"I hope not."

Hurrying to the computer, I typed *Daniel Aherne, pub owner, Ireland.* Nothing.

***

At half past four, Mathieu picked me up and we drove to the elementary school gym. Dressed in his dobrok, or white uniform, he assembled equipment for his class—several mats, a whistle, and a Styrofoam bat, which I later learned he used to strike the girls gently on their heads. The girls arrived, some singly, some in groups, wearing two-piece white uniforms. They removed their shoes and stood in two lines.

Mathieu sat on a mat and crossed his legs. After leading the girls in a brief meditation, he proceeded to warm-up exercises and stretches. Next came kicks and fist thrusts. The girls followed, rapt and lithe. How many had fallen in love with their instructor?

He did look magnificent. Always trim, he'd added muscle tone in the time we were apart. I'd always admired his gracefulness, but now he was sleek like a panther. I was warmed by the memory of the feel of his body next to mine.

The session ended at five-thirty. Mathieu and I returned to the inn and I paged through a copy of *Anthropology Digest*, while he showered and changed into street clothes.

"What are you finding at Ballygosteen?" I asked.

"Yesterday, we found a grave of ancient bones," he said. "A few items—a jar, a spearhead, some smooth stones that must have been used in rituals—perhaps to the sun. These people predated the Celts. They may have come from Mesopotamia."

"A long trip."

"It took centuries for them to cross Europe."

"I knew that. I was kidding."

He frowned at me. "That's one of the things you don't like about me: I can't tell when you're kidding. If only you'd give me a clue—like a teasing look, a smile."

"Sorry," I said. "If you want coquetry, look elsewhere."

"I don't want a coquette. I want you."

The bed lay between us, covered in a beige duvet with matching pillows.

"Let's go to the Gaelic Earls," I said quickly.

We left the inn and turned onto River Street. On the way, I explained that Danny Aherne and Iris Vale had once been married and had a child, who might have fallen into the sea.

"There's more to the story," I added. "I think Father O'Neill knows something. I tried to pull it out of him, but I fear he found out in the confessional."

Mathieu nodded, intent on finding the pub. "Is the restaurant on this side of the bridge?"

"On the other side."

The steel bridge loomed ahead. Mathieu drove across, and I looked upriver where the waterway narrowed slightly, the limbs of oaks and maples nearly touching from both sides. Two speedboats were moored at docks. Were they Danny's? This would be a perfect place from which to launch a boat to carry village girls out to sea.

Then we were across the bridge and Mathieu asked again where the restaurant was. I pointed out the pub, and he pulled into the parking lot.

"This is where the girl ran to the couple for help," I said, reminding him of the event two weeks earlier. "I could kick myself for not intervening."

He pressed the button to lock the car. "You could have gotten yourself killed."

"As far as I know, the girl hasn't left Ireland via the ports. If the Irish Naval Services is scaring off vessels at sea, she still may be here. So may Tessa, the Hardesty girls, and Katelyn."

"You're saying the girls could be imprisoned around here."

"I am. If we could find out who was identifying the girls, we might be able to locate them."

We went inside the pub. It was early, and the after-work crowd had congregated at the bar. The place was unchanged from the last time I ate there—broken hinge, seat yourself sign, stuffed owl, bearded waiter. Danny moved among the bar crowd, stopping to clap a friend on the back, to share a joke with another. Taking Mathieu's arm, I walked over to him. Danny's blue eyes gleamed. Was Elizabeth correct in saying he used drugs?

"This is my friend, Mathieu Broussard," I said. "He's working at the dig in Ballygosteen."

Danny extended his hand and Mathieu took it.

"Glad to meet you," Mathieu said.

"Ah, sure," Danny said. "How are you? Found anything interesting at the dig?"

"Each shard we dig from the earth is a find," Mathieu replied.

Danny turned to me. "Have you written any more poems for me to set to music?"

"Not yet. When I do, I'll call you."

We chatted for a moment, then Mathieu and I took a booth near the bar. Mathieu was strangely withdrawn. What was bothering him? I didn't ask, knowing he'd tell me when he was ready. When the waiter came, we ordered two pints of Guinness.

"I get bad vibes from Danny Aherne," Mathieu said.

"Why do you say that?"

"He reminds me of Pigpen in the Charley Brown comic strip. Always a cloud over his head."

"That's a cloud of dirt, not gloom—hence, the name, Pigpen."

Mathieu moved the slate menu to better view it. "I'll have the beef and Guinness stew."

"A good choice. That's what I had when I was here with Elizabeth and Judy."

I decided on lamb. The waiter returned and we ordered. A roar of laughter erupted from the bar. We could hear only the punch line of the joke: *Mary, put down that gun.*

"I wonder what went before," I said.

"It's an old joke," Mathieu said, back to his old self. "The priest asks the widow if her late husband had a last request."

I laughed. "How funny."

Our food came. Mathieu adored the brown bread and Irish butter.

"Kerry cows," I told him. "Their butter is the best in the world."

"Can we get it at home, do you think?"

"I've seen it in supermarkets," I said.

We'd begun to talk like...I didn't want to think about it.

Holding a microphone, Danny climbed on the stool. "The rain has put me in a melancholy mood," he said softly. "Though I laugh and make merry, sadness dwells within me. Let me sing 'Little Man Stone,' and try to get the sorrow out of my bones."

The red-haired woman stepped up to accompany Danny on guitar. His beautiful tenor conveyed a sense of unending grief. I brought his aura into focus: pale green. His energy was nearly depleted.

Little Man Stone
I wander alone.
See you in the sky,
Yes I do.
Little Man Stone,
I love you.
Yes, I do.
Alain...

The song went on for several verses. When he finished, there was no applause. People were struck silent—another demonstration of the village's communal feeling.

"Thank you for sharing my sadness with me," he said. "Now let me sing a ditty about Dublin town and cheer you up."

He sang a raucous folksong, re-establishing an upbeat mood. His aura was still green, which told me he could push himself through sadness.

"Did you tell me he tried to get custody of his son?" Mathieu whispered.

I nodded. "He wasn't a church-goer and Iris was. She got custody and then the child disappeared while in her care."

"And she also was Bridget Vale's mother?"

"Yes. A second tragedy to befall Iris Vale."

I thought of what Father O'Neill had said about Iris. She'd been too young, too unready for motherhood.

Danny bantered softly with people at the front tables. Then someone shouted a request for "Red is the Rose." Applause. Danny hadn't even sung the first words of the song.

Red is the rose that in yonder garden grows,
And fair is the lily of the valley;
Clear is the water that flows from the Boyne
But my love is fairer than any...

I was transported to an Irish past I never knew but had heard of from my grandmother. Throughout the harsh laws under British occupation, the famine, the deaths, the people sang of love and the beauty of the land. I had tried to capture that resilience in my poem about Cork Harbor. When Danny finished, we thanked him, paid our bill, and headed toward the door. A man seated at the bar turned to stare at us.

"Don't pay any attention," Mathieu said.

The man might be racist.

It was raining again, but still we paused to look back at the restaurant door. No one followed. We hurried to the car. As Mathieu pulled onto the cobblestoned street, I looked back again, saw no one.

Fog came in from the sea to mix with the rain. Street lights—dim glowing balls anchored by invisible posts—gave the night a spectral appearance. As we crossed the bridge, a fog horn sounded, warning small vessels away from the coast.

Then we heard a roar from behind. A pickup truck swerved around us and abruptly came to a stop. Mathieu slammed on the brakes. The pickup sped away, invisible in the fog.

"The pickup's right headlight is out," Mathieu muttered.

My cell phone rang. Inspector Finch.

"Ms. Pell," he said, "we've found a girl. Siobhan Hardesty. She's alive. She's at the hospital."

"Mathieu," I said, "one of the girls has been found alive. We must go to the hospital."

CHAPTER SIXTEEN

Sergeant Mary Potts stood guard outside Siobhan Hardesty's hospital room. Inspector Finch, Sergeant Gowdy, Father O'Neill, and a middle-aged man and woman, whom I took to be the girl's parents, had crowded into the small, adjacent waiting room. Mathieu and I quietly approached the group. Finch introduced us to Sean and Moira Hardesty. Moira had a peach-toned complexion and prematurely gray hair. She huddled next to her husband, a somber-faced man in workman's clothes.

"We'll get them all back," Moira said, referring to her other missing daughter and niece. "Siobhan will know where they are."

Finch pulled me aside. "We can't question the girl yet. The doctors say she's traumatized. They've given her a sedative."

"Where was she found?"

"In the cemetery by the church," Finch said. "Father O'Neill found her collapsed against the statue of St. Patrick."

"She had tar on her clothing," the priest said. "I can't think where she might have picked it up."

I edged toward the door and looked in. Siobhan Hardesty lay with her face turned toward me. Another girl with creamy skin and dark hair. Bridget Vale and Baby Doe flashed into my mind again.

But this girl is alive.

Siobhan had escaped from her captors, which meant the other missing girls could be in or near Coomara. Mathieu was talking to Finch. I returned to his side in time to hear that Siobhan had been grasping a paring knife in her left hand when the priest found her.

"We had to pry it away from her," Finch said.

The elevator dinged. Three people got off—a man in a tan jacket and two elderly women. The women hurried down the opposite corridor and the man went to the nurse's station, but no one was there. He stood for a moment, then glanced away, studied a painting on the wall, then went in the room next to Siobhan's and with a low, burred voice, spoke to the patient inside. A Scot. I thought no more about him.

An image of a paring knife blazed into my mind. Fixating on its handle and blade, my mind slipped away from my surroundings. I envisioned Siobhan crouched on an earthen floor, then crawling toward a strip of light beneath a crooked door with brass hinges. The light went out. She waited, then rose to touch the door. Slowly, it opened into shadowed darkness. I made out the shape of a stove, a sink...a knife block resting on the counter. She selected the paring knife because she could conceal it in her pocket. A noise—a cough. Knife in hand, she ducked under a table and waited. Then quiet. She crept up the stairs. Her heartbeat quickened and she darted into---

"Maria," Mathieu said, "did you hear what Dennis just said?"

I snapped to attention, directing my gaze to the inspector.

Finch turned to me. "I said we found fronds in Siobhan's hair. She ran through dense bracken, which is found in several places along the coast."

I hadn't smelled the sea in my vision. "What about the lakes?"

"Yes, there's bracken near the lakes. Why do you ask?"

Did Finch believe in visions? "I didn't sense she'd come from the seacoast."

"How would you...?" he said slowly. "You are psychic. That's why you're so quick to—why didn't you tell me? My mother and my youngest sister have the gift of second sight."

Since he was receptive to psychic phenomena, I fully described my vision.

He stared out the window. "What you describe sounds like an older structure—the hinges on the door, the dirt floor. I can think of several places. I'll send officers to check them out."

"Near lakes," I reminded him.

A doctor emerged from Siobhan's room and told the Hardestys it would be several hours before their daughter awakened. Finch told Sergeant Gowdy to take a position at the elevator and left. Siobhan would be safe with two officers guarding her. I looked in on her again. Her mother and father were sitting beside the bed. Mathieu and I prepared to leave the hospital. As we passed the room next to Siobhan's, I saw the Scot was gone. No one was in the bed, which was made. Who had the Scot been talking to?

Or had he been talking to himself? Had it been a ruse to get as close to Siobhan as possible? I touched Mathieu's arm and returned to speak to Sergeant Potts.

"Can you describe the man?" Potts asked.

"Scots accent, low voice...."

I thought of Mikey Scanlon's description of a man with a croaking voice.

"About six feet tall," I went on, "a strong build, tan jacket, brown hair."

Sergeant Potts called Finch and informed him about the Scot. I waited until she finished.

"He's sending over another officer," she told me. "The girl will be safe."

We said goodbye and left.

***

Outside, an ambulance had pulled to the curb. Lina Mulligan parked behind it in her husband's red Porsche. I paused to see who the patient was. The doors opened and the attendants rolled out a stretcher. Pearce Mulligan lay covered to his chin under a white sheet.

"Mrs. Mulligan," I called out. "What happened?"

She gave me a testy look. "My husband fell down the stairs."

Mulligan raised his head and yelled, "She pushed me!"

"No!" Lina cried, "You misunderstood, darling!"

I glanced at Mathieu. "How do you misunderstand a push down the stairs?"

Two garda officers fell into step behind the stretcher. Mathieu and I got in his rental car and pulled out of the parking lot onto the highway, heading toward the center of town. As we turned onto River Street, Mathieu looked in the rear-view mirror and said that a vehicle with one headlight was following us. I turned to look out the back window. He was right.

Mathieu turned abruptly onto a side street. The pickup followed, the glow of its single headlight menacing as it rose and fell with the bumps in the street. My blood chilled. This was the same pickup that had followed us from Danny's pub. Was this the man who shot at me?

Unfamiliar with Coomara's streets, Mathieu turned into a cul-de-sac and swerved into a hedge-flanked lane that ended at the rear of a two-story house. He turned off the lights and waited.

"Get down," he told me.

I ducked my head. The pickup driver slowed, nosed into the lane, and stopped, but did not come farther. He lingered a few seconds, then backed out. We waited too. Mathieu got out to see if the pickup was parked farther down the street, waiting for us to emerge.

"The street is clear," he said when he returned to the car. "You need to tell Dennis about this."

I got the inspector's voice mail and related the incident.

Mathieu slowly pulled out of the lane. "You must be careful, Maria. These people are dangerous."

"I'm extra watchful, Mathieu."

He turned onto the empty street. "Maybe you should carry a gun."

"I don't know what the rules are for foreigners."

"I'll wager there are a lot of unregistered guns here."

He was probably right. We did not see the pickup again and arrived safely at my cottage.

***

"I'm staying with you tonight," Mathieu said, as he got out of the car.

I didn't protest. Having a brown-belt karate expert in my cottage seemed sensible. When we went inside, Elizabeth was still up, sewing bangles on a crepe paper cloak.

"This is for the King of Mirth," she said. "One of the Finnegan boys needs it for the parade."

"Mathieu's staying the night," I told her, and then related our experience with the pickup truck.

"Sex traffickers," she said. "You've riled them by helping the police."

She seemed to have forgotten it was she who revealed I might have information about the crimes.

"Where do you want me to sleep, Maria?" Mathieu asked.

"Take my bed," I said. "I want to stay up. I'll sleep on the sofa."

I showed him where my bedroom was, took a nightgown from the bureau, and kissed him lightly at the door. Taking a pillow and blanket from the linen closet, I went downstairs, checked the locks on the doors and windows, and changed into the nightgown. Then I lay down on the sofa. My mind was pulsing. I reviewed what I knew about Bridget Vale's murder and the kidnappings.

Bridget had been viciously garroted in the chapel at the abbey ruins, which indicated a killer with a fierce personal grudge and perhaps, hatred of Catholicism. He—it was probably a he, although a strong woman could have killed her—was either a practitioner of Inquisition-style religion or someone who despised the Church. It had not been proven that Bridget was involved in drugs, but if she was, then her killer, with his sick mind, might have thought she had profaned the honor of May Queen. The vase of pansies at the graveside could have been part of his ritual. Valerie Anderson identified Bridget as the Miss Priss who paid attention to Albert Malone. It may have been him I saw in the cemetery. Had he left the pansies? Was he Bridget's killer, or simply an admirer?

I toyed with the notion that Bridget might have witnessed a violent drug deal and was killed to keep her quiet, but her murder seemed too ritualistic for that. But maybe not—if her killer had wanted to make an example of her death to frighten others. Was her body dragged to the rocky shore to hide the ritualistic aspects of her murder? Or did the killer want it found quickly for some reason I did not understand?

The woven bracelet probably came from Tim Hawkins. Though Inspector Finch said Hawkins had a solid alibi the night Bridget left her house, I still suspected him of something. His aunt was Grace Devereaux, the librarian. She had a solid reputation. If she said he was at home with her, then he probably was. Or was he? What was he doing in Ireland, anyway?

How did Valerie Anderson's observations fit in? She said she saw Bridget selling drugs. She also said the drawing of stick man represented the man who brought the drugs to Coomara.

I moved on to the kidnapped girls. Why did the kidnappers keep coming back to Coomara? It seemed something was at work besides random kidnappings. As Mathieu suggested, someone in the village could be selecting girls for the kidnappers. They were all bright, attractive girls. Then I remembered something Finch had said—he'd thought the Hardesty girls were related to Iris Vale. If that was true, then all the kidnapped girls, except Katelyn Scanlon, were related to Iris. That meant they were also related to Bridget.

There was the past to consider. Were Coomara's griefs caused by an avenger? There was the story of Deidre O'Malley's ancestor, betrayed by this very village. Did Deirdre want revenge? Could she have killed Bridget? She practiced Druidism. She also translated for Finch, placing herself inside the walls of the garda station. I had no doubt she would take risks.

Margaret Mulligan's father was killed by an unidentified hunter. Was the hunter from Coomara? Her twin sister was killed when a speedboat rammed a sailboat off the coast of Dublin. The pilot was never unidentified. Perhaps someone from Coomara was responsible. Was it too far-fetched to think that Margaret or her bumbling son could be exacting revenge on the village for one or both of those incidents?

Hector Perez-Conti was surely part of the sex trafficking gang. A ruby ring linked him to Katelyn Scanlon's abduction. Mikey said he saw him parked outside his house—he was stalking the boy. Fearing Mikey would identify him, Hector had fled to a country with no extradition treaty with Ireland. Hector had lived at Ravensclaw, which had an unobstructed view of the Irish sea almost to the Welsh coast. He could have signaled to sex traffickers in a seagoing vessel. And who *was* Hector?

Judy Moriarity, who told tales on everyone, was briefly married to an IRA member, who was killed in a skirmish with English soldiers. Was the killer from Coomara? Was Judy an avenger? She wasn't strong enough to garrote Bridget.

What about Brendan Calloway, my landlord? He'd had ample opportunity to watch Bridget as she worked in the garden. He'd pursued me because he thought he'd been placed under a curse. When he broke down the door and the garda intervened, he had been remorseful, and recently, he'd proven to be a friend. Was it all an act? If anyone had time for mischief, it was Brendan, who spent most of his time sunning on his porch. And staring out to sea.

Elizabeth yawned, finished the cloak, and went upstairs. Mathieu was probably sleeping soundly in his boxer shorts, one foot thrown over the side of my bed. I turned off the table lamp and lay in the darkness. My mind turned off. I went to sleep and did not dream.

***

I heard Mathieu coming downstairs the next morning.

"Don't get up," he said. "I have to go back to the inn to get ready for work."

"The least I can do is fix breakfast."

"No, thanks." He knelt beside the sofa. "What are you planning for today?"

"I hadn't thought."

"I've made several notes on the artifacts we've found. Would you type them for me? You could always make sense of my scribbling."

"Certainly," I said. "I'd be glad to."

One of his students could do the work. Mathieu was trying to make sure I stayed in the cottage. He went out to his car and returned with a legal pad.

"There are several pages," he said. "If you don't want to transcribe them all, I'll understand."

He left the pad with me, kissed me on the cheek, and said goodbye.

"Lock the door," he said.

I got up, locked the door, and went upstairs to dress. Mathieu had neatly made the bed. I laid my head on the pillow he'd used and breathed in his scent. Cloves. Mathieu always smelled of cloves. Hearing Elizabeth stir in the next room, I hurried into the shower and dressed, went downstairs, and fixed my breakfast. Elizabeth was taking her time getting up.

Danny Aherne's song about his son suddenly replayed in my mind. I stared into my tea mug. The amber liquid became the gray waters of the stream from which my father had lifted Baby Doe. Her small face appeared—staring blue eyes, skin the color of ashes.

What a terrible thing to do—throwing a baby into the creek.

Elizabeth put her hand on my shoulder and I jumped.

"What are you thinking about?" she asked. "You're so intent."

"Baby Doe."

Her eyes widened. "What made you think of her?"

"I've never forgotten her."

Elizabeth went to the cupboard. Her hand shook as she attempted to take down a mug. She *did* remember Baby Doe.

"Did your mother and father ever speak of her?" I asked.

"I can't remember." She poured tea from the pot into the cup. "I was only six or seven."

She was eight. I waited for her to say more, but she was looking out the window at a bluebird that had lit on a thorn bush.

"Look," she said, "he's back—the little bluebird I spoke of yesterday."

Years ago, my father had looked toward Elizabeth's house, as he carried the baby's body. Why had he asked where his brother was? What had Elizabeth heard in her house regarding the baby?

I walked into the sitting room, picked up Mathieu's notebook, and went to my study. Putting aside thoughts of Baby Doe, I spent the greater part of the day transcribing his notes. Toward evening, Mathieu returned from Ballygosteen and dined with us. I grilled pork chops and served them with asparagus, spiced apples and brown rice. Mathieu left for the inn around ten o'clock, and I went to bed soon after. Sleep eluded me.

Brendan's dock light provided sufficient illumination to shadow the leaves on the elm near my window. I watched them dance on the ceiling for a while, then went to sleep.

CHAPTER SEVENTEEN

Drowning girls haunted my dreams. They walked on the waves, which alarmed me, and I called them to come back. They tumbled into the froth of the waves and disappeared. I awakened before sunrise, grateful for the firmness of my bed. My next thought was of Siobhan Hardesty, who had escaped from the kidnappers. What story would she tell? Would she remember the way back to where she had been held?

I heard a door slam and scooted out of bed to look out the window. Brendan had exited his cottage. Hands on hips, he looked at the sky, no doubt speculating about the possibility of rain clouds. Did he plan to take the *Hawk* out?

Around eight o'clock, Finch called to say he was sending a car, asking me to come file a full report on the pickup truck that had followed Mathieu and me from Danny's pub. I leapt at the chance. Perhaps I could learn more about the garda's progress on the case. A half hour later, Sergeant Potts arrived.

I liked Sergeant Potts. Her given name was Mary and when Finch wasn't around, she had a sense of humor. As she drove to the garda office, we spoke about the weather—a thunderhead of clouds showed in the west—and the upcoming St. Kevin's Festival.

"My sister's children are terribly excited," she said. "There will be rides, you know. Everything has been so bleak in Coomara. We need some joy."

It was hard to find joy with three girls missing and Bridget's murder unsolved.

"Now that Siobhan Hardesty has escaped, we will find the other girls," she added confidently. "They must be close by."

"When will the inspector be able to question Siobhan?" I asked.

"Perhaps as soon as this evening."

Potts parked in the area designated for officers. As she and I approached the front door, two youths came out. Both had white blond hair. I hadn't seen many people with white blond hair in Ireland.

"The Fitzgerald brothers," Potts muttered. "Always up to some kind of mischief. I wonder what they've done this time."

***

Finch was at his desk, poring over a document. Waving me into a chair, he put the papers aside, poured a cup of tea, and handed it to me.

"Thank you," I said. "I saw Pearce Mulligan as he was admitted to the hospital night before last. He accused Lina of trying to kill him."

"Odd business, that," he said, scowling at the wall. "A domestic squabble. She said he'd tried to grab her when they were standing at the top of the staircase and she pushed him away."

"How did Pearce Mulligan describe the squabble?"

"He said they'd argued about her brother. He called Hector several uncomplimentary names." He turned to face me. "It seems certain that Hector is part of the sex trafficking gang, but I fail to see how he is connected to Bridget Vale's murder."

"Maybe through the drugs."

"Assuming Bridget was involved in drugs." Finch took a sip of tea. "I got your message about the man who followed you, and about the Scot who went into the room next to Siobhan Hardesty's."

"A man stared insolently at Mathieu and me when we left Danny's pub. He may have been offended because Mathieu and I are of different races. He could be the man who followed us."

"Can you describe his pickup?"

"It was dark. Mathieu might know what kind it was. It had a broken headlight."

Finch nodded, took a sip of tea. "It's fortunate you saw the Scot going into the room next to the Hardesty girl's. He might have meant to harm her."

"He was behaving strangely."

"I'll give this to you, Ms. Pell: you notice things others don't. If I can question Siobhan Hardesty this evening, I'd like you to come along."

My spirit perked up. "I'd love to."

"I'll stop by for you if we get word she's awake."

Finch has finally realized I am a help and not a hindrance.

"Have you received information about the hunting party that killed Margaret Mulligan's father?" I asked.

"Here's the copy of the report." He handed it to me. "I didn't see a Coomara name on it. Half of the men were Brits."

"And the other half?"

"Three Scots, two Irish, one Norwegian."

Sunlight played on the louvered blinds behind Finch's desk. A good sign. I remembered the thunderclouds in the west. Hopefully, sunshine would chase them away.

"I've been wondering about the relationship between the McMurrays and the Hardestys," I said.

"Moira Hardesty was a McMurray," he replied. "She is sister to Declan McMurray, father of Tessa. Families are interrelated here. People haven't gone far for mates."

"What about Katelyn Scanlon?"

"As far as I know, unrelated —but you never know. She could be a third or fourth cousin."

"Danny Aherne," I said quickly. "Who is he related to?"

"No one. He isn't from here. He met Iris in Dublin and came here when they married."

"What was she doing in Dublin?"

Finch scratched his head. "As I recall, she had run away from home. I was just a sergeant then. She was wild when she was young."

"Did she settle down after marrying Danny?"

Finch lifted one of the louvers to look out the window. "Some, but she was always a hard drinker."

"Even when she was pregnant?"

"I assume so." He stood up. "I'd like you to fill out a report on the pickup truck driver. The desk sergeant has the forms. If you'd stop by her desk..."

His cell phone rang and he answered it. I went to the front of the building, retrieved the form, and sat down to document the harrowing trip from Danny's pub with the pickup in pursuit. Before turning in the form, I read the report on the hunting accident. A note was stapled to the first page: *The third name on the list is the same surname as Pearce Mulligan's late first wife.* That name was Archibald Campbell. I'd assumed that Lina was Pearce Mulligan's first wife, but because of his age, it made sense that he'd been married previously. Taped to the second page was a copy of an obituary for the first Mrs. Mulligan, dated 5 December 1999

Laura Campbell Mulligan, wife of Pearce Mulligan,
passed away last Sunday after giving birth to a son.
Her funeral will be held at Grayfriars Kirk, Edinburgh,
Scotland on Friday.

What happened to the son?

Was Archibald Campbell related to Laura Campbell Mulligan? Was he the hunter who shot Margaret Mulligan's father? What possible motive could he have had? Perhaps he was an assassin, paid to kill a Nazi collaborator and his ties to the family gave him access to their comings and goings. That was too far-fetched. It was probably coincidence that Laura Campbell Mulligan and Archibald Campbell shared a surname.

I looked again at notes I'd made while researching Margaret and her father. Margaret married Pearce Mulligan in May, 1965—twelve years after her father was killed. How had Pearce's father made his money? I was determined to find out.

Potts asked if I was ready to go home, and I told her I was. The sun had vanished and winds were so forceful they shook the car.

"We're going to get a storm," Potts said. "It's a bad sign when the winds are this strong."

When we reached my cottage, I stepped out into a blast of wind that took my breath away. Ducking my head, I fought my way to the front door.

Something was pulling at my mind. It was the birth year of Pearce Mulligan's son. 1999. Alain Aherne was born the same year. Both boys seemingly disappeared. Another tug of memory—someone—probably Judy—had said Alain was born only a few months after Iris and Danny married. Did someone else father the little boy? Almost immediately, I cast the thought aside. Danny Aherne was deeply attached to the memory of the boy. Alain had to be his son.

***

The aroma of cinnamon rolls distracted me when I hurried inside the cottage. Elizabeth was baking. I went upstairs, turned on the computer and typed in Terrence Mulligan's name. The screen filled with his obituary, dated March 5, 2000:

Terrence Michael Mulligan of Coomara was lost at sea during a storm off the coast of Portugal. He leaves a wife, Margaret, and a son, Pearce. Memorial services will be held at St. Columba's Church on Friday.

A grandson was not mentioned. Though I continued to search for Terrence Mulligan of Donegal and Coomara on the internet, I got no additional hits. I called Judy.

"Why are you wanting to know about Terrence Mulligan?" she asked.

"Just curious." It wouldn't do to tell Judy I was looking for motives for murder.

"Mr. Mulligan was in shipping, as was his father before him," she said. "During the Second World War, he made a mint of money. Look up Rowan Tree Shipyards. That will tell you about the Mulligan family's universe."

Both Terrence Mulligan and Klaus Hess were in shipping. Did that fact have any significance other than coincidence?

I wanted to know about Pearce's son. "Judy, did Pearce Mulligan have a child with his first wife?"

"Not that I know of. Why do you ask?"

"It seems a shame that the Mulligan clan will die out. Who will inherit Ravensclaw?"

"Margaret will probably leave it to Pearce during his lifetime and then it will pass to the church."

Pearce's son was such a well-kept secret that Judy Moriarity knew nothing about him. Perhaps he died soon after birth. I looked out the window and saw the postman leave. It was raining heavily so I put on my rain jacket and went out to get the mail. Opening the mailbox, I grabbed the contents and ran back inside.

Mail consisted of an advertisement for the opening of a Coomara hair salon and a pastel blue envelope addressed to me. When I opened it, I found a drawing of a leprechaun with a malevolent face and the message, *Go Home, Poet*. Looking closely at the leprechaun's eyes, I saw the left one was filled in with concentric circles. A target. The pupil was the bull's eye. I had been served with a warning. Mathieu feared I'd been shot at by drug dealers. I didn't think they'd sent the leprechaun, as something about the drawing seemed personal.

My first impulse was to call Finch, but I hesitated—there had already been one attempt on my life. This anonymous threat would force him to bar me from the investigation. He had asked me to accompany him to the hospital to question Siobhan Hardesty, and I didn't want to give him a reason to change his mind. I hid the warning in a bureau drawer, not wanting Mathieu or Elizabeth to see it.

Returning to the computer, I looked up Rowan Tree Shipyards, and as Judy had said, it was a universe all its own. Margaret Mulligan was a billionaire.

Rain peppered the side of the house and a branch of an elm swiped against the window pane. I tensed. I'd been in tornadoes in Indiana. Did they have them in Ireland? Would the weather permit Finch and me to drive to the hospital to question Siobhan Hardesty? Downstairs, Elizabeth dropped a pan. The wind was getting to her, too. I went down-stairs, expecting to see cinnamon rolls on the floor, but the pan had been empty.

Elizabeth placed the baking pan in the cupboard. "I'm remembering tornadoes."

From the kitchen window, we watched the sea. Waves leaped high, pummeled the dock and the rocky coast.

"I've heard storms get so bad here the power lines go down," Elizabeth said.

"Let's hope they don't. I'd hate to lose the internet connection."

Mathieu called to say his team was covering the archaeological site with tarps and he would stop by to make sure Elizabeth and I were all right.

"Did you close the shutters?" he asked.

The shutters closed from the outside.

"No. I was away when the storm started and Elizabeth didn't think to."

"When I come, I'll close them."

Immediately after Mathieu's call, Finch called to say he was coming to pick me up before the river road closed.

***

The drive to the Coomara hospital was hazardous. Finch swerved to avoid standing water on the streets. He parked in front of the en-trance—a prerogative he enjoyed as garda inspector—and we dashed inside the building.

"Did your officers have any luck searching for the place where Si-obhan was held captive?" I asked, as we went up in the elevator.

"No, but we were able to rule out several sites," he answered.

The elevator stopped on the third floor and we got off. An officer posted between the elevator and stairway reported there had been no incidents. A female officer outside Siobhan Hardesty's door said the girl was awake and her mother was with her.

Siobhan was sitting up in bed, eating oatmeal from a tan bowl. Her hair was combed back from her face and secured with two red barrettes. Her face had been washed, and although pale, was recovering the same peach tone as her mother's. The bedside table held a vase of pink roses. Moira Hardesty met us at the doorway.

"Her sister Sinead and Tessa were with her in a basement," she whispered. "She doesn't remember where it was."

I turned to Finch. "What about Katelyn?"

He shook his head at me, then patted Moira Hardesty's hand. When we entered the room, Siobhan looked at us warily. After inquiries about her health, Finch sat down beside the bed. I sat down, as well, after looking at the card on the roses: *Best wishes, Margaret Mulligan.*

"Do you remember anything about the men who took you?" Finch asked the girl.

"They wore ski masks," she replied. "One forgot to pull it down over his hair and I saw it was white."

"He was older?"

"No, he was young. Another was a Scot. I could tell by the way he spoke."

I felt a surge of excitement. The net was tightening over the kidnappers. The Scot who went into the room next to Siobhan's had to be part of the gang. And where had I seen shocks of white hair on young men? It came to me. When entering the garda station, I'd encountered the white-haired Fitzgerald brothers. Was one or both of them involved in the kidnappings? Fitzgerald was the surname of the school custodian. When Elizabeth told her committee members I had information to solve the crimes, Rose Fitzgerald was present.

I turned my attention back to Siobhan. Once she began talking, words flowed from her lips like a waterfall. She, Sinead, and Tessa were kept tied up in an old cellar. She found a sharp-edged shell and frayed the ropes that bound her, and feigned sleep when the kidnappers came into the room. When one of the men roused Sinead and Tessa and marched them into another room, he left the door open, and she saw an opportunity to flee. Passing through the room where they'd taken their meals, Siobhan snatched a paring knife from the sink.

"It broke my heart to leave the girls behind," she said, "but I had a chance to escape and bring back help."

"What about Katelyn Scanlon?" I asked. "Was she there with you?"

"I didn't see Katelyn."

"Can you show us where the cellar is?" Finch asked.

"I don't think so. It was dark. I didn't stop to look when I got outside, but ran as fast as I could. The grass was slick and I slid down the side of a hill."

"Could you see the sea?" Finch asked.

"I saw nothing. I just ran."

Had she been molested? The question burned in my mind.

It was her mother who asked. "Love, did the men touch you?"

"When we were taken, a man came and told the men he would kill them if they laid hands on us. He said the traders paid a high price for virgins."

"And this man? What can you tell us about him?"

"He wore a ski mask, too. He was about Mum's height. He didn't have to duck his head when he came down the cellar steps."

"What about his voice?" I asked.

She thought for a moment. "He had a soft voice like Da's. Once I heard him speak Spanish. I think he was talking on his phone."

Hector Perez-Conti!

Inspector Finch thanked Siobhan and we got up to leave.

"Wait," the girl said. "He had a pale mark on his ring finger, like he had taken off a ring."

Most definitely, Perez-Conti.

A nurse came in with medication. She turned to us, saying the girl looked tired and needed rest. Finch and I said goodbye and ran to the car, getting soaked in the process.

"The storm is going to be a bad one," Finch said. "Where is Mathieu? Did he try to go to Ballygosteen this morning?"

"Yes. He had to put down tarps."

"I hope he gets back before the storm hits."

In the car, I wrote down Siobhan Hardesty's description of the man in charge: five foot two or three, soft voice, spoke Spanish, recently ringless. I read them aloud.

"Hector Perez-Conti," Finch said.

"Yes," I said, "And the other one—could that be one of the Fitzgerald brothers?"

"I hate to think so. Usually, they're involved in juvenile pranks."

When we returned to my cottage, Mathieu's car was parked in the front and he was securing the shutters on the front windows. I leaned into the wind and helped him. As we rounded a corner of the cottage, Mathieu pulled me back as a limb from the elm came crashing down.

"Close call," he murmured, holding me tightly.

I remained in his embrace long enough to recover my senses. Then we hurried into the house. The storm hit, full force. The lights blinked twice.

"We're in for it," Mathieu said.

I thought of the missing girls and prayed to the universe to keep them safe.

CHAPTER EIGHTEEN

For the next two days, the storm raged relentlessly. Fortunately, Elizabeth had gone shopping for groceries the day before. Always a worrier, Mathieu fought the storm to return to Ballygosteen to tighten the rigging on the tarps. He brought back a small cardboard box.

"What's that?" I asked.

"Something on loan."

He placed the box on the coffee table and opened it. "Voila!" he said, unwinding two yards of bubble wrap.

The four-faced goddess.

I fell to my knees. "Oh, Mathieu, you've brought her to me."

"I'll need to take her back when we re-open the site, but she can stay with you a day or two. Perhaps she'll speak to you."

I laid hands on her, traced her four small noses, caressed the top of her head. Closing my eyes, I felt pulled into her history. She had perched atop a slender column, each face calibrated dead center east, west, north, and south. People gathered in states of reverence and awe. Dea, goddess of rivers, fertility, creation.

Elizabeth paused in her festival artwork to look at Dea. "We should ask her to stop the storm."

The wind slammed the back of the house. Elizabeth dropped the jar of red paint she was holding.

"That will teach you make light of goddesses," Mathieu teased.

"That damned wind is making me crazy," she said.

"Nothing to do but weather it out," Mathieu told her.

"Elizabeth," I said, "you've been working all day on things for St. Kevin's Festival. Why don't you rest a while? Watch television or read a book."

"Yes," she said, "that might help."

She cleaned the paint from the floor, went to the sitting room, and turned on the television to watch a British comedy.

***

Mathieu drove through the rain to my cottage both days, reporting on washed-out roads and downed trees, and rechecking the shutters. He even climbed into the attic to check for non-existent leaks in the roof.

Elizabeth was in daily contact with fellow committee members. One intrepid woman drove through the storm from the far side of the village to deliver plastic banners, pennants, and other materials for decorations. Elizabeth worked on her projects at the kitchen table, and I found a niche in a corner of my bedroom where I listened to the pounding waves. Surrounding myself with reference books, I returned to my study of pre-Celtic history.

Without interruption, the wind battered the cottage, shaking its timbers and rattling the shutters. I thought of the fragility of life, and the enormous advantage of shelter. Shelter led to the importance of faith. Faith, in a way, was shelter. I saw myself girded by belief in myself and the universe, prepared to take on life's adversities.

The lash of the wind and upsurge of waves (a terrible swooshing sound!) also forced into my consciousness inexorable memories like Baby Doe and the deaths of my parents. Once or twice, I thought of Mathieu's infidelity but did not allow it to bear down on my spirit.

***

The second day, the power went out around seven o'clock in the evening. Elizabeth found candles and we sat in the sitting room. Flames created a spectral shadow dance on the walls.

"When we were children," I said, "we told ghost stories. Do you remember any of them, Elizabeth?"

"I was never fond of ghost stories. I remembered them at night and couldn't go to sleep."

"That's how finding Baby Doe affected me."

Elizabeth burst into tears. "Not tonight, Maria. Please don't talk about that."

She took her candle and went upstairs to bed.

Why do I keep tormenting her about Baby Doe?

I went to the back door, which had an un-shuttered windowpane, and looked out at the sea. The storm was savage. Waves heaved against the shore with a hideous roar. Tree limbs waved maniacally. And the wind...no wonder people went insane where the wind blew without stop.

What did primitive people think as they viewed the harsh weather from the mouths of their caves? Huts would not have withstood this storm. They would have huddled in fear, wondering how they had offended the gods.

As I watched the rampaging sea, a light appeared. A man in a rain-coat carried a lantern. It could only be Brendan. He must have been checking the ropes on the *Hawk*. If he weren't careful, he'd be swept into the sea. I watched him grip the railing as he climbed the steps back to his porch.

Reaching out, I caressed the head of the goddess.

"It's enough," I murmured. "It's time for calm weather."

Quiet settled in the room. I took my candle and went upstairs to bed.

***

Was that birdsong? I couldn't believe it—it *was* birdsong! *Bless you, Dea!* The storm had spent itself. The electricity came on. Elizabeth and I went outside to un-shutter the windows and assess the damage in the back yard, the fallen limb, and smaller branches from the elm and willow strewn across the grass. We ventured into the street. There was no flooding—the street was at the top of an incline. One tree had been blown down, and twigs and small branches littered the pavement.

Elizabeth muttered. "What must the churchyard look like? And St. Kevin's Bed at Glendalough? How will we ever get this all cleaned up by Saturday?"

A door banged. Brendan came outside.

"Quite a storm," he said. "It blew in from the Atlantic."

"I saw you last night, checking on the *Hawk*," I said. "I was afraid you'd be blown into the sea."

We chatted a moment. He asked us in for coffee.

"I'm not a tea drinker," he said. "I prefer a nice Colombian roast."

I accepted. Elizabeth did, as well. Brendan held open the door as we stepped into his vestibule. The pungent smell of coffee permeated the cottage.

The layouts of his cottage and mine were identical—sitting room to the left of the vestibule, kitchen-dining area straight ahead, and bedrooms on the second floor. Prussian blue dominated Brendan's paisley wallpaper. A faded Persian carpet covered the plank floor. White curtains hung at the windows. On the west wall, a glass case held a rosary collection. Each set of beads lay on a bed of black velvet. Elizabeth and I went to look at them.

"How many are there?" she asked.

Standing at the door, Brendan replied, "I haven't counted. They belonged to my late mother. She was fascinated by rosaries. Some she made herself."

"I adore the one with the gilt crucifix," Elizabeth said.

"That must be the most expensive," he responded. "It's saphiret—gold mixed with sapphire-colored glass."

"And the crystal one," Elizabeth said. "It's simply gorgeous."

While Elizabeth raved about the beads on the first and second shelves, I stared at the rosaries displayed on the bottom level. They were crudely made of wire, irregular metal beads, and twisted knots.

"What is the story of the beads on the bottom shelf?" I asked.

"Those are oddities Mother collected."

"The beads aren't smooth," I observed. "They'd rub the skin off your fingers."

Elizabeth was also looking at them. "That may have been the purpose."

Suffering for the faith. I left the display cases to sit on Brendan's camel-back sofa. Elizabeth joined me a few seconds later. Brendan went to the kitchen and brought back our coffee in three delicate porcelain cups. Elizabeth took cream and sugar. I took my coffee black.

"My mother and father lived in this cottage," Brendan said. "They enjoyed the view of the sea."

Sipping our coffee, Elizabeth and I agreed the view was splendid.

Then Elizabeth bent to her favorite topic. "Brendan, will you help with St. Kevin's Festival?"

She spoke of the need to clear away storm debris from the church grounds and set up tents and kiosks. Before we left, Brendan had agreed to head a subcommittee to clean up the cemetery and courtyard in front of the church. Elizabeth's recruiting skills impressed me. We thanked Brendan for his hospitality and returned to my cottage.

Mathieu pulled up to the curb soon after.

"You haven't come to take Dea, have you?" I asked, hoping to spend more time with her.

"You can keep her until the weekend," he said. "I'm off to Ballygosteen to assess the damage at the site."

He blew me a kiss and drove away.

***

Elizabeth wanted to see for herself the damage done to the church yard, where much of the festival would be held, so we drove to the downtown area. Village workers were already hauling away limbs and other debris. I parked near St. Columba's while Elizabeth went inside to discuss festival preparations with Father O'Neill. As I waited in the car, the sun came out. I saw Danny Aherne going through the cemetery gates on foot.

Curious to know what had brought him out so early in the morning, I got out of the car and followed him. He went straight to his son's grave and cleaned off leaves that had blown onto the headstone. Then he knelt, withdrew a rosary from his pocket, and began to pray. For a split second the sun glinted on the rosary and I saw that it was made of silver. Then my cell phone rang. Danny snapped his head around to glare at me, thrust the beads into his pocket, and hurried from the grave without speaking. I opened my mouth to apologize, but he was moving fast and would not have heard me unless I shouted.

I looked at my phone. A wrong number.

I walked back to the car and waited for Elizabeth. After taking her home, I drove to garda headquarters to see if officers had learned anything about the location of the kidnapped girls. Before I could speak with Inspector Finch, Sergeant Potts ran down the hall to his office.

"Inspector," she said, "there's a little girl here who says someone tried to pull her into a van. She's one of Dr. Broussard's karate students."

Finch and I rushed out to find a young girl with a blond ponytail and her mother sitting on a bench. The agitated girl was speaking to a female officer.

"This is Diana Drake," the officer said. "She has a story to tell."

Diana's knee was skinned, her blouse was torn, and tears of rage gushed down her cheeks. "It was horrible!" she shrieked. "He grabbed me off my bicycle."

Finch knelt, pulled a clean, white handkerchief from his breast pocket, and gently covered her knee. The girl calmed and gave an impassioned report of what had happened as she rode to school. A man had pulled up in a van, jumped out, and yanked her off her bike. She screamed and kicked him in the groin. A female officer patrolling the area came to her rescue. The man jumped in the van and sped away.

"I kicked him in the bollocks, I did!" Diana cried.

Her mother tried to shush her. "Diana Mary Drake!"

"What did he look like?" the inspector asked.

"He had hair like a Viking," Diana said. "It was white."

"Was he old?"

"He was young."

The girl went to the infirmary for the scraped knee. The female officer left to write a report. I called Mathieu to tell him Diana Drake's karate training had helped avert another kidnapping. He was thrilled that one of his students had used her new skills to save herself.

"Do you think one of the Fitzgerald brothers tried to kidnap Diana?" I asked Finch.

"I've asked Potts to call the Fitzgerald home to see if they are there."

Potts came back. "The Fitzgerald boys are out fishing with their da. They won't be back until noon tomorrow."

"When did they go fishing?" Finch demanded.

"Just after daybreak."

Finch looked at me. "Then they couldn't have tried to take Diana."

My dander was up. "Don't you get tired of dead ends, Inspector? Tim Hawkins surely lured Bridget out of her cottage. Yet he couldn't have because his aunt says he was at home. Now despite Diana's testimony that one of her attackers had whitish hair, which is unusual in this area, and the Fitzgerald boys have white hair and are in trouble most of the time, it can't be them because they went fishing."

His pale blue eyes darkened and I thought I had lost a friend. "They'll be back around eight tomorrow," he said. "I'll go talk to them. You can come along. I'll pick you up."

I drove back home. Elizabeth was gone. I sat down with Dea in my lap and caressed her with both hands. In a short time, my fingers began to tingle, and I felt myself slip into a kind of sleep. In my mind's eye, I saw a forest glen stippled with sunlight. People wearing animal skins gathered in a circle around a raised flat stone. A priest strode to the center of the circle, Dea, in his hands.

Reverently, he placed her on the stone, then bowed, and backed away. The crowd chanted. A baby cried. His mother suckled him and he was quiet. The chanting intensified. Gusts of wind rattled the leaves, lending a crisp staccato to the chant, which was in an unknowable language. In an instant, I knew the people lived in a world of fear and wonder. They expected wonder. I wrote the word *wonder* in my notebook.

Judy Moriarity called before bedtime. "Maria, you'll never guess what I found!"

"What is it, Judy?"

"It's a...a...oh, I must show it to you. I found it this afternoon, but then my food committee met, and I..."

"Tell me what you've found."

"You must come and see."

"I'll come now."

"No, you'll wake the Father. Come first thing in the morning."

"I can't. I'm going somewhere with Inspector Finch."

"Then come right after," she said and hung up.

What had Judy found?

CHAPTER NINETEEN

Finch picked me up soon after breakfast and we drove to Pollard Woods where the Fitzgerald family lived. The development consisted of ten medium-sized houses in various stages of construction. Most had bay windows. The Fitzgerald house was painted emerald green and sported an iron deer in the front yard. We rang the doorbell. A small Nordic-looking boy with white hair opened the door. Finch introduced himself and me, and asked to speak to Rose Fitzgerald.

"Mum!" called the boy. "Garda's here. Wants to talk to you."

Rose Fitzgerald came to the door in a blue dress with a ruffled white apron. She was an attractive woman, slender, with fine blond hair and blue eyes. From what I could see of the house, she was an immaculate housekeeper.

"Are your older sons here?" Finch asked.

"They're upstairs, getting cleaned up. I told your officer they went fishing with their da yesterday. They got back less than an hour ago."

"What time did they go fishing yesterday?" Finch asked.

"I told your officer that, too. At the crack of dawn."

"Do you have other sons?"

She indicated the boy who had opened the door. "There's wee Billy, here."

The front door opened and a young man with white hair entered.

"Who might this be?" Finch asked.

The young man turned to leave.

"Not so fast," Finch said. "What is your name?"

"Ewart Fitzgerald."

Finch turned to Rose. "Is this one of your sons?"

"He's the eldest," she said. "He'll be twenty his next birthday."

"Did you go fishing with your da yesterday?" Finch asked Ewart Fitzgerald.

"No, he didn't go," Rose answered. "He works at Ravensclaw."

Finch turned to Rose. "Please allow your son to answer my questions."

Footfalls clumped down the stairs. Two young men and an older man—all white blonds— appeared.

"What's this?" the father asked.

"I'm taking Ewart to the station for questioning."

Manfred Fitzgerald glowered at Finch. "Questioning about what?"

Finch ignored the question. "You're the school custodian. You may as well come too."

"Is this about those girls that have gone missing?" Manfred wanted to know.

"We'll talk at the station."

Manfred and Ewart climbed in the rear seat of the patrol car. I sat in the passenger seat.

"Drop me off at the priory," I said to Finch, wanting to keep my appointment with Judy.

He looked at me with raised eyebrows. I indicated with a slight shake of the head that I didn't want to explain with the Fitzgeralds in the car.

We drove back to Coomara and Finch let me off in front of the church. I went to the priory and knocked on the door. No one answered. Thinking Judy might be in the kitchen with a mixer whirring, I went to the back door and knocked again. No response. The priory seemed deserted. I walked to the church, went inside, and found Father O'Neill filling a basin with holy water.

"Hello, Father. I'm looking for Judy."

"She's gone to Glendalough," he said, "to make sure the grounds are ready for the visit to St. Kevin's Bed."

"I was supposed to meet her."

"The priest at Glendalough was supposed to check the grounds, but he was called away suddenly. Death in the family."

"When do you expect her back?"

"Later this afternoon."

I walked home, hoping Finch would call with an update on the Fitzgeralds. The call never came. Either the Fitzgeralds had furnished rock solid alibis or the interrogation wasn't over.

***

I prepared a salad for lunch, using lettuce, radishes, and green onions from the garden. In the sitting room, Elizabeth was bent over her missal, her lips moving silently.

What is she praying about at this hour of the day? Why is she praying in the sitting room and not in her room?

To me, worship was a private matter. That was one reason I avoided churches. It unnerved me to have someone mumbling over their beads in my sitting room. Twice, I thought about telling her to go up to her room to pray, but stopped myself. I looked at the clock. She had been praying for forty-five minutes. Something was deeply troubling her.

"Elizabeth," I said, "please tell me what's wrong."

"I'm praying, Maria. Can't you see?"

"What are you praying for?"

"That's private. I'm surprised you're asking."

"I've made a salad. Would you like some?"

"Thank you, but no."

She resumed her prayer. It was the sixth time she'd recited the Lord's Prayer. I went back to the kitchen and sat down at the table. Elizabeth wanted me to *know* she was praying. Why? I ate the salad, washed the dishes, and was drying my hands on a towel when Mathieu called.

"We've unearthed a female skeleton," he said, "and are sending it off to Trinity College in Dublin for genome analysis. She was buried with farming tools."

He was excited at the find and filled my ears with several theories about the woman's antecedents. Did she come from Spain? From the Fertile Crescent?"

I interrupted. "I thought we all came from the Fertile Crescent."

"There's the problem of blue eyes…"

He continued discussing the blue eye mutation and how it probably developed in the Black Sea region during the Neolithic Period. I grew impatient. Not that I didn't find his discourse interesting, I was simply too tired to listen to a scholarly lecture on mutations. He sensed he was losing me.

"You sound tired," he said. "How is little Diana Drake?"

"She suffered a skinned knee. The nurse in the infirmary fixed it up and she went home with her mother."

"Anything new on the case?"

"Diana identified her assailant as having white blond hair. There's a family here named Fitzgerald. All the males have that color hair. Finch is interrogating the father and one of the sons now."

"Fitzgerald. Wasn't that the name of the school custodian?"

"Yes, Manfred Fitzgerald. He's the father of the clan."

"Maybe this is the break Dennis has been looking for."

I waited until late afternoon to call Finch, but he was out. I left a message for him to call me.

***

During the night, I awakened twice. The first time was to shut my window, as a squall had come up and rain was wetting my face. Elizabeth's screams woke me the second time. I ran to her room in time to wrap my arms around her as she leaped out of bed.

"What were you dreaming about?" I asked, when she had come fully awake.

"Don't ask," she said. "It's too terrible."

I soothed her back to sleep and returned to my bed. Then at daybreak, I nearly fell out of bed when St. Columba's bells tolled. Another girl gone! I pulled on my clothes and drove to the church. People ran to the steps, poking their arms into sweaters and jackets. An old man bent to tie his shoe and was nearly trampled.

His hair uncombed, Inspector Finch stood on the top step. A twelve-year-old girl named Jacy Pew had been taken from her bed. Her older sister, Lucy, who was sleeping beside her, tried to fight off the assailant, and got a bloody nose for her effort. Lucy was not taken.

The ruckus had alerted the girls' older brother, Ian, and he had jumped in his pickup truck to give chase. Lucy said her sister was dragged into a yellow van, which turned onto a street leading to the highway, and Ian had been only a few minutes behind. Because it was dark, she could not identify the attacker, but had scratched his face as she pulled off his cap. The cap and scrapings from under her fingernails would be sent to Dublin to test for DNA.

"The girls must be kept somewhere close to town," Finch said. "Siobhan Hardesty said she was in a cellar. We've searched the empty buildings in town and on the hillsides without success. That means someone could be living in the house above the cellar."

"Maybe it's an old cellar like the smugglers used to use."

An American accent. I turned to see who had spoken: Tim Hawkins, the teenage poet with the shaved head and Mephistophelian beard.

"The paper said the Hardesty girl had tar on her clothes," Tim went on. "They used to paint cellar walls with tar because of the damp."

"I know what you're talking about," Finch said, "but there are none of those cellars around here. The old smugglers used caves in the cliffs."

I edged through the crowd to stand nearer Tim Hawkins. Finch had been too quick to dismiss the young man's suggestion. I found it credible. If there were no suitable caves in the cliffs, smugglers might have dug cellars to store contraband. DuMaurier's *Jamaica Inn* popped into my mind. Smugglers lured ships onto the rocks to steal their cargo, which they stored in a cellar.

"Where are you from?" I asked Tim Hawkins, moving next to him.

"St. Louis," he said. "What about you?"

"Fennville, Indiana. I teach poetry at the university."

His eyebrows shot up. "What kind of poetry?"

"All kinds, even your kind. I heard you at the Green Mountain Café."

"I remember you." He drew back to look at me. "What did you think of my work?"

"Full of metaphors," I said, being kind.

His face lit up, and I realized how very young he was. "Yeah. I'm known for wild imagery."

The crowd formed into groups, hurrying to beat on doors of houses with cellars. Albert Malone, the defrocked priest, walked into the shadows. No one wanted him in their group.

I'd been in Coomara long enough to know that many of the older cottages were built with cellars, but not the newer ones—with the marshy ground, they were too expensive to dig.

"They won't find those girls under the cottages," Tim said. "There's a smuggler's cellar somewhere."

"Siobhan Hardesty could have picked up tar from a road."

"She could have, but she didn't. My dad's in construction. I've seen how tar bleeds on cellar floors."

Tim walked away before I was ready to have him go. Without a doubt, he knew more than he was saying. Iris Vale had thought him an unsuitable friend for Bridget. On the night she was killed, he'd been alibied by his aunt, the librarian Grace Devereaux.

"Wait," I called out to him. "I'd like to talk to you again. Where can I find you?"

He shrugged. "I'm usually at the Green Mountain."

Though I wanted to go to garda headquarters to find out what had happened with the Fitzgeralds, I was concerned about Elizabeth's mood, so I hurried home to see how she was. As I approached my front gate, Brendan Calloway called to me from his front porch.

"Something's wrong with your cousin," he said. "I found her wandering in the street in her nightclothes and brought her inside."

I hurried to Brendan's cottage. Wrapped in one of Brendan's blankets, Elizabeth sat in her nightgown, staring into a cup of coffee. She looked up at me with eyes that were sullen and lifeless.

"What is it?" I asked.

"I was looking for you, Maria. I didn't want to be alone."

Whatever was troubling Elizabeth was none of Brendan's business, so I urged her to come home and she did, after thanking him for his kindness. When we returned to my cottage, I settled her onto the couch in the sitting room and tuned the radio to a classical station.

"Elizabeth, would you like French toast?"

"I'm not hungry."

"You should eat something. You'll feel better if you do."

"No, thanks."

I stood in the doorway looking at my cousin, who had lain down on the couch, her face turned to the back. She should go home. She wouldn't be alone there—she lived with her mother in the hilly town of Attica, Indiana. I toyed with the idea of calling Aunt Carol, but immediately discarded it. Aunt Carol was in her seventies. Why worry her?

What had made Elizabeth scream in the night? What was causing her religious fervor, her aberrant behavior? If she remained here, I would need to stay home more, and I resented that. I hadn't signed on as babysitter when I opened my door to her. Call me selfish. I would die if I didn't have freedom to go where I wanted.

"I think I'll go upstairs," Elizabeth said.

She pulled Brendan's blanket close and went to her bedroom.

I was sorry to have missed Judy and wondered if she was back from her visit to Glendalough. Dialing her number, got her voicemail.

"Judy," I said, "I was sorry to miss you this morning. If you're back from Glendalough, give me a call."

Shortly thereafter, I called Finch to find out what the Fitzgeralds had to say. He picked up the phone and I could tell by his tone that he was frustrated.

"Did your interrogation of the Fitzgeralds yield anything?" I asked.

"Very little. Both Manfred and Ewart were tight-lipped. I did get out of Ewart that he was mowing at the time Jacy Pew was taken. A field hand confirmed he was in the field."

Another dead end.

***

In the evening, Elizabeth shuffled down the stairs to sit in the rocking chair near the fireplace.

"I have a chill," she said in a tiny voice. "Could we have a fire?"

Her request annoyed me. Couldn't she put on a sweater? But I bit my tongue, went outside to find dry wood under the porch, brought it in, and lit a fire.

"Are you coming down with something?" I asked.

"I'm not sleeping well. I'm a jangle of nerves."

"Maybe you should go to a doctor and get something to help you sleep."

"I have something. I've been reluctant to take anything for fear I'd be groggy in the morning. There's so much work to do for the festival."

"It's only eight o'clock," I said. "If you take a pill now and go to bed, you can have a good twelve hours of sleep."

"I'll need to get up earlier than eight."

"All the more reason to go to bed now."

My argument won out and she dragged herself up the stairs. When I went to bed at eleven, she was sleeping soundly. Inspector Finch had not called. Had he released the Fitzgeralds? Had Ian Pew caught up to his sister's kidnappers?

I thought about Tim Hawkins' belief that the girls were imprisoned in a smuggler's cave. There were caves throughout Ireland, some along the coast, others near rivers. Since Siobhan Hardesty may have escaped from one, it had to be nearby.

St. Kevin's Festival was tomorrow. What kind of celebration could the villagers have with the girls still missing? If our theory that they'd been taken by sex traffickers was right, they could be in Hong Kong by now. The thought sickened me. Where was the energy I'd felt after participating in Deirdre O'Malley's ceremony to honor the waning moon?

I'd certainly felt something then. Did I think the search for the girls was futile? Why had I imagined them in some sex parlor in Hong Kong?

You have the answers.

Damn it. What are the answers?

CHAPTER TWENTY

DING DONG DING DONG! DING DONG DING DONG! The bells of St. Columba's rang joyfully. Switching on my bedside lamp, I stared at the clock. Two-fifteen in the morning. My heart leapt! Had the girls been found? Ian Pew had gone after Jacy's abductors. Had he found the girls?

I threw on my robe, thrust my feet into slippers, and ran down the stairs. At my gate, I bumped into Brendan, who was zipping his jacket.

"They must have found the girls," he said.

We raced to the church. Megaphone in hand, Finch stood on the top step. Beside him was a handsome young man, beaming broadly.

Finch saw me. "We've got the girls back!" He turned to the young man. "Ian found them. Tracked those devils straight to their lair."

I hurried up the steps. "Did you find all the girls? Did you find Katelyn?"

"All of them," Finch said. "We even found the girl who tried to get away in Danny Aherne's parking lot."

"Are they unharmed?"

"We took them to the hospital so they could be examined, but merely as a precaution. They seemed fine."

The resilience of youth! I fell to my knees, bowed my head, and thanked the universe for its mercies. A warm, hand touched my shoulder. Mathieu. He joined me in prayer. We were bonding again.

A crowd gathered.

Finch raised the megaphone. "A most blessed day," he said. "Thanks to Ian Pew, who chased after the scoundrels and phoned the station when he found their hideout, we have rescued Tessa McMurray, Sinead

Hardesty, Katelyn Scanlon, Jacy Pew, and Jane Doogan, who is from Liverpool. Though they seemed none the worse for wear, the girls are with doctors now to make sure they're all right." He smiled. "They *seemed* all right. Never have I seen happier faces on five girls."

An American voice. "Where were they?"

"Is that Mr. Hawkins?" Finch asked.

Tim Hawkins moved to the bottom step. "Yes."

"You were right," Finch said. "They were in a hidden smuggler's cellar at the far end of the valley. Weeds hid the door. We overlooked it more than once."

"Did you catch the kidnappers?" a woman asked.

"We caught three of them. One was homegrown—Ewart Fitzgerald. The others were from Dublin and Edinburgh."

Ewart's name rumbled through the crowd. "Ewart Fitzgerald? Manfred's son? That's Rose's boy."

I thought Ewart had an alibi.

"Do you know why the girls were selected?" Danny Aherne asked.

I glanced Danny's way. There was something in his voice I couldn't identify. Perhaps it was nothing more than he had a theory of how the girls were marked for kidnapping.

"We don't know yet," Finch answered. "We're hoping Ewart will tell us."

"How many more kidnappers are there?" Grace Devereaux asked.

"There are bound to be more. We know of one who fled after the Scanlon kidnapping."

Finch hadn't revealed Hector Perez-Conti's involvement in the kidnappings. Was that because he thought Mikey Scanlon's word was of no value? Mikey was only eight. Didn't he have legal standing as a witness because of his age?

Father O'Neill stood behind Finch. He stepped forward to offer a prayer of thanksgiving, adding at the end, "That the return of our girls should occur on St. Kevin's Day is yet another reason to remember the blessed saint for whom the day is named."

Then he told everyone to go home and go to bed. The festivities commenced in five hours.

I was too excited to go back to bed. Mathieu walked home with me and I invited him in. We sat on the sofa, talking about the girls' return and the relief expressed by their families. Two of the kidnapped girls had sisters enrolled in Mathieu's karate class and he described how they had broken down one day in class, fearing the worst. Gradually, tiredness caught up with us and we drowsed off until his wristwatch alarm went off.

***

The first thing I thought when I awakened was that I hadn't looked for Judy Moriarity in the crowd. I had to find her as soon as I went back to the churchyard. Mathieu returned to the inn to put on his dobrok. He and his karate class were marching in the parade, which would form after the ceremony at St. Kevin's Bed.

What do you wear to a saint's festival? I went to my closet and tried to choose.

"Elizabeth," I called out, "what are you wearing today?"

"The white dress with pink rosettes," she replied.

My green shirtdress with three-quarter-length sleeves beckoned to me. Green for life, green for growth. I felt buoyant. The girls were returned to their families. Despite not having solved Bridget Vale's murder, I was more hopeful than I'd been for days that we would soon find her killer.

After Elizabeth and I loaded food and children's costumes in my car, we drove to the church. I parked behind the priory. Mathieu was waiting for me by the statue of St. Columba. We briefly listened to a group of children singing about the saint.

Blest be Kevin of Leinster
He blessed the blackbird
who lent him her eggs;
he blessed the farmer
with milk for his cow.
Tra la Tar la Tra la la la

Around the corner, Danny Aherne was reading a poem to a group of avid listeners.

Summer has come, healthy and free,
Whence the brown wood is aslope;
The slender, nimble deer leaps
And the path of seals is smooth.

The poet, whoever he was, was lost to the ages. I had come across the poem, "Summer Has Come," in my research. It was written in the tenth century, no doubt by a monk or priest. Few lay people could read and write at that time.

Tents had been set up in the churchyard and bagpipers warmed up near the priory. Elizabeth and her committee sold ham and cheese jambons from a tent in front of the church. Thinking I saw Judy, I hurried toward the tent, but she wasn't there. A round-faced woman said she'd gone to the priory to fetch a carving knife from the kitchen. I started to follow, but Mathieu called to me, saying it was time to leave for Glendalough. The ceremony to honor St. Kevin began at ten.

He looked at his watch. "It's nearly nine-thirty. We should leave now so we'll be back in time for the parade."

"I really should try to find Judy."

It had been two days since she'd called, wanting me to see something she had found—perhaps related to Bridget's murder.

"She'll be at Glendalough," he said. "You can catch up with her there."

We walked quickly to his rental car, which had a large plastic shamrock dangling from the antennae. He got behind the wheel and pulled out into the street. Ahead were several cars, also bedecked with shamrocks, some green, some gilt and silver. Glendalough lay south, a distance of just under fifty kilometers.

We drove through the green, rock-strewn foothills of the Wicklow mountains. In the distance, the mountains were a hazy gray. Overhead, the heavens were blue with drifting clouds as white as newborn lambs. Thick forests, interspersed with meadows, ran up hillsides. The lyrics to "Danny Boy" played in my head: *the pipes are piping from glen to glen and down the mountain side...*

When we entered the Valley of the Two Lakes, Glendalough came into view. Reading aloud from a festival brochure I'd picked up at the library, I informed Mathieu that Kevin of Leinster had lived as a hermit in his cave for seven years, and had rejoined society to convert pagans to Christianity. Legend said that to gain land needed for the monastery, he'd given new life to King O'Tool's aging goose. He made a shrewd bargain with the king while the goose was old and weak, asking that his payment would be the number of miles the bird could cover in flight. O'Tool agreed, thinking his old goose was too decrepit to lift itself off the ground. One touch and Kevin invigorated the goose so that it flew several miles.

"That's legend, of course," Mathieu said.

I didn't reply, for a quiet peace had settled over me. Maybe the story was true.

We reached Glendalough. Cars pulled into parking spaces along the road and we followed suit. Elizabeth alighted from a friend's car. Since the opening to St. Kevin's Bed was in a rock formation accessible only from a narrow lake, we viewed it from the opposite side. Staring at the cave, I thought how lonely the saint must have been. But maybe not. Often one's best companions are birds and animals.

Father O'Neill was already at the worship site. Beside him were Pearce Mulligan on crutches, Lina, and his mother. I looked for Judy, but didn't see her. *Where could she be?* I was beginning to worry about her.

Father O'Neill turned to face us. To my right, the pedophile priest, Albert Malone, dropped to his knees, crossed himself, and began to pray. Freddy Vale, minus Iris, knelt and did the same. So, did the Hardestys and the McMurrays.

Elizabeth and two of her friends knelt beside us. Mathieu nudged me and we dropped to our knees. Father O'Neill began with the Our Father and led us in a long prayer of thanks for the girls' return. Then invoking the name of St. Kevin, he asked for peace in the village and in the world.

Judy wasn't among the worshippers. *Had she remained in Coomara?*

After the benediction, Mathieu wanted to briefly tour the monastery ruins, which included a once-grand cathedral, a tower for sighting Vikings, and several chapels.

"The stones tell a story," Mathieu said, always wistful for the past.

The ruins had a different effect on me, for I had been transported to a Viking raid that took place over a thousand years ago. In my mind's eye, brown-robed monks ran in terror, some carrying relics and holy books to hide in the tower. Helmeted Norsemen raised axes and spears, and clamored over the walls. One monk, before he was slain, stared me in the eye and said, "*Look upward to your Savior.*"

Mathieu touched my arm, saying he was going into the cathedral to better view the interlocking of the stones, leaving me standing beside a wall. I hardly heard him, reluctant to let go of the monk and the long-ago raid.

Then from above, a grating sound—rock against rock. I jerked my head upward in time to jump out of the way of a large falling stone. A short, muscular man in khaki-colored shorts and a white hooded sweatshirt ran the length of the wall, climbed down, and vanished into the forest. Valerie Anderson's stick man, with his short arms and legs, flashed into my mind. She said he brought drugs into the community.

"Hey!" I yelled.

The magnitude of what had almost happened stunned me. I could be lying dead on the ground, my head crushed by a massive stone. The monk—bless him—had given a warning: "*Look upward to your Savior.*" My heart pounded in my chest. Leaning against the wall, I quieted my body and blessed the universe for sending the monk.

Mathieu heard the stone crash and came running. "My god, Maria! You could have been killed. What caused the stone to fall?"

He hadn't seen the man atop the wall. I didn't tell him, nor did I plan to tell Finch. After I was shot at, Finch told me to do my sleuthing from home. If I reported this attempt on my life, he would bar me from the investigation. If Mathieu knew, he would, as he termed it, *lay down the rule.*

Mathieu peered up at the wall to see where the stone had come unmoored and shook his head. "They should place warnings that stones can fall," he said. "They should put up barriers."

The stone hadn't fallen. It had been deliberately dislodged.

Someone had tried to kill me.

Again.

Our fellow celebrants were returning to their vehicles, and so did we. My cell phone rang. Judy. I noted the time. Half past twelve.

"We seem to be having trouble getting together," she said. "I desperately need to talk to you. Come by the food tent when you return to the village."

"What is it you want to tell me? Can't you share it over the phone?"

"I want to show you something...Oh!"

"Judy," I said. "Judy! What's happening?"

She had ended the call.

"That was Judy," I told Mathieu. "She has something to show me. I don't know what it is. She was cut off."

"We'll be in Coomara in a half hour," he said.

On the way back to the village, I could think of nothing but the attempt on my life. A stone larger than my television set had missed my head by inches. I didn't recognize the man who ran away. I'd seen only his back.

I'd been warned with the evil leprechaun note. I'd been shot at. A branch had nearly fallen on my head—although that was caused by the wind. Now someone had tried to crush my skull with a large rock. The universe was hard at work keeping me alive.

Mathieu was discoursing again, and didn't expect any responses. He expressed wonder about the way stones fit together in the monastery walls. I heard words: *interlocking, carboniferous limestone, footing trench*...then he was talking about the Normans and how they destroyed monasteries when they invaded Ireland, then used the assets to form a diocesan structure for the church.

"The Normans were noted for attention to order," he said, continuing his lecture. "William the Mareshal was an able administrator."

"William the Mareshal," I said, "was one of my grandfathers."

He stared at me. "Yes, I suppose he was. You are descended from the Scottish kings."

"And Charlemagne," I said.

"Then I suppose you know all about William."

"Yes, quite a lot."

He told me about William anyway: "*twelfth century Anglo-Norman...served five English kings...crusader....*" I didn't mind. My mind was on Judy and the man who tried to kill me. I breathed a long sigh. Spirits watched over me. But I knew the danger of taking that too much to heart—it could make me reckless. Upon our return to Coomara, I headed for the food tent to find Judy.

Elizabeth touched my shoulder. "Have you seen Judy? She's supposed to help with the food."

"I'm looking for her, too. Isn't she at the food tent?"

"No. That's where she's needed."

Father O'Neill stood near the church entrance. I asked him where Judy was. He craned his neck, searching. "Why don't you try the priory?" he said. "She may have gone to the kitchen for something."

Hurrying across the court to the priory, I opened the front door and called for Judy. No answer. *Where is she?* Apprehension sent my heart tripping. I hurried down the hallway and entered the kitchen, passing the sitting room, which smelled of lemon. Judy had recently polished the furniture. The same scent lingered in the kitchen, but was overpowered by another smell—the acrid odor of nervous perspiration. Fear shot through me, and I thought of Bambi's mother scenting Man.

I smelled Man.

The back door was ajar. I went outside. Had it not been for a squirrel that ran down a tree trunk, I might have missed seeing her, but my eyes went to movement by the trees and I saw a woman in a blue dress with her apron pulled over her head, lying on the ground next to a statue of the Virgin Mary.

Judy!

I ran to her, praying she had not been harmed, then saw blood coursing from her neck. Like Bridget Vale, she had been garroted, the flesh on her throat deeply pierced. I felt for her pulse. She was dead, still warm. By minutes, I had missed her murder.

I sank to the ground and wept. What had Iris Vale and Dierdre O'Malley called Judy? A clatterfart? Despite her gossiping, I was fond of Judy. Truth be told, I often leaned in to hear what she had to say. Her life as a wife of an IRA man in Northern Ireland must have been fraught with worry and fear. Here in Coomara, she had, perhaps, found the peace she deserved.

But she talked too much. Did that lead to her death?

I ran to find a garda officer and led him back to Judy's body. Within minutes, other officers came, including Finch.

"Ms. Pell," he said, "they say you found the body. Are you all right?"

I wasn't all right. I wasn't used to seeing my friends garroted. Finch waited until I calmed.

"She's was killed the same way as Bridget," I said dully.

Finch knelt to examine the throat wounds.

"Judy called two days ago," I said. "She'd found something she wanted to show me. I've been trying to contact her, but she's been busy with the festival and my schedule was erratic. Today, she called at twelve-thirty to tell me to come by the food tent."

"Why didn't she go to Glendalough with Father O'Neill?" Finch asked.

"She must have been detained. If she'd gone to St. Kevin's Bed, she'd still be alive. If she'd only gone..."

"Her fingers are broken," Finch said sharply. "All ten of them."

Judy had been tortured! I stared at her hands. Her fingers and thumbs had been bent backward until they snapped. She must have screamed, but everyone had gone to Glendalough and there was no one to hear her.

Finch turned to Sergeant Gowdy. "Her killer tried to force her to tell him something—possibly the information she wanted to give to Ms. Pell."

The reality that Judy had suffered killed my spirit. This was Judy with the sparkling blue eyes, gray curls, plump little body. I could not bear to think....

Finch stepped away from the body. "Another savage murder."

Gowdy stared hard at me. "Do you remember what she said two days ago when she called you?"

"She said she found something that afternoon, and then the food committee met. She didn't elaborate, but I took it to mean that committee work distracted her from what she'd found. Then she told me I must come and see it—whatever *it* was."

Judy might have let something slip at the committee meeting. This was the same loose-lipped committee that Elizabeth told I knew who was committing Coomara's crimes.

"Maria! They won't let me through!" Elizabeth cried.

Officers had cordoned off the crime scene, but Elizabeth wanted through to find out what had happened. The officers allowed her passage. When she saw Judy's body, she fainted. Thinking uncharitable thoughts, I sat on the ground and held her head in my lap. Hysterics didn't help. Fainting didn't help. I wanted to smack Elizabeth. She revived without my smacking her, and Mathieu returned from the parade in time to get her to her feet and take her home.

I didn't want to leave the murder scene.

Did the man who tried to kill me at the monastery ruins return to Coomara and kill Judy? The stone fell from the wall about an hour before Judy's call—plenty of time for the killer to return to Coomara.

Finch narrowed his eyes. "We should look in her room at the priory."

"Can I go with you?"

"Come along."

He summoned an officer with a camera, and we went inside the house and up the stairs to search Judy's room. Father O'Neill had a suite, whose windows looked out on the church. His door was open. The furnishings were dark, as was the bedspread—brown and black. A crucifix was nailed to the wall above the bed. He had no rug on the floor and I imagined the planks were cold on wintry mornings. A center room, its door closed, served visiting priests.

At the end of the corridor was Judy's room, curtained in dusky rose with matching bedspread. Before we touched anything, we paused at the door, and waited until the man with the camera stopped snapping photos. Judy's room was neat, feminine, grandmotherly. How else would one expect it to be?

Rage nearly blinded me. The sensation lasted for only a moment, but I determined then and there to find her killer. Nothing would stop me.

CHAPTER TWENTY-ONE

Finch handed me plastic gloves.

Judy's missal lay on a bedside table. The dresser top was covered with religious statues and window sills held pink African violets in bloom. Dickens' *A Tale of Two Cities* lay on the seat of a floral-slipcovered easy chair. A bookmark had fallen to the floor. Judy's robe, a thick pink chenille with raglan sleeves was draped over the back of a straight chair near the door.

At the back of the room was another door, partially ajar, leading into a bathroom. I opened the medicine cabinet. Judy took blood pressure medication. Other than that, the contents were the usual hygiene items and products: toothbrush, toothpaste, deodorant. Under the sink were cleaning supplies. There seemed to be nothing in Judy's bedroom to suggest a reason for her death.

I went downstairs to the kitchen and stood at the window. The sky had clouded up and I heard distant thunder.

The universe is reacting to Judy's murder.

In the yard, people enacted rituals and carried out the practicalities of death. Father O'Neill knelt beside Judy's body, sprinkling holy water, saying the prayer for the departed. Officers and bystanders made way for men from the medical examiner's office, who placed Judy's body in white body bag and lifted it onto a stretcher. An officer pulled a piece of paper from his jacket pocket and unfolded it. The wind caught it, sent it spiraling across the grass.

I blinked my eyes. The piece of paper multiplied, sending several sheets gusting across the yard. I had leapt into another dimension, as Judy's spirit attempted to communicate with me. There was pressure on my shoulders, my upper arms, as if she had caught me in an embrace. *What did all those flying pages represent? A book? Letters? Records?*

Then she released me.

Mathieu returned from taking Elizabeth back to the cottage. "You look lost, Maria."

"I can't bear it that Judy had to endure torture."

He rubbed my neck, took my arm, led me out of the priory.

"Is the parade over?" I asked.

He nodded. "It was a grand parade. Such a sad ending."

"I'm sure your girls looked formidable."

He patted my arm. "They did."

We walked out into the afternoon sunshine. I felt the warmth on my skin, but inwardly, was chilled to the bone. I had spoken to Judy minutes—perhaps seconds—before she died. What happened when she abruptly ended the call?

The person who killed Judy also killed Bridget.

Parade participants were dispersing. Bagpipers unshouldered their pipes. Dancers, still with spring in their muscles, hopped about in the courtyard. Youngsters and oldsters held their pets on leashes and in cages. Wearing a black and silver cloak, Deirdre O'Malley stood beside her two Afghan hounds; an old woman held a fat goose.

Mikey Scanlon grasped a small metal birdcage with a green parakeet inside. Mathieu led me to admire Mikey's bird. I tried to engage, but my mind was on Judy. Mathieu's students, dashing in their dobroks, were still lunging and kicking, and expecting a reaction. I tried to smile, but my lips felt frozen.

Father O'Neill left the priory, bearing the weight of the world on his sagging shoulders. I felt his pain. Each morning, he had breakfasted with chatterbox Judy and when he retired at night, hers was the last face he usually saw. She'd been with him for many years, keeping house, performing secretarial duties, and bringing him village news. I hated to disturb him, but Judy's message about the sheets of paper was foremost on my mind. I left Mathieu's side to speak to the priest.

"Father," I said, "Judy has tried to tell me something."

He stopped, took a moment to focus on me. "I heard she called you."

"No, I mean she has tried to send a message from beyond."

"I'd forgotten—you have second sight. What did she say?"

"She sent a vision of pages flying through the air."

"What was written on the pages?" he asked.

"I couldn't see."

He thought for a moment. "She was upstairs looking through old records, but that couldn't have had any bearing on her death."

"Did you ask her to find something?" I asked quickly.

"We had requests for baptismal certificates from America—people trying to find their ancestors."

"Do you recall the names?"

"No, but the requests will be filed away."

"By date?"

"By name. She keeps a log of people who write. It's not always current. With the festival, she may have delayed logging in the names."

"Thank you, Father."

I went to inform Finch, but he had returned to the garda station. Then Elizabeth called, wanting me to come home. It started to rain, and Mathieu drove me back to the cottage. He returned to the inn for a telephone conference with his archeological team members.

***

Elizabeth was stirring a roux of vegetables for soup. She looked tired. She had been close to Judy—perhaps closer than I had been. They had worked together planning the festival, and team effort bonded people. I brewed a pot of tea so we could sit by the window, watch the rain, and talk.

"I heard Judy got in touch with you," Elizabeth said. "What time did she call this morning?"

"This afternoon. Twelve-thirty."

"That must have been when she went to get a carving knife for the hams. I was busy accepting food people brought and didn't notice she hadn't returned."

We sat, staring out the window at the rain.

"What time did your committee gather at the tent?" I asked.

"Around eight," Elizabeth answered.

"Was everyone there?"

"Yes. Why do you ask?"

"Did Judy mention anything about Bridget's murder?"

I was on dangerous ground. Elizabeth had been the talebearer who may have unleashed the passions of the person who shot at me.

Elizabeth stiffened. "Are you saying something might have been discussed at the meeting that led to Judy's death?"

I bit my lip. "Perhaps."

"What a ridiculous assumption." Elizabeth shot me a baleful look and stomped upstairs.

She left her notebook behind. Opening it, I found a list of food committee members and their contact information: Blair, Fitzgerald, Hennessey, Murphy, and O'Toole. Rose Fitzgerald was the mother of Ewart, who had just been arrested as part of the kidnapping ring. Had Rose disclosed something to Ewart that marked Judy for death?

Ewart Fitzgerald was in jail. His cohorts, however, remained free.

I called Finch. "Judy might have let drop to committee members that she'd found information about Bridget's murder—or about the kidnappings."

"I thought of that," he said. "Mrs. Moriarity was often indiscreet. Sergeant Potts has gone to question the women on the food committee."

"Will you let me know what she finds out?"

"Stop by in the morning," Finch said.

***

The next morning was Sunday, June 4. I went to the garda station right after breakfast. As I eased into the chair beside Finch's desk, I asked him if Ewart Fitzgerald had identified others in the kidnapping ring.

"Not yet. We're hoping his dad and mam can convince him to. They're here now, talking to him."

I moved on to Judy's murder. "Were Bridget and Judy killed with the same kind of weapon?"

"It would seem so. We still don't know what was used for the garotte."

A door slammed. A woman cried out. Inspector Finch hurried into the hallway. In a moment, he returned with Rose Fitzgerald, who sat down next to me. Her shoulders shook with great heaving sobs. Finch handed her a box of tissues.

"What happened, Mrs. Fitzgerald?" Finch asked.

"Ewart refuses to give up his mates," she said. "We told him he'd have a better chance with the law if he did, but it made no difference. He says he's no squealer. Manfred thought he might be able to persuade him with me out of the room."

Finch agreed. "Perhaps, he will. Could we chat a bit about what Mrs. Moriarity talked about at your last committee meeting?"

"I spoke to Sergeant Potts last night."

"She's not yet on duty this morning, so tell me what you told her. When the food committee first gathered, what did you talk about?"

"We discussed the arrangement of food on the table. The fish and chips and lemonade vendors were coming. We decided where their stands would be placed."

"Any gossip?" I asked.

Rose Fitzgerald shook her pretty blond head, then remembered. "We discussed a recent newspaper story. Ten years ago, a man accidentally ran over his little boy with his automobile. His wife said she forgave him. Last Sunday, she aimed her car at her husband as he pulled weeds from their garden and killed him. Though she said it was an accident, the police arrested her for murder."

"I saw the story in the paper," Finch said. "It happened in Belfast. Why were you discussing it?"

"It was topical. Someone said the woman's act of revenge was served cold."

"What was Mrs. Moriarity's contribution to this discussion?" Finch asked.

"I can't...oh, wait. I do believe she commented...what was it? I can't remember exactly, but I think she said something about old sins not being forgotten. Then she said she'd been looking through records and..."

I moved to the edge of my chair. "And what?"

"Your cousin spilled her tea and since we'd just put down a clean paper tablecloth, someone made a fuss and we changed the cloth. That's all I remember about the meeting."

"Did you tell anyone about the conversation?" Finch asked.

"No. The boys and their da are always gone. Who would I tell it to? Billy? He and I barely talk now that he's growing up."

A grim-faced Manfred Fitzgerald appeared in the doorway. "It's no use, Rose. Let's go home."

Rose burst into tears again. Her husband put his hand on her shoulder and steered her out of the building.

A few minutes later, Sergeant Potts entered the room. Finch asked her what the committee members had to say.

"Mrs. O'Toole said she repeated Mrs. Moriarity's remark about old sins when discussing the Belfast case with a friend who bought a croissant from her," Potts said. "Others stood close enough to hear, while waiting for their jambons."

"Oh good." Finch's tone was sarcastic. "The whole village could have heard her."

"Did she also repeat the information that Judy had been searching through old records?" I asked.

"She did."

"Potts," Finch said, "go to the priory and find out what Judy was researching. Take Ms. Pell with you. I have phone calls to make."

***

Sergeant Potts and I drove to the priory, catching Father O'Neill between services. When we explained that we wanted to know what Judy was looking for in the church records, he let us into her office, which was at the back of the priory. It was a sunny room with chintz curtains at the windows. Her desk was in immaculate order, putting me to shame as I thought of my own disarranged desk.

I sat down and began looking through drawers. A black notebook, labeled *Correspondence* lay in the bottom drawer. The first entry was dated June 1: Sophie McMurray, 1022 Skylark Street, Lorraine, Ohio. Tessa's last name was McMurray. So was Iris Vale's maiden name. Judy had made a notation: *Wants information on Michael Sean McMurray, born circa 1876.* There were two other entries made on June 1—Jessica McLeod and Everett Kane, both wanting information on ancestors with the same surname as theirs. I called the sergeant over to see the entries.

Father O'Neill came down the stairs, on his way to the church.

"Are the files upstairs?" Potts asked him.

"At the top of the stairs."

He took a moment to look at Judy's notebook. "For Michael McMurray, you'll find a file referring you to one of the old maroon record books. Anyone baptized before 1920 will be found in those books."

The priest left. Potts and I went upstairs and opened the cabinet marked H to M. In the McMurray file were several baptismal certificates. For Michael Sean McMurray, I was referred to Book Number Eight in the maroon series. While Potts looked there, I riffled through the McMurray file and found nothing that seemed relevant to the investigation.

"Nothing here," Potts said. "Just an entry for Michael McMurray's baptism."

"Maybe the church records have nothing to do with Judy's death," I said. "She could have been referring to another type of record."

"Let's look in her bedroom again," Potts said.

We went into Judy's bedroom. Dickens' novel had been moved from the chair to the dresser top. Someone had retrieved the bookmark from the floor and placed it beside the book. Potts said I could touch the items, so I picked up the bookmark, which was made of thick royal blue paper. Embossed on the front was a Claddagh—a three-quarters circle ending in hands with a heart and crown. On the back, in tiny script was a date, 15.1.2000, and the letter, E.

I showed it to Potts. "What does this mean?"

She shrugged. "Something that happened on January 15, 2000. Maybe the letter E represents someone's name."

As I picked up Charles Dickens' *A Tale of Two Cities*, it fell open to a page with its corner turned down. The chapter was titled "Knitting." Madame DeFarge wove the names of victims destined for the guillotine into her knitting, starting with the St. Evrémondes, who had destroyed her family. Her husband counseled her to curb her enthusiasm for death. She replied, *Tell the Wind and the Fire to stop, not me!*

Revenge. A list of victims.

"Maybe Judy was going to tell me she'd thought of a list," I said.

"There's the list of the men in the hunting party that shot Margaret Mulligan's father," Potts said.

A feeling of certainty energized me. "That happened in the Fifties. This list pertains to something that happened in January, 2000."

I ran down the stairs, the bookmark in my hand. Potts followed. We returned to garda headquarters and found Sergeant Gowdy in Finch's office.

I took the Claddagh bookmark from my purse. "Judy was using this bookmark in Dickens' *A Tale of Two Cities*. On the back, she wrote *15.1.2000 E*. Sergeant Potts and I believe the numbers are a date. Can you tell me what the *E* stands for?"

I passed the bookmark around.

Sergeant Gowdy said, "It could stand for the defunct newspaper—the *Eolas*—means knowledge or information."

"Where would I find the *Eolas* archives?" I asked.

"The current newspaper, *The Daily Sun*, surely has it," Finch said. "I'll send Sergeant Murphy to *The Sun* to look it up."

My heart skipped a beat. We were surely on the verge of finding out what Judy Moriarity was trying to tell us.

CHAPTER TWENTY-TWO

As I was leaving, Tim Hawkins walked into the station and said he wanted to talk to Inspector Finch. I waited a moment, hoping Finch would call me back to listen to what Tim had to say. He didn't.

Instead of going home, I went to Miss Molly's Tea Room and ordered a raspberry scone and a cup of tea. I was a jangle of nerves. How long would it take Sergeant Murphy to search through the newspaper archives? Why had Tim Hawkins come to see Finch?

My telephone rang. Finch wanted me to return to his office. I hurried back. Looking as if the starch had gone out of him, Tim Hawkins sat in the chair next to Finch's desk.

The inspector looked daggers at the young man. "Mr. Hawkins' conscience has been troubling him. He's confessed to his part in Bridget Vale's murder."

Tim slouched in his chair, his eyes glued to the floor. "I was the one who got Bridget to come out of her house."

"For what purpose?" I asked.

"It's not what you think," Tim said.

His explanation—that she was so beautiful he needed to see her to create his poems— fell on my deaf ears. I doubted Tim wrote love poetry.

I still had my doubts about Bridget. How had she acquired the two-hundred and fifty euros found in her room? Had she been involved with drug dealers as Valerie Anderson had suggested?

"So you got her to come out of the house," Finch prompted. "Then what?"

"We walked along the street, then went down to the shore. A man called for help and I thought he was drowning. I raised the flashlight and went closer to the water, but I couldn't see anything. When I turned back for Bridget, she was gone."

"Did you recognize the voice of the man you thought was drowning?" Finch asked.

Tim shook his head.

"Did you tell anyone you were going to Bridget's house?" I asked.

Tim frowned. "I might have. I was with friends at Green Mountain. I might have said I needed to see my muse. Several people knew Bridget was my muse."

Inspector Finch asked for the names of his friends and Tim duly wrote them down on a sheet of paper.

"Your aunt lied for you," the inspector said.

Grace Devereaux had claimed Tim was home with her the night of April 30.

Tim's face clouded. "She didn't lie—she thought I was home."

"But you weren't. Why did she give you a false alibi?"

"That's not what she thought she was doing."

Tim looked helplessly at me, as if I could rescue him from the snare of lies he'd told. I gave him a steely look. He'd have to extricate himself and Grace Devereaux. As far as I was concerned, I didn't believe a word of what he said, except that he lured Bridget from her house.

As his story—this part, hopefully truthful—unfolded, it turned out that Grace Devereaux was away from home the night of April 30, but had called Tim on the landline around ten to remind him to let the dog out. Tim answered. She thought he'd been home all night.

"Where was your aunt?" the inspector asked.

"She'd gone to Deirdre O'Malley's house."

"When you realized Bridget was gone, did you try to find her?" Finch asked.

"Of course I did. I searched the beach and both sides of the road, but she was gone."

Finch scowled. "Did you see anyone?"

"Only that old priest nobody talks to."

"Albert Malone?"

"I don't know what his name is. He's short and thin and has a bald head."

I thought of the sketch of the priest in Valerie Anderson's notebook. *What does Miss Priss see in him?*

There was a question I wanted to ask Tim Hawkins. "Why are you visiting your aunt during your school term?"

The teenager's face reddened. "I'm taking a layover year."

I raised my eyebrows. "Isn't that usually between high school graduation and college? You're only sixteen."

"A person can take layover whenever."

"Did you get kicked out of school?" I asked.

"What does that have to do with Bridget?"

"Maybe a lot," I said, my temper rising. "Maybe if you'd stayed in St. Louis, she'd be alive."

A bleak look crossed his face. Inspector Finch cleared his throat loudly, and I understood he felt I was being too hard on the young man.

"When can I go?" Tim asked.

Finch looked down at his desk. "You can go now, Mr. Hawkins."

When Tim had gone, the inspector called Potts in. "Bring in Albert Malone. I want to talk to him." He turned to me. "Perhaps you should leave while I speak to Mr. Malone."

It was my own fault—I'd shown antagonism with Tim Hawkins. Finch didn't want me near Albert Malone when he questioned him. As I drove home, Margaret Mulligan called, asking me to tea the following afternoon at three and I accepted.

What could Margaret want? I was puzzled. Did she want to discuss her daughter-in-law, Lina? Or Hector? She had invited me to tea—a sociable act that suggested she might want to talk about something unrelated to Coomara's recent crime wave. Had she composed new poems and wanted me to critique them? If that was the case, I felt honored.

***

The cottage was quiet. Elizabeth napped on the sofa. Wondering what to prepare for supper, I looked in the refrigerator and found leftover broccoli and boiled potatoes. I could make a frittata. A quick meal. I closed the refrigerator door and walked to the window.

I was in a state of high anticipation. If it could be proven that Albert Malone murdered Bridget and Judy, the village would rest easier. I would rest easier. Coomara's girls were back and some of the kidnappers were in jail. The rest of the human trafficking ring was probably spread throughout Ireland. The ring leader—at least in Coomara—was undoubtedly Hector Perez-Conti, who had hightailed it to Venezuela, where there was no extradition treaty.

I needed calm. Hurrying down the stone steps to the sea, I settled into a nook some distance from the dock. Waves lapped at the rocks below my perch. Gradually, the mist faded, allowing afternoon sunlight through. Scanning the horizon, I saw a ship pass, then another.

Breathing deeply, I felt my body relax. My mind lay fallow like a harrowed field, waiting for random thoughts. When they came, I wrote them down: *ragwort, secrets, grim, tunnel, rock-bound sea.*

I concentrated on *secrets*, for not only did the term excite me poetically, it could also lead to a motive for Bridget's and Judy's murders. The villagers had secrets. Why had the village suddenly become the target of sex traffickers? Judy was a teller of secrets. Her death possibly meant she'd told one too many secrets.

I, too, had secrets. Dark memories I didn't want to share with anyone.

Grief over losing my parents.

The despair I'd sunk into upon discovering Mathieu was unfaithful.

Finding Baby Doe, who had been discarded. In some twisted way, I thought finding her might have made it difficult for me to forgive Mathieu.

***

When I returned to the cottage, Elizabeth was reading her missal.

"Do you know the Our Father?" she asked.

"The Lord's Prayer? Of course, I do."

"You know the part, *Do not lead us into temptation*? Why was it translated that way? A merciful god would not *lead* his children into temptation."

"Is God merciful?" I asked. "He created Lucifer, didn't he? *Lead* is appropriate. You should pray to God to lead you away from every temptation he places in front of you."

She was quiet. I hadn't given her the answer she wanted.

"I thought I'd make a frittata for supper," I said, after a moment.

"I'm not hungry. Don't cook anything for me."

"Have you eaten today?"

"Yes, yes," she said impatiently. "I had toast and orange juice this morning, and a boiled egg for lunch."

"I'll fix a frittata. You can eat it or not," I said, going into the kitchen.

Early in our relationship, Mathieu had taught me how to make frittatas. He had assembled ingredients on my kitchen counter: olive oil, diced cooked potatoes, half a green pepper, minced onion, cooked broccoli, eggs, cheddar cheese. I had listened intently as he explained how hot the oil must be. As I leaned in, the heat of his body had excited me. My heat affected him. Backing away from the counter, he turned and kissed me deeply. I remembered how strong his arms felt, how smooth his skin....

We had forgotten about dinner and hurried to my bed, where we flung ourselves at each other. Hours later, we returned to the kitchen, where he finished the frittata and put it in the oven. Later we took a red Chablis and the food to the bedroom and dined in bed, listening to Miriam Makeba sing "Pata." The memory made me smile. In the beginning, Mathieu and I had created magic. I supposed that was true of all lovers when relationships were young and full of lovely surprises.

I baked the frittata and sat down to eat. Elizabeth did not join me. After cleaning the kitchen, I went in the sitting room.

"I just hate it here now, Maria," Elizabeth said.

"Why don't you go home?"

"You're just trying to get rid of me."

I counted to ten. "Not so. I understand that the village has lost its charm. Two murders—three, if you count Franco Milton."

"I don't feel safe here."

She didn't feel safe? There had been two attempts on *my* life. I didn't feel safe either, which was why I locked the cottage doors and windows every night.

"What do you want me to do?" I asked.

"You're out and about so much. I'd like you to spend more time with me."

"I can't do that, Elizabeth. I have things to do. Tomorrow afternoon, I'm having tea with Margaret Mulligan at Ravensclaw. Why don't you ask someone to stay with you?"

As if on cue, Brendan came to the door. Elizabeth had left her slipper at his cottage. I thanked him, and as he turned to leave, Elizabeth called out to him.

"Brendan, I have a favor to ask."

He stepped into the vestibule.

She rose from the sofa. "If you aren't busy tomorrow afternoon, could you come and sit with me? Maria has a commitment and I'm feeling unsure of things...with all the killing."

"I'd be glad to keep you company," he told her. "What time?"

Elizabeth looked at me.

"My appointment is at three."

Brendan promised to come over at half-past two the next day. Elizabeth smiled at him and daintily offered her hand in parting. She was flirting with Brendan! I was baffled. Perhaps she saw him as a rescuer— he had found her wandering in the street and taken her into his home where he wrapped her in a blanket. He had taken care of her.

There had been few men in Elizabeth's life. She was engaged once for two months when she was twenty, but returned the ring, saying she was unready for marriage. A few years later, she kept company with a history professor at the university, but they drifted apart. As far as I knew, there had been no one since the professor. Would Elizabeth stay in Coomara to be near Brendan? This thought drove me into the kitchen where I cleaned the refrigerator, a job I hated, to distract myself.

Mathieu stopped by and said he'd need to take the four-faced, stone goddess back to the dig in the morning.

"So much has been happening," I said. "I haven't been able to devote as much time to Dea as I wanted. Could you let me have her a little longer?"

He agreed to extend Dea's visit for a few more days. I told him that Tim Hawkins had seen Albert Malone in the vicinity the night of April 30 when Bridget disappeared.

"Finch was bringing him in for questioning when I left the station," I said.

"I saw Dennis in the pub a few minutes ago," Mathieu said. "The interrogation must be over."

Why hadn't Finch called me?

***

Finch hadn't called by noon on Monday, so I drove to his office. He was buried in a stack of papers. Record-keeping. I remembered that from my teaching days.

"Did Albert Malone confess?" I asked him.

"He told a most peculiar story," Finch said. "He admitted he was out walking the night of April 30, but said he had neither seen nor heard Bridget Vale. He said he had been fond of her because she had offered him friendship. He called her a saint."

I thought of the drawing of the priest in Valerie Anderson's pink notebook and the words, *what does Miss Priss see in him.*

"Furthermore," Finch said, "he said she was trying to model her life on that of St. Clare of Assisi, who was a follower of St. Francis. His first follower, if I recall correctly."

"How can that be true? We know she was fond of Tim Hawkins. What about the money you found in her bedroom?"

"We don't know how Bridget felt about Mr. Hawkins. According to Albert Malone, Bridget took in outcasts. She counseled those who used and sold drugs to stop, saying it wasn't Christ's plan for them. Tim Hawkins may have been one of her projects. He'd left high school and had no plans to continue his education."

"But...but the money in her bedroom..." I stammered.

"Albert said she'd been saving money earned from odd jobs to send to an African mission."

I had been wrong about Bridget Vale. Finch stared at me. My face grew hot with embarrassment and shame.

"Do you believe Albert Malone?" I asked.

"I have no reason to disbelieve him."

I swallowed hard. "I'm ashamed that I doubted Bridget."

For a moment, neither of us spoke. I was squirming, trying to remember if I'd shared my suspicion that Bridget was leading a disreputable life with anyone. Mathieu. I thought I'd said something to him. No one else. Thank heavens I hadn't said anything to Elizabeth.

CHAPTER TWENTY-THREE

Around two-thirty, I stepped from the cottage, preparing to leave for Ravensclaw. In the sitting room, Brendan sat beside Elizabeth on the sofa, watching an old Peter O'Toole film. Within reach on the coffee table were soft drinks and a bowl of freshly popped popcorn. In his shaggy way, Brendan looked harmless. Elizabeth looked content.

My rental car wouldn't start. I headed back inside to ask Brendan if I could borrow his car, but remembered he drove a stick shift, and I'd never driven a stick shift. What to do? I didn't want to cancel my appointment with Margaret Mulligan.

From its niche by the side of the house, I glimpsed my bicycle handle bars. I looked at my cell phone for the time. If I hurried, I could get to Ravensclaw by three. Grabbing the bike, I rolled it onto the street and headed for the Mulligan estate. Traffic was rarely heavy in Coomara, so I covered the distance through town in less than ten minutes. The coastal road to Ravensclaw sloped slightly upward. I felt the strain on my thigh and calf muscles, and was glad to reach the crest where the land leveled out. Though the sun was shining, a few gray clouds streaked the sky and I warned myself to keep an eye on the weather.

After parking my bicycle near the front entrance of the Mulligan manor, I ran up the steps and lifted the stag's head door knocker. The butler opened the door at the second knock and stepped aside so I could enter.

I had never been inside the great house. The foyer was octagonal, with scarlet tapestries embroidered with snarling lions, peeved otters, and jolly shamrocks, which I assumed comprised the Mulligan coat of arms. An archway opened onto a gallery sprouting an emerald green circular staircase. At the bottom, a maid met me and led me to an upstairs sitting room done in pale lavender and moss green. I glanced around the room. In addition to statues of the Virgin Mary, delicate ceramic birds perched on shelves flanking the bay window.

Dressed in royal purple, Margaret Mulligan shuffled in, leaning on a cane. She invited me to join her at a tea table topped with a silver urn and two bone china cups. As she poured the amber liquid into the cups, another maid brought in a salver of warm scones, butter, and fresh strawberries.

Margaret came straight to the point. "I've invited you here, Ms. Pell, to seek your help in organizing a poetry retreat—something small and intimate. I also write verse and am lonesome for like-minded people."

"I'm struck by how close you are to the natural world in your poetry," I said.

"That was my early work. Now I write sonnets about the past. Among my late husband's ancestors are the old Irish kings. I visit the stones and wait for them to speak."

Her writing process intrigued me—it was much like my own. "May I read your current work?"

She went to her bureau desk, which was decoupaged with scenes of Irish saints—Patrick, converting a heathen king; Kevin, holding a blackbird in his hand; Columba, rescuing a man from a sea monster. From the top drawer, she withdrew a slim book, covered in brown leather, and handed it to me.

"I have other copies," she said. "Please take it. It is signed."

"Thank you," I said. "I'd be honored to help you with a retreat. When would you like to hold it?"

"Next month. We could set up a tent by the sea."

"Will that give us time to get people together?"

"I think so. I know poets at Trinity College who'd be glad to come and lead discussions. There is plenty of room here for guests to stay overnight."

She shared her vision, which included comfy chairs, evening bonfires, and delicacies from her kitchen. As she spoke, her plan took shape in my mind. I would certainly benefit from a retreat—my mind had been so overtaxed with worry about the missing girls and the murders, I had not been able to write my verses.

We were sitting quietly, discussing whether the retreat should last two or three days, when a woman's shriek pierced the walls.

"Don't leave me!"

A male voice yelled, "Release my arm!"

The shouts came from the corridor. Margaret raised her patrician eyebrows and hobbled to the door, pushing it open. "What is the meaning of this?"

Lina Mulligan appeared in the doorway. "Forgive us for disturbing you, Mother Mulligan. Hector was saying he was leaving and..."

Hector Perez-Conti had returned? How had he gotten past airport officials? Had he used an alias? He probably had multiple passports.

Someone dashed past the door.

A blond Hector!

Lina ran after him.

Margaret Mulligan rolled her eyes at me. "I'm so sorry, Ms. Pell. There's no accounting for the rabble my son brings into this house."

Rabble. An interesting word to use to describe one's daughter-in-law and her family. My fingers itched to call Finch and report that Hector was at Ravensclaw, but I hesitated to do it in front of Margaret Mulligan. Did she know about his crimes? The noise in the hallway had disconcerted her, and I politely brought our discussion to an end and promised to get back in touch about the retreat.

In the hallway, a door creaked open. Pearce Mulligan looked out, tucked a crutch under his armpit, and waved. Running down the emerald staircase, I flew through the vestibule and dashed outside. Lina was hanging onto Hector as he tried to get into his BMW. Not only had he bleached his hair, he had shaved off his mustache. He and Lina spoke in a torrent of Spanish. Twice, I heard the word *Paris*.

Paris? Was Hector going to Paris? Ireland surely had an extradition agreement with France.

"Si, si!" cried Hector, tearing himself out of Lina's grasp.

He roared off in his car. Pushing past Lina, who was doubled up with weeping, I ran to my bicycle and called the garda station to report Hector's return. Sergeant Potts said she would come straightaway. I kept my eye on Hector. He didn't turn onto the highway but headed for the coast. There was no way I could catch up with him, so I pedaled to a promontory where I could observe the coastal road.

The BMW vanished behind a hill. Though the sky had darkened, I made out the shape of a vessel at sea. As it neared, I saw it was a large yacht—the kind you see in magazines featuring celebrities. How I wished for binoculars!

Something important was about to happen. I hoped Sergeant Potts would hurry. Minutes later, a squad car careened around a bend. Potts was behind the wheel. In the passenger seat was Finch.

"Get in," Finch yelled.

I got in. We rounded a curve in time to see Hector speeding toward the yacht in a motorboat. Potts braked at the wharf and got out her binoculars.

"The yacht is the *Isala*," she said. "That's Arabic."

"You know Arabic?" I asked.

"Some."

Finch made a call. Soon coastal patrol boats were pursuing the motorboat. A speedboat burst free of the yacht, carrying two men who opened fire. The patrolmen shot back; the men went down. Within a short period of time, the patrol had captured Hector and the wounded men, and were piloting both boats to shore. I watched open-mouthed as an ambulance came, followed by another garda car. *Inspector Finch moved quickly when it counted.* The wounded went to a hospital and officers hustled Hector into the car. The yacht disappeared in the mists.

Sergeant Potts surprised me with a high five. "You have a knack of being in the right place at the right time, Maria Pell."

"Aye, for sure," Finch said. "Where is your car?"

"It wouldn't start. I had an appointment with Margaret Mulligan and rode my bicycle."

I braced for a lecture, but it didn't happen. Finch let his hand rest for a moment on my shoulder and then took it away.

"Good lass," he said.

I felt like a golden retriever.

But the Irish love their dogs. Did his gesture mean he had forgiven me for my grievous error about Bridget?

***

The night rain washed Coomara clean. Next morning after a tow truck had hauled my 2005 Mazda back to the rental agency, I got behind the wheel of a 2015 blue Mazda and drove through puddles to garda headquarters.

Wrapped in a black fringed cape, Deirdre O'Malley sat in a chair in the inspector's office. She smiled when she saw me. Finch was on the telephone. He ended the call just as I appeared in the doorway.

"The men from the *Isala* are Greek," he said. "Deirdre speaks Greek, so we took her to the hospital to translate. They want a priest."

Deirdre raised her eyebrows. "They are most contrite but they're not admitting anything."

"Did the yacht get away?" I asked.

"Fortunately, not," the inspector said. "The patrol stopped it. Two young girls from Scotland were in the hold. They'd been taken from the Edinburgh area. There was a crew of five. All were arrested."

I sat down beside Deirdre.

"The Greeks say they are not part of a larger organization," Finch went on, "but of course, we don't believe them. The *Isala* is registered to a shipping company in Hong Kong. If the men don't talk, there will be no way to trace them to the ringleaders."

"And Hector?" I asked. "What is he saying?

"He's asked for a solicitor," Finch said. "Since the Greeks aren't talking, we have nothing to hold him on, so we're releasing him."

"But Mikey Scanlon identified him as one of his sister's abductors," I said. "He told us Hector followed him and his mother from the petrol station."

"Though I believe young Mikey, he is only eight years old. We haven't been able to confirm his allegations."

The front door opened and closed. Lina Mulligan rushed into Finch's office. "What have you done with Hector?"

Escorted by an officer, Hector Chavez-Ponti came down the corridor. Though Hector's bespoke suit was rumpled, and he needed a shave, he had pulled himself up to his full height—probably five feet and two inches—and walked out like a fair-haired Spanish grandee. Lina linked her arm in his and spoke in a soothing tone.

Deirdre asked if her services were still needed, was told no, and made a telephone call. Soon after, Grace Devereaux picked her up.

At last the inspector and I were alone. "What is the real relationship between Lina and Hector?" I asked.

"He said they are step-brother and sister," Finch replied. "Hector's father and Lina's mother married when their children were in their early teens."

Lina's and Hector's frolic in the aspen grove was only adulterous, and not incestuous as some people, including me, had suspected.

"Will Hector's arrest be in the newspaper?" I asked.

"Probably. A reporter was alerted to the arrests."

I thought of Margaret Mulligan in her lavender sitting room, brooding among her lovely ceramic birds. Was she lambasting her son for bringing Lina and Hector into their lives?

"What happened to Pearce Mulligan's son by his first wife?" I asked.

"A son?" Finch said. "Pearce doesn't have a son."

"His first wife's obituary said she died after giving birth to a son."

"The child may have been stillborn. How long ago did the first wife die?"

I consulted my notebook. "She died in 2000."

"That was sixteen years ago. I remember her dying, but didn't know she'd had a son."

"She was buried in Scotland."

I asked if Sergeant Murphy had made any progress searching through newspaper archives for the cryptic date on the back of Judy's bookmark. Finch replied that the records were disorganized and he'd found nothing yet.

"There are no indices," he explained.

Father O'Neill would know about Pearce's first wife. He might even know about the son. I got up from the chair, told Finch goodbye, and drove to the priory.

***

Father O'Neill received me in his office.

After exchanging greetings, I got straight to the point. "Father, did Pearce and Laura Mulligan have a child?"

The priest stared at me as if he'd stepped into a nest of spiders. "Yes, a son. Laura Mulligan died when he was born and her family, the Campbells, took him to raise."

"Margaret Mulligan gave up her grandson?"

"It's best to leave this alone, Ms. Pell. You'd be wise to stop your sleuthing and return to your fine poetry."

"Why can't you tell me why the Mulligans let the Campbells raise the boy?"

"The reason has no bearing on present day concerns."

At that moment, I saw myself as he saw me: a meddler. He was partially right. I *was* insinuating myself into the lives of the villagers, most of them innocent of any crimes. Yet the dilemma! Someone was killing people, and the motive was surely buried in someone's past. With her focus on records and comment that old sins were not forgotten, Judy had substantiated that.

"It is interesting you would say that, Father," I said. "As the spiritual leader of nearly all the people in the village, you would know, through the confessional, nearly everyone's secrets. I know you can't reveal them, but..."

My next words would have been: *how can you possibly separate what would be relevant to solving the crimes and what is not?* I didn't say them. A shiver went through me. The only way he could make the statement was if he knew who killed Bridget and Judy.

He saw the truth dawn in my eyes.

"If I were you," I said, "I would be very careful."

Father O'Neill's aura was cloudy, dark blue with a gold fringe. He was troubled by something he couldn't control, and his angels—represented by the gold—were moving in to protect him. He was a spiritual man, faithful to his church, but he was afraid.

The priest shook his finger at me. "Ms. Pell, villagers are grateful for the help you've given Inspector Finch in the apprehension of those involved with the human trafficking ring. However, there's no need for you to continue prying into our lives. Families have been living together in this village for centuries. We know the warp and weft of our fabric."

He was telling me I was an outsider. There was also something he was not saying and I thought it had to do with Judy. I felt the personal animus he had toward me.

I took a deep breath. "Do you think that if Judy had called the garda instead of me, she would still be alive?"

His eyes narrowed. "What do you think?"

Judy had called me because she felt no barrier in sharing whatever it was she wanted to share. I supposed she didn't call the garda because she felt her information insufficiently worthy of Inspector Finch's consideration. Or maybe she feared the garda because of her late husband's violent death in Northern Ireland, at a time when one couldn't be sure which side the police were on. It surprised me that Father O'Neill, with his understanding of the village's warp and weft, didn't know that.

I changed the subject. "Elizabeth is unwell."

"What is the matter?"

"She broods."

"Shall I call on her?" he asked.

"She'd probably benefit from your guidance."

I told him goodbye and left the priory.

***

"Mother of God," Finch murmured. "I wonder what the Campbells had on Pearce."

That was his response when I passed on the information that the Campbells had taken Margaret Mulligan's only grandson to raise.

"The son would be around sixteen years old now," I said.

"He'd be preparing for his A-levels."

"It seems a shame that if Margaret Mulligan has a grandson, she isn't able to see him."

"Yes, but we'll leave that to the Mulligans."

I said no more about the Mulligan heir, but I wasn't done with it. Since his birth year was the same as Alain Aherne's and both boys had vanished—one to Scotland and the other into the sea—I sensed a connection.

"Inspector," I said, "could we review what we know about the murders? It's been difficult to separate them from the kidnappings."

Finch pursed his lips. "Let's start with Franco Milton. His killing was surely connected to the kidnappings. My guess is he was murdered because he'd been inept—or maybe he angered his boss. Whatever the reason for his murder, he wasn't worth keeping around."

"Maybe the men you arrested will shed light on who murdered him."

"Possibly," he responded. "Now let's take a look at what we know about Bridget Vale's murder."

"She was as she presented herself—a virtuous young teenager," I said. "She was modeling herself after St. Clare. Like the saint, Bridget connected with Coomara's outcasts, which brought her in contact with a pedophile priest, drug users and dealers, a malcontent American poet, and God knows who else."

Finch tapped a pen on his desk. "Now we come to Tim Hawkins, who must have suffered a guilty conscience by not admitting he persuaded Bridget to leave the Vale cottage the night of April 30. According to him, they walked along the beach, where he heard a man crying for help. When he left Bridget's side to investigate, someone abducted her."

"But I don't wholly believe Tim Hawkins' story."

"Neither do I," replied Finch, "but it does present a reason the body was taken to the beach. Bridget was taken to the abbey ruins and garroted in the chapel. Now that we know she was with Tim Hawkins before she was murdered, the killer must have taken her body back to the beach to implicate Tim. The garrote was unusual," he went on. "It wasn't made of cord or rope. It left gouges in the flesh as wire would, but the coroner doesn't think it was barbed wire because the thorny parts were too close together. Whatever it was made of, it was used in the Vale and Moriarity murders. The women were probably killed by the same person."

"Poor Judy," I said. "She'd found evidence implicating someone in Bridget's murder or the kidnappings in records of some type, and tried to get that information to me. I feel terrible that I didn't go to her when she first called."

I hadn't told Finch—or anyone else—about the attempt to kill me in Glendalough—and decided to disclose the incident. "Inspector, on St. Kevin's Day, someone tried to kill me at the monastery ruins an hour and a half before Judy called. A man pushed a large rock off the wall, which narrowly missed my head. I didn't report it because I was afraid you'd stop sharing information with me."

Finch scowled. "I might have put you in a cell. I still might."

I tried to look contrite.

The inspector swiveled his chair to look out the window. "Did you see the person who tried to kill you?"

"A man. He wore a hooded white sweatshirt and khaki shorts. He was short and had a muscular build."

"Hector is short," Finch said.

"This man was taller than Hector—maybe five feet seven or eight. He had broad shoulders, narrow hips, like Sergeant Gowdy."

Finch turned to face me. "The attempt on your life occurred before the killer garroted Mrs. Moriarity. I wonder why he went after you before he killed her—since she was the one with the incriminating information."

"Maybe he thought she had already given me the information. The ruins were an ideal spot to kill me. If he'd succeeded, it would have looked like an accident. Inspector, has it occurred to you that the murders of Judy and Bridget might be unrelated to the kidnappings?"

"It has," he replied, "but I'm left with the fact that Bridget and some of the kidnapped girls were blood relations. Tessa McMurray was a cousin, and the Hardestys were connected in some way."

"But not Jacy Pew and Katelyn Scanlon?"

"Not that I know of." Finch picked up the pen, clicked it a few times.

"I think Father O'Neill knows who killed Bridget and Judy," I said. "He may have found out in the confessional."

The pen dropped to the desktop. "Then his life could be in danger."

I nodded. "He's afraid of something. He has a protective aura around him. The universe is trying to protect him."

"I'll send a man to keep watch over him," Finch said.

"Better safe than sorry," I said.

The last thing Coomara needed was a murdered priest.

CHAPTER TWENTY-FOUR

A parcel from Trinity College rested on the front porch when I returned to my cottage. I opened it to find a copy of the twelfth century *Lebor Gabála*, a compilation of Celtic biblical and historical writings. Despite all I had on my mind, I was drawn back to my reason for coming to Ireland—composing poetry—and took the book to my room to thumb through the pages.

This text, which concerned Ireland's waves of invasion, began with the biblical flood. After the waters receded, Bith, son of Noah, took his daughter, fifty women, and three men to Ireland, intending to populate the island—but they all perished. The Partholonians, Nemedians, and Formorians came next, followed by the Fir Bholg people, who were small and dark, and settled on the Aran and Rathlin islands. Descending from a dark mountaintop cloud (and not from the sea), the Tuatha Dé Danann became the gods of the pre-Christian Irish pantheon reduced to human form.

Then came the Milesians. Noah's grandson, Fénius Farsaid, the Milesian leader, was present at Babel when Jehovah, in a power grab, confused human language and scattered the tower-builders over the face of the earth. I closed the book and stretched. Enough for now. The stories, written by Christian monks, sought to bind biblical stories to Irish myth. However, they didn't pull the stories out of a hat. Kernels of truth were present, taken from ancient oral histories. For the purpose of my poetry, I needed to isolate those kernels.

Glancing out the window, I saw the sun sparkling on the sea and decided to take Brendan's boat out. Elizabeth was in the kitchen poaching an egg. When she finished eating, I asked if she wanted to join me. Though I had to coax, she tied a scarf over her hair and came along.

***

Taking the helm, I headed out to sea. An image of a garrote crashed into my mind—a wire or cord with barbaric thorns. Unconsciously, I touched my throat. I couldn't free my mind from the murders. As the *Hawk* skimmed over the water, I wondered what the garda would learn from the men taken from the yacht. Was the yacht used to transport girls to brothels in other countries? Would Finch be able to connect Hector to the kidnapping ring?

Opening the throttle, I roared past Innis Cove, jostling Elizabeth, who complained. I slowed, taking in the sea, the rocky cliffs, the green mountains and meadows. Glancing back at my cousin, I saw she was looking at the coast. Did she find the sight restful?

I turned the *Hawk* toward the coast, then swiveled to ask Elizabeth if she was ready to return home. To my horror, she was balancing on the gunwale, ready to jump!

"Elizabeth!" I cried, lunging to grab her by the waist.

She struggled, nearly pulling me overboard. Meanwhile, the boat started to run in a crazy arc. I had to regain control of the boat and I had to restrain Elizabeth. What could I do? I drew back my fist and struck her. She fell to the deck, weeping. I straightened the boat, Elizabeth stayed put, and we went home.

Brendan saw us dock and Elizabeth crumpled out on the deck, and ran down the steps to help. "What on earth happened, Maria?" he asked.

"She fell," I said shortly.

He helped me carry Elizabeth up the steps to the cottage.

"Why didn't you let me jump?" Elizabeth cried.

"Because you're a valuable human being and I care about you," I said.

"She tried to jump?" Brendan asked.

I looked at him. "It is time for you to go home. Please don't tell anyone about this. It will embarrass Elizabeth."

He looked at me meekly and left.

Elizabeth sat up. "You hit me."

"I'm sorry. I didn't know what else to do." I sat down in the rocking chair. "You must tell me what's troubling you. I know you have night terrors, you're moody, and now you've tried to kill yourself."

She shook her head. "I can't tell you, Maria."

"Why don't you talk to Father O'Neill?"

"I've tried, but the words won't come."

"But you're a practicing Catholic, Elizabeth. You go to confession regularly. If you tell him what's on your conscience, perhaps he can help you."

"Ten 'Our Fathers' won't work. A hundred wouldn't work."

"Father O'Neill is an intuitive man. He will know you've already prayed over this—whatever it is—and recommend something."

She looked at me with interest. "What could that be?"

I shrugged. "I'm not Father O'Neill. He's sure to know how to be helpful."

"What I did—it happened a long time ago."

I glanced at her quickly, wondering if she'd done something as a child. Viewed in an adult light, it could be nothing at all. For years, I chastised myself for planning to make pinpricks in my father's condoms, hoping for a brother or sister. Fortunately, my mother caught me with the box of condoms and took it away from me. She'd not needed to say anything: her look of disappointment seared my soul. I cleared my conscience by denying myself lemon drops for a month. But it could have been worse. What I didn't know at the time, was that Mother's heart would not have withstood another pregnancy. I shuddered. How would I have felt if I'd carried out my plan, and Mother had conceived and died in childbirth? I no longer felt guilty about my selfish plan. I had been saved by my mother's vigilance, and time had diminished feelings of guilt.

What had Elizabeth done?

"Talk to Father O'Neill," I said, leaving the room. "He's heard about all kinds of sins. Recent sins, old sins..."

Old Sins. I went away with the two words ringing in my ear. If someone was seeking vengeance over the shooting accident (or was it an accident?) that killed Margaret Mulligan's father Klaus Hess, that could be considered retribution for an old sin. Or did Deidre O'Malley wish to cause suffering because her ancestor, planning to alleviate the effects of famine by robbing a granary, was betrayed by someone in Coomara? Pearce Mulligan had a son by his first wife, but her family took the boy to raise. What had Pearce done?

I went out onto the back porch to think. The sky was darkening. The scent of rain was in the wind. Thunder clapped and loosed a memory into my consciousness, which had to do with Baby Doe. My grandmother, suffering from dementia, had been visiting when I found the baby in the creek. After my father took the corpse into our house, my grandmother, a devout Catholic, baptized her with holy water she kept in a vial. She called the child her grandchild.

Grandchild.

Did she mean the word literally? Or was her poor mind confused?

***

Mathieu came around seven o'clock. I was so glad to see him that I kissed him on the lips.

"Well," he said, "what a lovely greeting."

We sat on the front porch in wicker chairs and looked out on the village street. Elizabeth had gone upstairs to bed, so I told him about her attempt to jump in the sea.

"She should talk to Father O'Neill," Mathieu said.

"I've told her. She says she's tried but the words won't come."

"Maybe she should go back to the States."

"I've suggested that. She said I was trying to get rid of her."

He reached over and took my hand. "Have you written any poems today?"

I shook my head. "The poems aren't coming."

"Maybe they would if you let me make love to you again."

I slid my eyes at him. "What a bold remark."

"You need to let me back in your life."

"Don't push, Mathieu."

"All right."

"I was terribly wrong about Bridget Vale," I told him. "According to Albert Malone, she was modeling her life on that of St. Clare and was spending time with Coomara's outcasts, which included him. Tim Hawkins admitted he lured Bridget out of the house the night she was killed. He says she was his muse." I looked at Mathieu. "Tim wasn't telling the whole truth."

"Did Dennis believe him?"

"No."

"Maybe we should find the lad and have a talk with him, Maria."

"Finch would disapprove. He became irritated with me when I told Tim that Bridget would probably still be alive if he had stayed in St. Louis."

"Maybe Dennis has handled him too gingerly."

"That's a thought. What time is it?"

He looked at his watch. "Nearly ten o'clock—too late to try to find Tim tonight."

"Let's talk to him first thing in the morning," I said.

"I'll come by at nine."

Mathieu left and I went to bed.

***

I had just finished my blueberry scone and scrambled eggs when Mathieu knocked on the door the next morning.

"Do you know what day it is?" he asked.

I thought. "It's June 7, the anniversary of when we met."

"You fell in my lap."

I laughed. Thirteen years ago, I had walked past Mathieu in a campus restaurant, stumbled over a student's stack of books, and fell on top of him.

"I spilled my coffee," he reminded me.

Mortified, I had struggled to get up. In doing so, I fell against him again. He had said, "You are not meant to leave, mademoiselle."

I smiled at the memory and offered my cheek to be kissed.

"Let's find Tim Hawkins," I said.

Where was Tim likely to be at nine o'clock in the morning? It was too early for him to go to the Green Mountain Café. His aunt, Grace Devereaux, would know. Since I didn't know where she lived, we decided to try the library.

Grace was behind the checkout desk when we went in. Mathieu and I had decided she might be uncooperative if we asked bluntly where Tim was, so I wandered around the stacks while Mathieu chatted her up, using his charm, hopefully softening her so that when I returned, she'd reveal Tim's whereabouts. She clearly found Mathieu interesting, and was laughing at anecdotes about his native Togo when I rejoined them.

"...and then my papa shook hands with the orangutan and invited him in to tea," Mathieu was saying.

His stories were mostly made up. He believed white people wanted to believe Africans were on the same level as the beasts that roamed the jungles. One of the reasons I'd fallen in love with him was that he was even more cynical than I.

"Grace," I said, "I'd like to talk to your nephew about his poetry."

"Do you think what he writes is publishable?" she asked eagerly.

"Definitely. Where does he hang out?"

Grace looked at her watch. "He likes to write at Eddie's Nook over on Kildare Street. You can probably find him there. If not, here's his cell number."

She wrote the number on a piece of paper and handed it to me. We thanked her and left.

Mathieu pulled the car out onto the street. "Where is Kildare Street?"

"Go to the intersection and turn left," I said. "It's two streets over."

We found Eddie's Nook, which was set in a red-painted building with lattice windows. A bell jangled as we opened the door and behind the counter, an old man looked up from his newspaper to say good morning. Tim Hawkins sat alone in a booth, a laptop plugged into a socket and open in front of him. He had pushed his cup of coffee and a golden-crusted croissant next to the wall.

Mathieu went to the counter and ordered two teas. I slid into the booth opposite Tim. He glanced up, surprised.

"How nice to see you," I said. "Your aunt told us we might find you here."

He closed his laptop and looked at me belligerently. "I don't have anything to say to you."

"How is your poetry coming along," I asked, "now that you've lost your muse."

The barb hit home. Tim winced. Mathieu came with the tea and sat down on the bench next to Tim, trapping him. I introduced Mathieu, who clapped him on the back, saying it was good to meet a man from home.

"Are you writing something?" I asked.

"I have writer's block."

"Is that because you're troubled by the lies you're telling?" Mathieu asked.

"I don't know what you're talking about," Tim said, his mood growing dark. "Get out of my way. I want out."

"I imagine you do," Mathieu said. "Your conscience is troubling you that you lured poor Bridget out of the house and someone killed her."

Tim tried to stand up. The old man behind the counter didn't look up from his newspaper. *Was he hard of hearing?*

Mathieu pulled Tim back down. "But maybe you didn't know someone wanted to kill her," he said in a kinder tone.

A look of uncertainty passed over the teen's face.

Mathieu pushed on. "You were fond of Bridget. You didn't want anything bad to happen to her."

That's all it took for Tim Hawkins to break down. Terrible sobs erupted from the boy, and it was then that I saw that his ill humor was a mask for fear. He revealed his part in Bridget's murder, saying he'd been standing outside the Green Mountain Café with a group of boys when his marijuana supplier—a man he called Lord Joffrey—joined the group. They had been discussing a soccer game when the talk turned to the village girls. Someone said most of the girls had taken a vow of chastity, and their parents had set strict dating rules.

Lord Joffrey said something about the May Queen and what a triumph it would be to take Bridget Vale's cherry. Someone said Bridget had a crush on Tim. Lord Joffrey laid a wager that Tim couldn't get her to come out of the house and stand in the circle of the moon for an hour.

The circle of the moon was an arrangement of Druid stones in one of Pearce Mulligan's fields—a favorite place for lovers.

"It's too far out to Pearce's," Tim had argued. "No one wants to walk that far in the dark."

"I'll send a driver with a panel truck," Lord Joffrey had said. "He'll take you and the Vale girl there."

Tim took the bet. Off he went to the Vale cottage and knocked on the door. Bridget called out "Who's there?" and when he identified himself, she told him that her mother would have a fit if she opened the door. Knowing she had a soft heart, Tim began weeping, saying he was going to kill himself.

She opened the door. He reached in, grabbed her arm, and pulled her out onto the street. The panel truck drove up with two men inside. Tim had never seen them before. One of the men pushed Tim to the ground; the other grabbed Bridget and the truck roared away.

"Who is Lord Joffrey?" Mathieu and I asked in unison.

"I don't know his real name. I've seen him around the village. He ..."

The old man behind the corner rumbled to life. "Is everything all right over there?"

"Tell him," Mathieu said.

"I'm fine," Tim said.

I looked at the man. "We're just sorting something out."

He nodded and returned to his newspaper.

Mathieu looked at Tim. "What were you about to say?"

"He's the guy who sings at festivals."

Mathieu and I stared at each other.

"Danny Aherne?" I asked.

"Danny—I think I heard someone call him that."

I was shocked to the core.

Mathieu touched my arm. "I told you there was something sharky about him."

He meant *fishy*. I didn't correct him. I was trying to wrap my mind around Danny Aherne, whose gorgeous tenor voice had brought the words of my poem to life, as a ruthless killer who had garroted Bridget and Judy.

I wanted to cry out to heaven. Rage replaced shock. I wanted to kill Danny with my bare hands. He had manipulated Tim into luring Bridget outside her cottage, and then someone had hauled her away and killed her. Garroted her. Was that Danny, as well? I gripped the edge of the table with white knuckles.

"You have to tell Inspector Finch," Mathieu said. "You have to do it now."

Tim didn't argue. We drove him to headquarters where he told his story to Finch.

Finch scowled. "So there was no drowning man?"

"I made that up," Tim told him.

In the second telling of his story, Tim said Bridget pleaded with the men when she was taken. A vision overtook me: Bridget, still in her school uniform, standing inside her parents' cottage.

"I can't come out," she said.

"Please, Bridget," Tim whined. *"I'm so depressed I'm going to throw myself off the cliff."*

She opened the door. He snatched her arm, dragged her outside, and proposed a visit to the circle of the moon. A panel truck pulled up and two men jumped out. One knocked Tim to the ground, the other grabbed Bridget and shoved her into the van. The van door slid shut.

In my mind's eye, I saw the garrote; it was a rosary, not unlike Brendan's mother's primitive beads. It had barbs, just like hers, to tear the flesh off a penitent's hands.

It's rarely fun being an empath. I went limp. I felt no bones in my body. I was grievously sad, but suddenly a great strength pieced me together and I burned with fury. I wanted to destroy Danny Aherne. I ran from Finch's office and out of the building.

Mathieu came after me. "Stop, Maria!"

I didn't stop. I wouldn't stop. I had to find a place where I would be free of ugliness and men. The sight of them sickened me. Even Mathieu. He grabbed my arm.

"Get away from me!" I screamed, tearing myself away.

I was farther away from my own humanity than I had ever been.

But I still wondered: Why did Danny Aherne kill Bridget Vale?

CHAPTER TWENTY-FIVE

Mathieu tried to hustle me into his car, but I broke away, running to Innis Cove. Flying down the stone steps, I headed for my secret place hidden among the great stones, and cradled myself. Waves crashed against the rocks below me, sending up a cool spray. Overhead, the sky began to darken. Lightning flashed in the distance. Was the coming storm as fierce as my hatred for Danny Aherne?

"Maria! Maria!"

I heard Mathieu calling as he stumbled over unfamiliar terrain. At last, he appeared, his face strained with worry.

He was my salvation.

"Don't talk," I said, raising my arms.

He stepped into my sanctuary, sat beside me, and lifted me onto his lap. I was on fire, wanting him, wanting assurance that I hadn't gone mad. I needed him, needed to connect with him. I undid his zipper, removed my underpants, and thrust him into me. "Make me sane." I whispered. He wrapped his arms around me and we began to rock. I felt union—I didn't have to face the pain of existing alone in a world where monsters killed little girls. My tears flowed. We kissed—my need for him intensified. He stood, with my legs wrapped around his hips, and we ground against each other until we climaxed in an explosion of belonging.

"I love you, Maria."

His voice was rough and sensual. Was this love? I knew he wanted me to say I loved him and so I did. Something primal existed between us. I could go to him for healing, which meant I trusted him. For the first time since his dalliance with Zara, I felt we might return to the life we had shared.

He drove me home.

***

That night, I slept peacefully. Sex was the ultimate relaxant, but I knew that intimacy with Mathieu was more than relaxing—he had restored my emotional core. Some might say he was my soul mate, but I felt the soul was a solitary principle of humankind. I could not expect anyone to match the uniqueness of what traveled in my soul; nor could I match anyone else's. That Mathieu was at the core of my being was singular and sufficient. I was glad—even relieved—that he and I had come together again. We could progress to the next level.

I had just finished my morning shower when Inspector Finch called.

"Maria, come to the station at once. We've got the motive for the killings."

Had Sergeant Murphy located the record in the archives of the *Eolas* newspaper? Heart thumping, I threw on a pair of jeans and a plaid shirt, ran to the car, and drove to the station.

Sergeant Murphy, looking jubilant, had returned from *The Sun.* In the archives of the defunct newspaper, the *Eolas*, he had found the record Judy cited on the bookmark. On January 15, 2000, an inquest had been held to determine custody of the infant Alain Aherne, Danny's son with Iris Vale. Those testifying for Iris were Declan McMurray, Gertrude Scanlon, Moira Hardesty, Bella Pew, Jenny Drake, and Astrid Mulrooney—a list that must have started wheels turning in Judy's prefrontal cortex when she read *A Tale of Two Cities*. Madame Defarge's lust for revenge could have triggered her memory of the inquest.

Judy put it all together then. Madame Defarge's family had been destroyed and so had Danny Aherne's. Defarge wove the names of the aristocrats responsible for ruining her family into her knitting so they would be sent to the guillotine. Danny set about killing Bridget and kidnapping the daughters of people whom he regarded as tormentors to avenge the death or disappearance of his little son, Alain.

The newspaper reported that friends and relatives of Iris Aherne (later, Vale) had praised her motherly attributes while expressing doubts that Danny, a single man, could provide a suitable home for his child. Some expressed concern that the pub was an unsavory environment to bring up a child. The fact that Danny had no family was held against him—there were no grannies and aunties in Coomara to help him care for Alain. Danny was also an irregular churchgoer.

Finch looked at me. "Except for the Mulrooneys, who have no children, the folks who vouched for Iris are parents of the abducted girls. The kidnappings were revenge against them for testifying against Danny."

Sergeant Potts shook her head. "He killed Bridget to take Iris's child from her as she had taken his."

"Why did he wait so long?" I asked.

"Bridget was chosen May Queen," replied Potts, "and that could have put her on his radar."

"As the mother of the May Queen, Iris would have been honored," I added, remembering the new dress and shoes Iris had purchased for the ceremony. "Danny couldn't bear to see that."

"It's a sick mind that carries out such a diabolical plan," Finch said.

"What really happened to Alain Aherne?" I asked, remembering Father O'Neill's warning to leave the matter alone.

My question was met with silence.

Finch rubbed his head. "We don't know. Danny and Iris were living apart. She left the child alone in her cottage and went to a pub. Neighbors heard the child crying and went to fetch Iris. The next morning, the baby was gone."

"His blanket was found near the cliff overlooking the bay," Potts said.

I was incredulous. "Did Iris say she had taken him to the cliff?"

"She had no memory of what she did that night. She was drunk."

I tried to picture what happened. "The baby was in her care. When he vanished, his blanket was found on the edge of the cliff."

Potts grimaced. "It's a sheer drop to the sea."

I looked at her sharply. "Iris could have thrown him into the sea."

"If she did, there was no way to prove it," Finch said.

"What did she say happened to the baby?" I asked.

Finch cleared his throat. "She said the faeries took him."

In mythology, faeries were an older race of people, dwindled gods—perhaps the Tuatha Dé Danann or the Fir Bholg—who retreated under Ireland's mounds to hide.

I frowned. "And you accepted her answer as credible?"

Finch did not smile. "She believed in faeries."

If Iris believed in the faeries and thought they took her child, that was, perhaps, her version of the truth. Her explanation would not have satisfied Danny.

"Iris had an unfortunate childhood," Finch said. "Her parents died in an automobile crash when she was very young and she was raised by an uncle who abused her. She took to drink as a teenager."

Finch and his staff were watching me carefully, measuring my reaction to the unfortunate tale of a drunken Iris Vale, who believed the faeries took her son.

"We don't arrest people without proof of their crimes," Finch said in a reasonable voice. "There was no real evidence to arrest Iris. It's possible the boy crawled off the cliff."

"Don't you have a crime called child endangerment?" I asked peevishly.

The room went silent again. *Careful, careful. It will do no good to alienate the inspector and his staff over the handling of Alain Aherne's disappearance, which occurred sixteen years ago.*

I took a deep breath, then matched Finch's tone to ask if he was making cases against the men who were caught red-handed with the girls in their hold.

"Yes, of course," Finch answered pleasantly, "and Danny Aherne, too. He was involved in the kidnappings, and now that we have a motive, probably killed Bridget Vale and Judy Moriarity—though we can't prove anything yet. We're hoping to track down the van used in Bridget's kidnapping. Officers are headed to Danny's establishment now."

"Let's hope you find the van," I said harshly.

I left in a negative mood. Would Bridget and Judy still be alive if Danny had gained custody sixteen years ago, or if Iris had been prosecuted for not supervising their child?

***

It was noon when I returned to the cottage. On the kitchen table was a note from Elizabeth, saying she had gone to Danny Aherne's pub. Instantly, I knew Danny had set a trap. He'd been behind all the attempts on my life. If he hadn't fired the gun as I came down the steps, he'd hired the man who did. In retrospect, I saw that he could match the description of the man who loosened the stone that nearly killed me at the abbey. Now he had lured Elizabeth to Gaelic Earls, knowing I'd come after her.

I bit my knuckles. Elizabeth was in a vulnerable state with whatever was troubling her conscience. Finch was on his way to Aherne's place to find the van and there could be gunfire. Elizabeth would be in the thick of it. I had to find her.

Mathieu was sorting his laundry when I called. He came at once to the cottage and I was standing at the curb when he drove up. I slid into the passenger side of his car. We made our way through town and across the river to Gaelic Earls. No garda patrol cars were in sight. Mathieu parked on the cobblestones near the entrance and we ran inside.

The restaurant was deserted, except for a man behind the bar who was polishing glass mugs. Elizabeth's floral scarf lay on one of the tables.

"Where's the woman who was wearing this?" I demanded.

He pointed to a metal door at the back of the room. I seized the scarf, dashed toward the door, and threw it open. Mathieu was directly behind me. Immediately, a man smelling of sweat and whiskey clamped rough hands on my throat. Another slammed the door, leaving Mathieu on the other side. The last sight I had of him was when he burst open the door and was tackled by two of Danny's brutes.

Holding my upper arms, the men hustled me through the building and out to a van, which had been used in the pilgrimage to St. Kevin's Bed—a gilt and silver shamrock still dangled from the antenna.

Where is Finch?

One of the men, dark-haired, wearing a gray pullover sweater of Nordic design, ripped my bag from my shoulder and took my cell phone. Then he pushed me into the rear seat and got in after me. The other man, ginger hair, denim jacket, got in on the other side. I'd never seen either of them before. Both were tall, muscular, and smelled of tobacco. Ginger Hair leaned forward to whisper to the driver whose identity was concealed from me—he wore a black hooded sweatshirt pulled close to his face, but from the set of his shoulders, I knew he was Danny Aherne.

As we veered onto the street, two garda cars came from the opposite direction. I tried to turn my head to see if Mathieu had thrown off his attackers and was following, but the man on my left boxed my ears. What was my next move? I'd have to wait to see where the men were taking me.

We headed into the mountains. Danny was speeding and the landscape streaked past, making me dizzy. Leaving the paved road, we swerved onto a bumpy one-lane road that wound up into the foothills. Foliage raked the sides of the car. With every twist of the road, I bounced against my captors.

So far, I'd been silent, searching for avenues of escape. No physical match for the men, I was trapped between them. I weighed whether I should continue to be quiet or speak out. Keeping quiet made the men think I was afraid, which I was. I decided to speak out.

"Where's my cousin?" I demanded. "What have you done to her?"

The man on my left hit me in the mouth. "Shut up."

He wore a ring, which cut my lip.

I spat blood. "Where is she?"

He drew back to hit me again, but Danny said something in Gaelic. The man put his hand down. As we rounded a particularly harrowing curve, Nordic Sweater got sick.

"Stop!" he gasped. "I've got to puke."

"Jesus! Don't puke in the van!" Danny cried.

He hit the brakes, which threw me forward. The sick man opened the door, dashed into the brush, and vomited. The sound of his retching exacerbated my own nausea. I gagged. Ginger Hair opened the car door on his side, dragged me outside, and pushed me onto the ground. Danny also leaped out, apparently to get away from the stench of vomit. He stood by his antenna, with the shamrock glinting gold and silver in the sun.

My stomach calmed. I raised my head slightly to see where I was. We had stopped on top of a hill, with mountains rising above us. Danny said something in Gaelic to the sick man. He muttered a reply. I wished I were fluent in Gaelic. I wished I had signed up for Mathieu's karate class.

Then I had an idea. I feigned gagging. Ginger Hair turned his head away. The dark-haired man and Danny exchanged words. I took a deep breath and inched toward the crest of the hill. I gagged again.

Below, black-faced mountain sheep moved out of the shadows to graze. Behind them was a small, black dog, which wove back and forth. If I bolted now, could I outrun Ginger Hair? The downward slant would also help him and his legs were long. I calculated how far I might get. The sheep kept the grasses short, but a few shrubs dotted the green. Ancient rocks, jolted from beneath the Irish soil, scattered over the green. No place to hide—at least, not for very long. A stream wandered through the valley. Could I reach the stream? Beyond was a dark forest. I might have no other opportunity to run.

"Get her back in the car!"

I lifted my head as Danny spoke, just in time to see a peregrine falcon, apparently annoyed by the sun glinting on the shamrock, plummeting downward, diving toward Danny's head. He was coming fast— I'd read they could dive at a rate of over two hundred miles an hour. Ginger Hair drew a gun, shot at the bird, missed. The bird, which must have had a wingspan of nearly four feet, reached out with its talons and scraped Danny's face.

Danny screamed. Ginger Hair fired again. The falcon screeched. I got to my feet and ran.

CHAPTER TWENTY-SIX

I expected to be shot in the back. Heading for the flock of sheep, I raced by patches of gorse and chunks of granite. My heart beat frantically. The stream was narrow—I leaped across, landed wrong, twisted my ankle. The sheep scattered, causing the dog to bark and run to do his job. I limped to a low stone fence and climbed over. Could I make it to the forest? I looked back. Danny was climbing the fence. He was right behind me.

Ignoring the pain in my ankle, I dashed into the trees. As a girl, I'd been a tree-climber and I put that talent to practice, scaling a tall oak. Aware that the same low hanging branches that boosted me up would also boost Danny, I crouched in the crook of a branch where leaves gave cover. My ankle pulsed with pain.

Mind over matter: the pain does not exist, Maria.

I had hardly settled myself when Danny appeared beneath me. His face was streaked with blood from the falcon's talons. He appeared to be trying to puzzle out where I'd gone. Circling the tree, he moved to its neighbors, an elm, another oak.

"Maria Pell, you can't get away from me. I know you're here."

I held my breath, not moving.

He was muttering. "Why couldn't you have stayed out of it? Coomara is no business of yours. You should have stayed in the States. You should have rested in the shade of a willow tree and written your poems."

Once or twice he looked up, but I had concealed myself well.

"I know you're here," he said. "I'll find you. You can't hide. I know the terrain better than you."

Where were Danny's men? If I turned my head, I feared I'd make a sound. I stayed where I was, still as Lot's wife inside the pillar of salt.

Where is Mathieu? Where is Finch? Where is the wail of sirens? How long until dark? Danny's sick henchman had taken my cell phone. I tried to calculate the time. It had been noon when I returned to my cottage. Then Mathieu and I drove to Danny's pub in search of Elizabeth. After that, the men threw me into the van. How long had the drive been? Thirty or forty minutes? It must be after three o'clock—maybe three-thirty.

Hours before dark. My ankle ached. *Mind over matter.*

On the ground, Danny paced like a disgruntled beast.

"Gerald," he said, "It took you long enough to get here."

I ventured a peek downward. The man in the Nordic sweater stood under the tree.

"The garda's here," Gerald said. "Just one patrol car. Rip's still up there. He was trying to get rid of the falcon."

"Oh, shit," Danny said. "The fuckin' falcon."

"Aye, and the garda will likely make a fuss about it."

European Union laws forbade the killing of peregrine falcons. I turned my head slightly toward the hill where the falcon had died. A second patrol car pulled up behind the first.

"Look," Gerald said. "Another patrol car. They'll be looking for us. I got a call from Sweeney. He said Finch was trying to find the van. He told them we were trying to make it to Belfast."

"You washed the van down," Danny said. "Did you use bleach?"

"Some."

"What do you mean *some?*"

"There was only a quarter of a gallon in the jug."

"You eejit!" Danny yelled. "You could have bought another jug. Why did you have to pull off her earring anyway?"

"I didn't know she'd bleed like a stuck pig."

Danny stared down at the ground, then grabbed Gerald by his collar and slammed his head against a tree trunk. They were talking about getting rid of traces of Bridget's blood in the van. Tearing her earring from her ear, ripping her clothes from her body—I thought of that poor innocent girl and my jaw clenched.

Moments later, Danny spoke. His voice was deadly calm. "We've got to find the poet."

"I don't understand why she has to die," Gerald said. "She had nothing to do with your losing your boy."

"She has to be punished."

"You seemed to like her. You put her poem to music. Grand song it was, too."

"She's been nosing around, meddling," Danny said. "The priest's housekeeper told her things. She's been working with Finch."

"That nephew of the librarian knows what happened. He was there when..."

"We'll take care of him when we go back to the village," Danny said. "The woman's here somewhere. I hear her breathing."

I stopped breathing.

"Listen," Danny said, "do you hear her?"

"You're imagining things," Gerald said. "I don't hear a thing. There's one of those faerie mounds over east. Are you sure she didn't run there? Some of those mounds have openings, places to hole up."

Danny walked away. I couldn't hear what he said next.

Now, silence. I tried to stand, keeping my weight on my good ankle. A twig cracked. I held my breath and waited. Nothing happened. I stood again, slowly, this time. *Where were Danny and Gerald? What was happening on the hill?* Parting the leaves, I saw the garda cars were gone. So was the van.

I was on my own.

Always, I'd felt protected by the power of the universe—but now I wasn't so sure. I'd had no sense that the peregrine falcon had given up his life so I could escape. If anything, I thought the falcon had died because he found the sparkly shamrock on Danny's antenna disturbing and dive-bombed it, losing his life in the process. Either I was losing my magical thinking or the universe was telling me it was time I thought things out on my own.

For another hour or so, I remained in the oak tree, then cautiously climbed down. Each movement sent agony shrieking through my lower leg. I found a stick to lean on and moved deeper into the forest, smelling the yeasty odor of fallen leaves, hearing the wind rustle in the canopies.

You could get lost. I had read that when people can't see the sun, they walk in circles. Researchers thought this was due to the uneven lengths of a person's legs and tricks of the undominant eye. With my twisted ankle, I would be even more off course. My right eye was dominant, so every few steps, I refocused that eye on objects ahead and tried to adjust.

My ankle had begun to swell. The best plan would be to find concealment near the edge of the forest and stay put. *Good thing Danny doesn't have a dog to sniff me out.*

How large was the forest? I had no idea, but knew that only ten percent of Ireland was forested. Waves of immigrants had cleared the land for farming.

Where was Danny? I wished I could run. The pain nauseated me. The arch of the trees loomed behind, above, in front of me, shading the bracken, lichens, and fungi. Here and there the sun broke through, sending shafts of greenish light onto the bed of the forest. The trees looked thrust up from ancient times. *Mysterious. Ethereal. Vaguely dangerous. A narrow-leaved helleborine, a white orchid, clung to a tree trunk. Was it a rarity?*

"She came through here!"

Oh, God!

Danny's voice. He was closer than I thought. Fear left a metallic taste in my mouth. With my dragging foot, I was leaving a trail anyone could follow. *Where could I hide?*

Dusk was falling. The undergrowth was so thick I had trouble making my way forward. Vines hung from the trees. Using all my will power, I lifted my throbbing ankle and hobbled on. Ahead was a stunted oak. Its trunk was massive. Around the tree, vegetation grew tall and dense. *A place to settle.* I crawled into the thick of it, reaching to smooth molting leaves to cover my tracks. Then I waited.

In the fairy tale, "Babes in the Woods," children ran to the forest to escape from assassins and died. Benevolent birds covered them with leaves. In some versions, the children became little risen Christs and went to heaven.

I had never felt so defenseless. If I had the use of my ankle I could run. I could fight. I could set cunning traps. Though I had exercised mental discipline over the pain, my ankle was useless. I could do nothing but wait.

Danny and Gerald burst through the tangle of weeds and bushes. "Where'd she go?" Danny yelled. "I know she came through here."

"She went to the left," Gerald said. "See the opening."

"No, I don't think so. See. She stopped right here."

The men were less than ten feet away. They were tromping around, disturbing the bracken. I knew they would find me. Danny would garrote me and no one would ever find my body.

To my horror, Gerald sat down. "I'm starving," he said. "It's nearly six o'clock. I haven't eaten since morning."

"You eejit!" Danny screamed.

Gerald stood up. "I'm going back to town."

"You can't do that! The garda is looking for us."

"They don't have anything on me," Gerald said.

"You're the one who picked up Bridget Vale," Danny yelled.

"That was Sweeney and Rip. I just drove the van."

"That makes you an accomplice."

"Tim Hawkins didn't see me."

I heard a shot, but didn't dare look out. Who had shot whom?

"Fucking moron!" Danny yelled. "Now look what you made me do!"

He had shot Gerald. All was quiet. I hardly dared to breathe. A bit later, I heard the sound of Danny's footfalls on the leaves. He seemed to be walking away.

I sat motionless under my cover of weeds and leaves. Darkness swooped down like the final curtain on a Greek tragedy. I resigned myself to spending the night buried in the undergrowth like the children in the fairy tale.

The sound of a bird—perhaps a pine marten—penetrated the wind-tossed bowers. I began to listen to the leaves. Shh-shh. Shh-shh. They were telling me to keep quiet, to appreciate the stillness. Now and then the flutter of wings and the furtive pattering of small animals broke the quiet. They could smell me, but must have known I was no threat—they went about their night-time business, leaving me alone.

I felt exhausted; I was cold, in pain, and had no idea what I would do next to try to save myself. Perhaps Danny would go away. He had killed Gerald. Why would he return to the scene of his crime? Then I remembered his monstrous rosary. If he was religious, he might want to bury Gerald's body.

I hoped Elizabeth was safe at home.

I had charged into Danny's pub like an overaged Nancy Drew, feeling impervious to danger. Stupid! I devolved into self-pity. Tears ran down my cheeks. I'd thought I was at my most vulnerable on my bike, particularly after the sun went down. I'd tried to be vigilant regarding my surroundings, but reason fled my mind when I saw Elizabeth's scarf on the chair, and she was nowhere to be seen.

I should have been more cautious. Now I might die. Whom should I pray to? God of the universe, do you hear me? Keep me safe. Please. God of the universe, forgive me the nastiness I released into the world: impatience with Mathieu; inward gloating when besting a colleague; egotism; self-indulgence; lack of family feeling—which may have resulted from being an only child whose parents died years ago. Don't make excuses, Maria. My impatience with Elizabeth—I was tired of her and wanted her to go home.

There wasn't much of me to like by the time I'd enumerated all my sins. In need of solace, I willed my Druid spirits to come to me and they did, soothing me with soft touches and murmurings. If I died, they promised to take me to the next realm. I relaxed, slid onto the ground, and fell asleep, my face against the leaves I'd soaked with tears.

***

When day broke, I heard the messages of birds, cheerfully greeting the morning. The night's rest had given comfort to my ankle. I reached down to touch it. The swelling had subsided. I brought myself into a sitting position, holding onto the tree, then stood on my good leg, then tried both. Pain knifed through my ankle. I gasped.

I heard something—or someone—scraping around on the leaves and looked out.

"Ohhh...."

It was Gerald, groaning. He was partially sitting up with his head resting against a tree trunk. He pressed his left hand against his shoulder.

Danny hadn't killed him. I had not forgotten that Gerald had a gun. He'd shot the falcon.

"The devil take you, Danny Aherne!" Gerald shouted. "I see you there in the thicket."

Danny had returned?

Gerald fished the gun out of his pocket and shot in the direction of a moss-covered elm. He shot again. Again. He had used one shot to kill the falcon. I had no idea how many shots he had left. As if in answer, a bullet whizzed by my hiding place.

"Danny Aherne, you gobshite, you've killed me. I'll rot here in the woods..."

He shot again. That was six shots.

"I see you," Gerald said.

His voice was growing weaker and I realized he was hallucinating. I chanced a look at him. He had passed out. Or died. I eased out of the vines and leaves, and crept past Gerald. I'd gone only a few feet when I heard someone approach and crouched beneath a dead tree that was slanted against an oak.

Two heads appeared: Danny and the man called Rip. They carried spades.

CHAPTER TWENTY-SEVEN

"There he is," Danny said. "We'll bury him and cover the grave with sticks and leaves. No one will ever find him."

The men thrust their spades into the ground. I sneaked away, finding the trampled trail marked by Danny when he entered the forest. That was the way I was going out. That was the way he would go out and I needed to stay ahead of him.

My progress was slow. I moved at an ungainly lope, favoring my bad ankle. Ahead was a thick patch of Irish spurge. I didn't pause to appreciate the pink and white flowers, but plunged through, the leaves slapping my arms. As I broke free of the shrub, I heard a gunshot.

Had Danny shot the man he brought to help bury Gerald?

Danny Aherne was a madman who made me shiver. In my mind's eye, I saw him tumble the man's body into the grave on top of Gerald's and begin the job of piling earth on top. I hastened my step. My ankle protested. I slowed down.

Then, daylight! I was leaving the forest.

When I stepped out of the trees, the sunlight was an assault. I'd been in darkness or semi-darkness for hours. It took several moments before my eyes adjusted to the light. Shaggy sheep still milled around the hillside. The faithful border collie rested on his haunches. At my appearance, he stood, watching to see what I would do. I sent a prayer upward that he wouldn't bark. He kept his eyes on me as I stumbled past the flock, but didn't see me as a threat. Possibly, he sensed how helpless I was.

I continued on, occasionally ducking behind a boulder to turn and see if Danny was behind. Not yet. Burying Gerald and the other man was taking time.

Heading east into the morning sun, I looked toward the mountains, trying to find the place where Danny had stopped the van a day ago, but the terrain all looked the same. I couldn't find it.

My head ached and my throat was parched. My lips felt gummy. How long had it been since I had anything to drink? The stream, with its beautiful clear water, was tempting. I studied the water—it seemed clean enough. There were no villages located above to contaminate. I hesitated. The sheep drank the water, the little dog, too.

Was I becoming deranged? I was neither a sheep nor a dog, whose digestive systems absorbed unclean food and water. *I am human. I could get sick. I could die.*

I started to trudge on, but was racked by a sudden fit of coughing. My body convulsed. I struggled to the stream, lowered my face into the water, and drank like the parched animal I was. *Microbes, be damned.* I swallowed, swallowed again.

While on my knees, I peered up again in a fruitless effort to locate the mountain road. If I found it, I'd have some idea of the direction I should take to return to Coomara. As it was, I could only head into the morning sun. Westward lay the forest and Danny.

Where is Finch? Why weren't officers scouring the hills looking for me? Where is Mathieu? Where is Elizabeth?

I felt abandoned, sorry for myself, and sobbed aloud. If I managed to escape from Danny, how would I ever find my way back to Coomara? My mind filled with dark, hopeless thoughts. From the position of the sun, it must be eight or nine o'clock. A whole day lay ahead. Would I live through it?

Deeper into the valley, I went. My headache disappeared. Whatever microbes were working their way through my system, my thirst was slaked, and so far, I felt no stomach rumblings. The heavens were a wave of cerulean blue smeared with feathery clouds. *Cerulean,* from the Latin *caeruleum,* meaning sky or heaven. All sorts of miscellanea swam through my mind—the bones of a female Celtic warrior buried with her sword in Scotland, my rent payment due to Brendan Calloway, a poem I'd written about Kerry cows.

That pail of milk!
Hosannas of fat
rise to the top...

What I wouldn't give for a sip of milk!
The sun burned brightly for Ireland. Usually, clouds or mists obscured that mighty orb. I breathed in the scent of heather, which bloomed in a field to my right. The pain had left my ankle. I trod lightly, respectful of my injury.

I felt the majesty of my surroundings—the sky above, green grasses, and mountains rising. The Wicklow range—heaps of granite pushed up during the Caledonian orogeny, or mountain building era, when continents collided. The mountain sides were covered with the greenest ground cover I'd ever seen and ancient boulders rose up like sentinels.

Druid spirits, where are you? I need you.
In the distance, a clump of trees appeared. I thought of the thorn tree the Druids had danced around in the Mulligan field. Deirdre said some called the tree a *faerie tree*. People didn't mess with faeries. According to tradition, they could be vengeful. Pearce had protected the tree. He could just as well have cut it down, expanded his field, made more money from his crop.

Faeries should be feared. Iris thought they took her baby. In some people's minds, faeries were real. I could use a faerie right now—a helpful faerie.

Nearing the trees, I wondered if it was a sacred copse. Certainly, the people who owned this land had left it undisturbed. When I saw the trees arranged in a circle, my heart leapt with hope. This was the faerie mound of which Gerald had spoken. Magnetized, I headed toward it. Here was refuge.

Inside the copse was an earthen mound surrounded by large, irregular boulders. Circling the mound was a ditch or trench from which the builders had dug up soil to construct it. I crossed the ditch, muddy from the rains.

I hadn't read of a burial mound near Coomara. I had, of course, visited the ones at Newgrange in County Meath. This seemed a fine example of Ireland's famed mounds. Why wasn't it on the mound circuit? Perhaps the location was too distant from major cities and towns to attract tourists.

The west entrance was piled with heavy boulders. There would be another opening, facing east, because ancient people built to catch the power of the sun as it rose and set. Moving around the structure to find the second entrance, I saw it half-buried in the earth with large stones on top. I pushed against the stone nearest me. It didn't budge. *What was inside?* I couldn't see.

Then I heard a slight sound coming from the ring of trees and whirled. *Danny!* Fear churned my stomach, and I tasted metal again. He paused to tear the paper off what looked to be a candy bar. *Candy bar.* My stomach growled from hunger. My heartbeat quickened. I didn't think he'd seen me.

Better the devil you know than you don't know. The old adage zinged through my head. *I would take the dark uncertainty of a burial tomb than crazy Danny Aherne with a gun any day!*

Eyeing the opening, I thought I could squeeze through and did, scraping my forehead in the process. My feet fell on solid ground. Pitch black. I couldn't stand without bumping my head on the ceiling. In prehistoric times, people were smaller. Not knowing if I was standing on a ledge or on the floor, I got down on my hands and knees and crawled away from the entrance.

I had never been afraid of the dark, which was a blessing in this circumstance. Darkness had always seemed a covering to me—protection, in a way. I did worry about placing my hands on something dead—a bird that had flown inside and become trapped, a small furry animal.

The tomb smelled pungently of mold and not of death. The air was cool and clammy on my face. I crawled slowly, testing with my outstretched hands for unexpected openings in the floor. Surely, I wasn't the first human in modern times to enter this burial mound. Whatever bones were found were undoubtedly resting in one of Dublin's museums.

I crawled on, grateful that I'd worn jeans. My ankle throbbed occasionally, but did not bother overmuch. The hard, grainy soil irritated my palms, but that was a small price to pay for safety.

Flashes of light appeared where the outside boulders did not quite mesh together, but that was of little help, for it did not disperse far into the tomb. Wsssh! *What was that? An insect of some kind? A lizard?* I didn't have to watch for snakes. Ireland was an island. During the Ice Age, it was connected to the European landmass, but it was too cold then for reptiles to survive. When the ice melted, it poured freezing water into the seas and oceans, isolating Ireland.

No snakes.

Bugs.

From the feeble light, I saw I was about to turn a corner and go down an incline. Other than my friend, the insect, there was no sound except that of my breathing and the scuffing sound I made dragging my body.

Then all light disappeared. I was again in total darkness. The incline became steeper and I worried where it would end. Suddenly, I plunged downward, landing on a pile of rubble. At one time, the earth had shaken loose some of the stones, which must have been a wall. I climbed over the pile of rocks, fell into a pit, and landed hard. I rubbed my tailbone. When I stood, I guessed the pit to be nearly six feet deep. I could easily reach the edge.

I knelt. My fingers touched something hard, rounded. *A skull.* I reached out. Another bone—this one could have been a leg. I had fallen into a pit of bones. Perhaps this burial site had been hidden from archaeologists when they originally excavated the burial mound. The wall had crumbled afterward.

Were the bones human or animal? Were they ancient or only the bones of some hapless wayfarer who got himself trapped inside the mound in recent times?

A scraping sound.

Danny is at the entrance!

Hiding wasn't proactive. I should be thinking of ways to save myself. Danny would surely wedge himself inside the aperture I came through. He was bulkier than I, but he'd find a way. How could I rig a trap? The only weapons I had were bones. I'd left the stick I'd used as a crutch inside the entrance. It was too late to fetch it. Danny might already be inside.

If the bones were ancient, there might also be artifacts—perhaps a weapon. Reaching out, I felt the skull again. It had all the contours of a human skull—though in the dark, I might confuse a wolf's skull with a human's. *How I wished for a flashlight! If I had my cellphone, I'd have one.*

My fingers played over the skull. There was the opening for the nose, for the eyes. It *was* a human skull. If it was the skull of a warrior, his weapons could have been buried with him. His axe, for instance, would come in handy. I felt around. Bones. More bones. Then at what must have been the edge of the pile, I found a hard object.

The iron hilt of a sword.

My fingers curled around the pommel as I lifted and pulled it toward me. The cross-guard was still intact. Corrosion had eaten away the sharp blades and tip, but it would serve as a defense weapon against Danny Ahearne. I was in a pit of ancient bones and now armed. But Danny had a gun.

I waited.

***

The sound echoed, a scrambling of pebbles. Danny had pushed himself through the opening, dislodging stones. I heard his shuffle as he moved toward my hiding place and waited to see the beam of his flashlight. It came, a flare against the walls above my head, then lower to guide his path. When the light played upon the collapsed wall, he paused and an exclamation erupted from his lips.

"Holy Mother of God."

I braced myself against the side of the pit directly beneath him. The flashlight played lower, shining directly on the skeletons. It was also my first sight of the contents of the burial vault. I saw a human skeleton, possibly that of a female because of the wide pelvic girdle. I saw the bones of several four-legged animals that looked like wolves. They may have been beloved dogs. I saw a time-encrusted dagger and a torc—a gold neck ring with two bulls at the opening. Beads of all colors. A comb. A cooking urn, the remains of several pots. This was the grave of a Celtic warrior princess—maybe a queen. *Would a male have been buried with cooking pots?*

"Holy Mother of God," Danny said again.

I heard him drop to his knees, then murmur words I'd heard before—the Lord's Prayer in Gaelic:

Ár n-Athair atá ar neamh,
Go naofar dainim
Go dtagfadh...

He started to weep. In between his sobs, he spoke the prayer of contrition in English: "O my God, I am heartily sorry..."

He named his sins, which gladdened my heart, because I wanted to hear them.

"I repent that I took Bridget Vale's life," he said. "I measured her goodness against my selfish desires and the devil won, but I used my rosary to give her back to you. It was already stained with my blood, shed as I recounted my sufferings."

"Did you not know, God, how much I loved my boy?" he went on. "My Alain was so sweet, so soft, so innocent of all that goes on in the world. I would have made the boy a priest, so gladly did he lay his pretty hands on mine, and indeed, on all who came in contact with him. Did you not see that on his christening day, he did not bawl, he did not utter a fretful sound?"

His voice rose. "I craved revenge against Iris for letting my boy fall into the sea. How I hated the town for taking sides against me. Yes, I took young girls from their families to sell them into slavery—all to avenge the lies people told to keep my boy from me. I would have kept my boy alive."

It did not escape my notice that as he prayed, he trained his flash-light on the bounty at the bottom of the pit.

He began wailing. "The killing—it has no end—Mrs. Moriarity, Tom, and Rip..."

The killing has no end.

I tightened my grip on the hilt of the sword.

"And the poet!" he screamed. "How well I love her verses! I'm thankful she has escaped into the mountains and that You have brought me to this place to..."

Heat poured through my bones like liquid steel. I imagined her, the warrior princess, as she had been in life—tall with long tawny hair, the color and texture of a lion's mane. She'd worn a leather body covering and had used her sword in battle.

I looked up. The sun, as it set, illuminated the passageway. Danny Aherne leaned over the pit, his gun in his right hand. His eyes widened demonically. He did not see the princess—he saw her treasure—the torc, the beads, the shining urn.

God had favored him at last.

He slid down the rubble as I had done. I raised the sword and swung. Craaaack!

That was the sound of the blade striking his head. I had surely killed him. Adrenalin pumping, I reached in his jacket pocket, grabbed his cellphone and flashlight. Using his crumpled body to boost myself up, I made my way out of the pit. Forgetting my twisted ankle, I crouched through the passageway to the entrance and squeezed through the aperture leading to freedom.

CHAPTER TWENTY-EIGHT

There was just enough charge left in Danny's cell phone to contact the garda station.

"Where are you?" the officer asked.

"By the faerie mound near a stream and a field of heather."

The connection went dead.

Was that sufficient information for Finch to find me? I prayed it was. I sat on the side of the hill to wait. And then it hit me. I had just killed a man. Should I have waited for Danny to train his gun on me before I struck him? Had I committed murder? At what point does an act of violence become self-defense? Danny would surely have killed me. When the garda arrived, I'd tell them what happened and let Finch sort it out.

I was too tired, too hungry, too thirsty to think about what killing someone had done to my soul. Instead, I thought about the lady warrior who had been buried inside the mound. I would write about her. I thought of Boudica, queen of the British Celtic Iceni tribe who led an uprising against the Romans. Before she was defeated, she had won several battles. Roman historians disagreed on the manner and location of her death. Tacitus wrote that Boudica was tall with golden hair that hung below her waist—like the warrior entombed in the pit.

I lay down on the hill to rest.

***

The sun was low when Brendan found me walking down the hill. Like a knight of olden times, he came riding on a stallion—not white, but a deep brown, almost black—with white fetlocks.

Sir Lancelot of the Lake.

"There you are, Maria Pell," he called. "I've been looking for you all day."

"That's good of you, Brendan. I'm so glad you found me."

"You look none the worse for wear—except for that abrasion on your forehead."

"I'm thirsty and hungry," I said.

He handed me bottled water and an apple from his saddlebag.

"Is Elizabeth safe?" I asked, after draining the bottle.

"She's at the church," he said. "She went to light a candle for your safe return."

He called Finch to say he'd found me, then reached down to give me a lift onto the saddle behind him. I felt the solidness of the saddle, the warmth of the animal on the insides of my legs. The pain in my ankle had nearly gone away. With relief came exhaustion. I put my arms around Brendan's waist and rested my head against his back.

"Ready?" he asked.

"Yes."

The horse started down the hill. I felt the swaying motion of his gait.

"Elizabeth was never in danger," Brendan said. "A young woman took her on a tour of the wine cellar. Likely, Elizabeth was there when you arrived. Danny never meant to harm her. He wanted *you*."

"I killed him," I said. "I hid in the burial pit inside the mound. When he slid down the rubble, I hit him with a sword."

"Sword?"

"There's treasure inside the mound, Brendan."

"You say? We'll tell the proper people when we get back."

"Shouldn't you phone Inspector Finch and tell him I killed Danny?"

"We'll tell him when we return to Coomara, Maria."

His voice was soothing. I leaned my face against his back. His shirt smelled faintly of pipe tobacco. He told me his horse was named Paddy O'Toole. I smiled.

Downward we went, the horse picking its way around the stones on dainty hooves. When we reached level ground, Brendan stopped at a stream so Paddy could drink. Then the horse broke into a trot and we rode across the fields.

It was twilight when we reached Coomara. Paddy's hooves clop-clopped on the paved streets. I was happy to see the village again. Though Brendan wanted to take me to the hospital, I said I wanted to go to the garda station.

***

Mathieu and Dennis Finch met us at the curb.

Mathieu helped me down from the horse. "I lost you," he said. "I couldn't see where the van went. I tried several roads out of town. I went crazy..."

"I know," I said, patting his arm.

"Thank God, you're safe, Maria. I..."

We embraced. I smelled his scent, cloves tinged with worry, and rested against him. Here was Mathieu, security, sanity, normality.

After a few moments, I turned to Brendan. "Thank you so much."

He smiled down at me, and I saw in his eyes that we would be friends forever. He rode off, the sound of Paddy's hooves reverberating on the street.

"Do you need medical treatment for your forehead?" Mathieu asked.

"It's just a scrape," Finch said. "Come inside. I'll fix it for her."

We went inside to Finch's office. He had a first aid kit in his desk drawer.

"It's started to heal," Finch said, as he cleaned the scrape with an antiseptic.

"Brendan said Elizabeth went to the church to light a candle," I said. "Is she still there?"

"I took her back to the cottage," Mathieu said.

When the inspector completed his ministrations, he put his hands on his knees and stared at me. "I don't mind telling you that we were afraid Danny Aherne had killed you. Thank God, you have nine lives like cats."

His statement was interesting—the Almighty paired with superstition.

"I spent the night in the forest, buried under leaves like the children in the fairy tale."

"Did your Druid spirits come to you?" Mathieu asked.

I thought of the peregrine falcon, which attacked Danny and gave me an opportunity to escape, and of the forest that hid and sheltered me, and the faerie mound, which provided concealment and the buried warrior who lent me her sword. Too quickly I had moved from one to the next without thanking the universe for its providence.

"Yes," I said, answering Mathieu, "I think they must have."

"We thought Danny had gone off with you to Belfast," Finch said. "We talked to a man named Sweeney—that's what he told us."

"He's one of them," I said.

"He sent us on a wild goose chase," Finch said. "Do you know where Danny is?"

"He's at the bottom of a burial pit inside the faerie mound," I said. "I think he's dead. I had fallen into the pit, found a sword, and struck him. I heard his head crack."

Finch nodded. "He would have killed you if you gave him the chance. Did you say you found a sword?"

"A female warrior was buried in the pit along with treasure."

"That mound was excavated years ago," Finch said.

"I'm guessing the treasure was behind a wall that collapsed after the excavation."

"I'll send men out there first thing in the morning."

Mathieu touched my shoulder. "Let me take you home."

I was tired, but I had questions. "Inspector, did you find the panel truck used in kidnapping Bridget? Did you find traces of her blood inside? Danny worried that his men hadn't cleaned it thoroughly."

"We found the van and traces of blood in the back," Finch said. "Also, articles of clothing and the braided bracelet, which Iris Vale identified as Bridget's. We've sent the blood samples to the lab in Dublin."

"Does Ireland have the death penalty?" I asked.

"No. The last man to be executed was hanged in 1954."

"What a pity. I had hoped the men who kidnapped Bridget would be executed."

"They will be locked up for a long time," Finch said. "One of them confessed to the kidnappings. He was wanted for a string of crimes and was quick to accept a deal. Danny Aherne was connected to a network of international sex traders. Virgins go for a high price, so he was trying to kill two birds with one stone by breaking the girls' parents' hearts and profiting from their sale."

"Why did he keep the girls so long in the cellar?" I asked.

"The yacht couldn't get close enough to the shore to get them. Patrol boats kept them away. Danny was waiting for the surveillance to end."

"Tim Hawkins said Danny was his supplier," I said. "Danny must have been dealing drugs."

"He was, but not so much that were breathing down his neck," Finch replied. "His goal was to carry out revenge against Iris's supporters."

I yawned.

"You should go home and rest," Mathieu said.

"I could use a shower."

Mathieu and I left for my cottage. As I went out the door, Sergeant Potts gave me my handbag and cell phone, which she said were found in the van.

***

The lights were off at the cottage. I hurried up the walk, anxious to talk to Elizabeth. The door was unlocked. I entered, calling her name. No answer. I searched all the rooms. She wasn't there.

"Did you say you brought her back from the church?" I asked.

"I did," Mathieu answered. "Has she gone next door to Brendan's?"

I called Brendan. Elizabeth wasn't there. I went back to her room and opened the door to her closet. Several empty hangers. One of her suitcases was gone. I opened her top bureau drawer and found her passport.

"She hasn't gone back to the States," I said.

"Maybe she went to see Father O'Neill," Mathieu said. "She seemed preoccupied when I brought her back from church."

"Why would she pack to go see Father O'Neill?"

I called St. Columba's, heard the phone ring several times. With Judy gone, there was no one to answer the phone. Mathieu and I returned to his car and drove to the priory. Father O'Neill wasn't home. We tried the church. He was working late in his office.

"Ms. Pell!" Father O'Neill exclaimed. "The police are looking for you."

"Yes, I know. I spent the night in a forest. I'm trying to find Elizabeth. Have you seen her?"

The priest gave me an uncertain look and glanced at Mathieu. "May I speak to Ms. Pell alone?"

"Is Elizabeth all right?" I asked, suddenly panicking. "Is she safe?"

He nodded. "Sit down, please. I need to speak to you." His gaze moved to Mathieu. "Alone."

Mathieu went out, closed the door.

"Elizabeth is with the sisters in the convent," Father O'Neill said. "I made arrangements for her to stay there."

"What happened?" I asked. "Did she try to kill herself again?"

"No. There is something she feels she must tell you, and it will be hard to hear."

What could it be? Aware of most of Elizabeth's foibles, I could think of nothing she had done that hearing about it would be unbearable. But she was safe. Father O'Neill had said she was. I calmed down, began to think rationally.

"When does she plan to come home?" I asked.

"In a few days. I know you weren't raised in the Catholic faith, but if you want to come and talk to me after she speaks with you, my door is open."

Now, I felt jittery. What on earth could Elizabeth say that would send me to a priest for comfort?

"I'll go home and wait for her."

He showed me out. Mathieu tugged at my arm and we got back in the car.

"What did he say?" Mathieu asked.

"Elizabeth's at the convent. She'll be home in a few days."

We didn't talk the rest of the way home. My stomach growled. I looked at my watch and saw it was nearly midnight. Rummaging in the refrigerator, I found a slice of ham, placed it between two slices of rye bread, and washed it down with iced tea. Then I went upstairs and showered. My heart was uneasy. What had troubled Elizabeth so deeply that she tried at least one suicide attempt—there may have been more—and sent her to a convent? I put on pajamas and rejoined Mathieu in the sitting room.

We sat in silence.

"All this mayhem—over a custody battle," Mathieu said.

"It was more than that. Iris let the baby die."

The events of the past forty-eight hours bore down on me and I dozed off on the sofa. What were my dreams? They were jumbled. Baby Alain Aherne lay in sea water, plankton streaked across his face. Baby Doe lay in an Indiana creek. Mother crying, "Whose child is this?" Bridget's dead white face. Her mother grieving drunkenly. Danny singing "Red is the Rose." A poem running through it all about how quickly hope is lost. I felt myself drowning, unable to complete my book of poetry. Seaweed covered my eyes, filled my nostrils and mouth. I woke doubled up with coughing. Mathieu, who had slept in the recliner, held me in his arms for a long time. Then it was dawn.

"Let's go out in the boat," he said. "I'll take the helm."

We did as he suggested and it was a blessing to be on the sea, watching clouds hurried by a west wind. Each cloud told a story—a fat goblin pursued by a dragon; a woman's hand, fisted to defend her virtue; a squalling child.

The sun was rising, a great orange reflection in the sky. A bird flew lonesome. Auras were everywhere—the energy of life. I bowed my head to the universe, humbled by my blessings. Raising my eyes, I saw the glimmer of a rainbow in the eastern sky. I wept, grateful and pleased.

Mathieu stood at the helm, straight and strong. Though I wondered what he was thinking, I didn't ask. The silence was golden.

He pulled into a cove, set the anchor, and came to sit beside me.

After a while, he said, "You must come home, Maria, so we can rebuild our life together. It's what you need. You haven't written a word since all this trouble began."

I reached over and held his hand. We stayed there watching the sun make its upward arc, and then went back to the cottage. I took him to bed with me that night and we made love with the quiet joy of old lovers who'd put to rest their differences and accepted a devotion that had become part of their lives.

But did I really want to settle down? It was the word *settle* that stopped me.

CHAPTER TWENTY-NINE

Inspector Finch called the following day to say officers had found Danny Aherne's body at the bottom of the pit. His right hand still gripped his gun.

"Self-defense," Finch said. "No doubt about it."

He had contacted an archaeological crew to take charge of the warrior maiden's bones and treasure. They named the location Pairc na Fraoch (Field of Heather). Using a map drawn by Finch, Mathieu went to the mound, returning with a list of artifacts, which included Byzantine coins.

"Proves there was trade with the East," Mathieu said. "Those longboats of the Vikings went all over. They sacked the suburbs of Constantinople in 860, but failed to reach the city walls. At the time, some attributed their withdrawal to the intervention of Mary, the mother of Jesus, but it was more likely they wanted to return to their homeland before winter set in."

"How old do you think the warrior maid is?" I asked.

"Around twelve hundred years," he answered. "That would place her at the beginning of the Viking raids, which occurred in 793."

"Where will she go?" I asked.

"My guess would be the National Museum in Dublin," he replied.

"Could you tell if she was killed in battle?"

"There was a slash mark on her collarbone," he answered. "I'd say she died fighting."

"When I was in the pit, I saw her. She was magnificent. A lion of a woman."

"You must write a book of poetry about her."

"I want to go to Newgrange to see the tombs again. Would you like to come?"

He said he'd arrange his work schedule so he could accompany me. It would be good having Mathieu with me. His knowledge of prehistory would add cultural dimensions to the stones and their positioning.

***

Three days passed. Elizabeth did not come home. I hoped she was finding peace at the convent. Mathieu began spending evenings with me. The third night, he checked out of the inn and moved into the cottage. His presence filled the rooms with new energy.

On June 20, the day before we left for Newgrange, I was reading Seamus Heaney's poetry when a car stopped in front of the cottage. I looked out the window and saw Elizabeth alighting from a tan station wagon driven by a nun. In the back seat were two more nuns. Elizabeth spoke to them a few moments and then came up the walk, carrying her suitcase. The car sped away.

Not wanting her to know I'd been watching, I moved to the sofa with the Heaney book and pretended to read. Elizabeth opened the door quietly, then paused to intuit whether I was upstairs, downstairs, or outside. She took a few steps toward the sitting room and peered in.

"Maria," she said.

I heard in her tone that she'd not wanted me to be there, preferring to have more time before seeing me. But she came in the room anyway and sat down in the easy chair next to the sofa. She'd had little sleep. There were circles under her eyes and new lines in her forehead, and I felt sorry for her.

"Father O'Neill said you had something to tell me that would be hard for both of us," I said. "Whatever it is, Elizabeth, I don't need to know. Sometimes people need their secrets."

With trembling hands, she smoothed her wrinkled skirt. "Maria, I *have* to tell you."

"Why?"

"For the sake of my soul."

That was different. If she needed to unburden her soul, I could listen.

She began. "When we were children..."

I leaned forward. What had happened when we were small? So many things, good and bad. Though younger than I, she had been a bossy child. Her tantrums had been more of an annoyance than anything else. When she didn't get her way, she would scream and kick, and I would take my dolls and go up to my room, or run to the orchard and climb to my treehouse.

"Baby Doe had a name," she said. "It was Emma."

I was surprised. "How do you know her name was Emma?"

"She was my father's child with a woman who lived in a white bungalow south of town. He called the woman Sandy. I went there with him a few times."

I felt like I was stumbling through a jungle with hanging vines. "Emma was your half-sister?"

Then words gushed from her mouth so fast they were jumbled: Sandy had called incessantly and once showed up on the front porch, and her mother, my Aunt Carol, had become hysterical. Aunt Carol packed to leave, planning to take Elizabeth with her, but Uncle Robert had begged her to stay. *All this was going on next door and I never knew.*

Elizabeth spread her hands. "When we went to Sandy's, she screamed and threw beer cans at Father. Emma howled nonstop. It was like a horror movie."

"Why did your father take you with him?" I asked, grappling with the image of an eight-year-old girl thrust into a messy adult drama.

"Maybe he thought if I was there, he could leave quickly."

"How dreadful for you!"

"I had to do something," Elizabeth said, "so I took Emma to the creek and threw her in."

Threw her in.

She said the words as casually as she might have said *washed my face* or *tied my shoes.*

"To me, she was the cause of it all," Elizabeth went on, "and if she were gone, our world would right itself again. I didn't dream you'd be the one to find her."

Something was out of kilter. The problem wasn't me finding the dead baby. The problem was throwing a helpless baby in the water!

Elizabeth shrugged her shoulders. "She was in the way. Sandy wanted money and Father didn't want to give it to her. Mother wanted Sandy to go away."

"But you *did* know it was wrong to throw the baby in the creek..."

She gestured impatiently. "I don't know what I was thinking. Maybe I thought she'd just float away and someone would find her and take care of her."

If I were listening to the confession of someone who was not my own flesh and blood, I might have understood more readily, but I cleaved to the notion that Elizabeth and I were raised with the same values.

I calmed myself. A little girl, distraught over family troubles, had tried to fix everything by drowning a baby. Yet she hadn't intended to drown her. She thought someone would rescue her.

How much did my parents know? I ran the scene in my mind—Father had lifted the dead baby from the water. Mother asked whose baby she was. Father looked toward his brother's house, and asked where Robert was. Grandma baptized the corpse, saying she was her grandchild.

They all knew.

After the baby was buried, I didn't remember anyone mentioning her.

"Did your father know what you did?" I asked.

Elizabeth shook her head. "Not at the time. When I took the baby from her crib, he was trying to make peace with Sandy. When they realized she was missing, I was outside sitting on the porch swing. Father asked if I'd seen anyone come in the house and I said I hadn't. Then he hustled me back into the car and we drove home. I think he stopped to buy me an ice cream cone."

An ice cream cone.

"What did Sandy do?" I asked. "Didn't she call the police?"

"I don't know. I think she was drunk. She may have passed out."

"What did Uncle Robert think happened to the baby?"

Elizabeth shrugged.

An infant vanished. No one cared. I found it incredulous that Uncle Robert, my father's brother, didn't search for the baby. *His* baby.

"Years later," Elizabeth continued, "I thought he must have known what I did. It was the only logical answer. She was too little to climb out of her crib and crawl down to the water by herself."

I held my head in my hands.

"I'm so sorry you found her," Elizabeth teared up. "I know it created problems for you."

Me? What about little Emma?

In my mind's eye, I saw the body of the infant, no longer nameless, but now identified. My cousin, Emma Pell. I saw her pale skin, her dark curling hair, her tiny fists, her blue eyes, and knew I was linked to her now more than I had ever been. As it turned out, she belonged to *us*— the Pell family.

"What are you going to do?" I asked.

"I'm returning to Indiana to tell the sheriff what happened. I may be sent to jail, but I don't think so. I was only six when it happened."

"Eight," I said. "You were eight."

"Can you forgive me?" Elizabeth asked, her lip quivering.

I turned away. "It's not for me to forgive, is it? It's Emma's life you took."

She stared down at the carpet. I went outside and took the boat out to sea where everything seemed clear and clean.

***

Hours later, when I returned, Elizabeth was gone and Mathieu was in the kitchen, making an Irish stew. Elizabeth had left a note on the kitchen table, saying she'd asked Brendan to take her to the Dublin airport. She was returning to Indiana.

"I figured you and she must have had a falling out," Mathieu said, as he peeled a potato.

"That's not quite right," I said.

He saw the pain in my eyes and came to sit beside me at the table. Since the beginning of our relationship, he had known about the nameless infant that haunted my dreams. Now, as Emma Pell's sad story poured from my lips, he covered my hand with his.

"Will this lay Emma to rest?" he asked.

"How can it?"

We sat, silent. I was thinking that when I went back to the states, I would go to Emma Pell's grave and say a prayer, hoping the universe had gathered her in. I would put up a headstone with her name on it.

"I don't know that I want Elizabeth in my life," I said.

One of Mathieu's great strengths was that he was non-judgmental; whereas I tended to condemn—not only others, but myself, as well.

He stared out the window. "You've mentioned that Elizabeth was a disagreeable child. Perhaps she was picking up on the tensions between her father and mother. When she realized the baby was a source of pain for her family, she may have felt compelled to get rid of her."

I didn't reply.

"Was she a murderous child?" he went on. "Did she tear wings off bugs, kick puppies, or pull cats' tails?"

"No, she was nothing like that."

"Then her killing the baby was an aberration."

"I suppose."

"Think what she must live with. She killed her own flesh and blood."

"I don't think that bothers her very much," I said. "I couldn't live with myself if I'd done what she did."

Then I remembered I had taken Danny Aherne's life. But it wasn't the same. Danny would have killed me. Emma was innocent. Danny was a stone-cold killer.

Mathieu pressed his lips to my forehead.

"She asked if I forgave her and I said it wasn't for me to forgive her."

"That's true. It wasn't for you to forgive."

I slid my eyes at him. "But perhaps I should have been kinder to her."

He didn't answer. My mind was in a state of great confusion, and I knew I could not reorder it using my intellect. I went outside, sat on the back porch, and listened to the voice of the sea.

A passage from Shakespeare's *Macbeth* drifted into my mind:

Canst thou not minister to a mind diseas'd,
 Pluck from the memory a rooted sorrow,
Raze out the written troubles of the brain,
And with some sweet oblivious antidote
Cleanse the stuff'd bosom of that perilous stuff
Which weighs upon the heart.

I thought of Danny Aherne's son, Alain, who had vanished off a cliff. Almost certainly, his death was caused by Iris' carelessness. Elizabeth's father had been reckless in involving her, an eight-year-old child, in his extramarital affair. In killing Bridget and kidnapping the girls, Danny had sought to set right the order that had denied him his son. Elizabeth had tried to restore peace in her family by getting rid of Emma.

Revenge, wrote Sir Francis Bacon, *is a kind of wild justice...*

Wild Justice might be a good title for a book.

***

I heard that few people attended Danny Aherne's funeral. A week after his body was buried near the back fence in the church graveyard, Iris Vale came to clean my cottage. After she finished her work, I invited her to sit down and share a pot of tea. Usually, she said no, saying she had to hurry home, but this time she accepted. As we lingered at the kitchen table, with a lovely sunset bursting through the window, she said she had something to share.

"What is it?" I asked, thinking she was going on holiday for a week or two.

She selected an oatmeal cookie from a plate. "If I had been truthful years ago, Danny wouldn't have gone on a killing spree."

My mug was halfway to my mouth. I put it back on the table. "How so?"

"Danny wasn't Alain's father."

"What did you say?"

"Danny wasn't Alain's father," she said again. "Pearce Mulligan was. He got me pregnant, then gave me money to leave town. I went to Dublin, where some of Da's people lived. They turned out to be a bunch of holy joes, called me a whore—though I was only a girl of sixteen—and kicked me out in the street."

I didn't know what to say, so I said nothing.

After a few seconds, Iris continued, "I had nowhere to go, so I called Pearce and told him I needed more money." Her eyes filled with tears. "He said he was a married man and there was a limit to what he could do. He did come to Dublin and give me money to rent a room in a rooming house."

I looked hard at Iris. "Did his wife find out about you?"

"She was listening in on a phone extension when I called." Iris bit her lower lip. "She was pregnant too. She called her father, who was a preacher. He came and took her back to Scotland. She died in childbirth there and her family kept the child to raise."

I had an image of a no-nonsense Presbyterian pastor with little tolerance of sin.

"Not long after I'd returned to Coomara," Iris continued, "Pearce saw me coming out of the grocery store with Alain. We spoke. That's how I know about the baby staying in Scotland."

"Did Pearce show any interest in Alain?" I asked.

"He touched my boy's chin with his finger and said he was a fine lad."

I envisioned the scene: The lord of the manor passing the time of day with a young village mother and chucking her baby's chin. Noblesse oblige.

Shaking my head, I asked, "How did you convince Danny the child was his?"

Iris slid her eyes at me. "I slept with him the night we met, which was about a week after Da's folks kicked me out. A bit later, I told him

I was pregnant. He assumed it was his and married me. I never corrected him. Alain weighed only five and a half pounds at birth. Danny thought he was premature."

I felt both horror at a deception that altered the course of a man's life and pity for teen-aged Iris, who had been alone and desperate.

She stared at me, waiting for me to speak.

"It was shrewd of you," I said, slowly, "to find a way to save yourself and Alain. You must have felt you had no other choice."

"But look what it caused," she said, looking toward the sunset. "If I hadn't lied to Danny..."

If she hadn't lied to Danny, he probably would have left her. He would have had no attachment to the baby, and would have been gone by the time she gave birth. She would have been a teenager with a fatherless child. Perhaps she would have given him up for adoption. Since she had run away from Coomara to hide her shame, she probably would not have come back and married Freddy Vale. Bridget would not have been born. Judy would still be alive.

So many *would haves*. I glanced at Iris. She had tied a blue scarf around her head, knotting it at the nape of her neck to keep her red hair in place while cleaning. Though only in her late-thirties, lines showed around her mouth and chin. She would have jowls by age forty. Her fingers, which were holding her mug of tea, were red and thickened from hard work, and perhaps incipient arthritis. Her life had been difficult and would continue to be so.

Iris turned to look at me. "I should have told Danny the truth."

"Someone," I said, "maybe some filmmaker, said 'Hindsight is always twenty-twenty—'"

She nodded. Soon after, she gathered up her sweater and handbag, and left. I sat at the table until the tea in the teapot grew cold.

***

The next day, the *Irish Independent* reported on a body washed up in Killiney Bay. Hector Perez-Conti had been shot execution style and thrown in the sea. After his arrest, he had holed up in a flat in Blackrock, a Dublin suburb, no longer welcome at Ravensclaw. The paper reported his arrest in Coomara and speculated that he was a member of a sex trafficking ring that had been targeting Irish girls.

***

Mathieu worked throughout the summer at Ballygosheen, spending at least three days a week in Coomara. It was difficult for me to move into a contemplative mood necessary to express myself in poetic form. I had dwelt too long in the world of dead and missing children, and harrowing escapes.

I needed calm. I needed work and a feeling of accomplishment.

At first, I puttered around the cottage, adapting rooms for male occupation, moving a large recliner from the corner into the light, making room for Mathieu's belongings in the closet and dresser drawers, putting another glass on the bathroom sink.

When Mathieu was at home, I prepared meals, trying native Irish recipes like boxty and colcannon. I learned how to make soda bread and scones.

I spent hours on the sea, walked the hills, and relaxed in Innis Cove. I frequented the library, keeping in touch with the Celtic maid from Pairc na Fraoch. Working with people from the museum, Grace Devereaux created an exhibit around the maiden warrior with replicas of the artifacts. Over time, the hard edges of my emotions disappeared into the Irish haze.

In July, I assisted Margaret Mulligan with her retreat. Poets came from nearby colleges to lead discussions, which attracted people from all over Ireland who wished to hold the poetic quill between their fingers. How lovely it was to sit under a large tent on a promontory overlooking the Irish Sea and speak of Yeats. For me, it was healing and I began to write.

EPILOGUE

Eight Months Later

It was time to leave Coomara. My leave of absence from Midwestern University was nearly over. The study I'd undertaken was completed and I had written several poems—not enough for a chapbook, but several. The rest, I would compose from memory and notes.

Mathieu and I threw a farewell party at a village park. He presided over the barbie, coating chicken breasts and a sirloin of beef with a secret tomato-Worcestershire sauce that sent up a marvelous aroma. I made a vat of potato salad from my late mother's recipe, as well as genuine Boston baked beans. Our guests furnished pies, breads, and dips, as well as crudites and potato crisps. Libations flowed with the conversations.

Nearly everyone who mattered joined us: The Vales and families affected by the kidnappings, Inspector Finch and officers not on duty, the girls in Mathieu's karate class, and members of his archeological team.

Father O'Neill came. He didn't ask about Elizabeth, and I guessed he and she were communicating by mail or email. She would have revealed to him that I had not been supportive when she confessed to murdering Emma Pell.

I hadn't heard from her, so didn't know what her fate had been with the county sheriff. It was doubtful that she would serve time in jail. When I returned to Indiana, I expected to look in on her.

Margaret and Pearce Mulligan arrived late. (Lina had returned to Peru.) Accompanying them was a handsome young man whom Pearce introduced as his son, Douglas, who was visiting from Scotland. Some-one had decided it was time for Margaret to get to know her grandson. I'd heard Pearce had filed for divorce from Lina and was courting a woman his age who owned a Dublin tea room. Perhaps he was finally turning over a new leaf.

Deirdre O'Malley and Grace Devereaux came. Tim Hawkins, Grace's nephew, had returned to St. Louis, at Inspector Finch's suggestion. Brendan Calloway helped Mathieu with the barbecuing. The two men had become friends since Mathieu moved into my cottage.

I hated breaking ties that had sustained me for over a year. Mathieu was so good at dealing with farewells, making them seem as if they didn't exist.

I sat in a lawn chair, trying to conceal my sadness at leaving. My attention was drawn to Mikey Scanlon and three boys playing a game of croquet. Mikey, I knew, had just had his ninth birthday. He was smaller than the other boys. One of his friends kept knocking his ball out of bounds. He made fun of Mikey, called him "Girly." Mikey's cheeks grew red with fury. When his tormentor bent to send, yet again, Mikey's ball to the other end of the court, Mikey gripped the handle of his mallet and raised it above his head. Just as he swung at the boy's head, I screamed "No!" and ran to intervene.

Mikey dropped the mallet.

In his dark eyes, I saw fear and confusion. He ran into the trees. I followed him, found him sitting on the ground at the foot of an oak. He was crying. As I put my arm around him, I thought of Elizabeth: maybe I could find the grace within myself to forgive her.

ACKNOWLEDGMENTS

I'm deeply indebted to beta readers R.G. Ziemer and Laurie Scheer, book designer Kevin Moriarity, cover designer William Pack, and marketing specialist Valerie Biel of Lost Lake Press.

ABOUT THE AUTHOR

Lynne Handy is a librarian, genealogist, poet, and author of the Maria Pell mystery novels. In "Old Sins," she once again creates characters, who carry out acts of "wild justice," a term used by 17th C. philosopher, Sir Francis Bacon. Handy combines a love of history and nature to provide dramatic settings, whether it is the American South or the eastern coast of Ireland. Her work has been nominated for the Pushcart Prize.

Made in the USA
Monee, IL
02 September 2022

12113489R00173